Wicahpi Wi
(Star Woman)

Mitakuye oyasin
(We all are related)

Bonnie Jo Hunt

Lawrence Ahrnt

LAND WITHOUT A COUNTRY

IT WAS A GREAT LAND COVETED BY MANY BUT HELD BY NONE. WHO WOULD HAVE THE COURAGE TO CLAIM IT AS THEIRS?

----

by

Bonnie Jo Hunt

and

Lawrence J. Hunt

Every part of this country is sacred to my people.
Every hillside, every valley, every plain and grove
has been hallowed by some fond memory or
some sad experience of my tribe.
Chief Seattle, Duwamish

A Lone Wolf Clan Book, Vol. V

LAND WITHOUT A COUNTRY

First printing, 2000

Library of Congress Catalog Number: 00 090334
International Standard Book Number: 1-928800-04-1 (Vol. V)

Cover *"Hallowed Ground"* is from original oil painting by Betty Hunt.

Cover design by ORO ENTERPRIZES. Visit their Online Gallery at http://www.oroenterprizes.com

Map, Umpqua Canyon and Ms. DeMoss photos reprinted from Catherine Cornwall DeMoss research collection.

"Whitman's Home at Waiiltpu" from MARCUS WHITMAN AND THE EARLY DAYS OF OREGON, Wm A. Mowry copyright, 1901, reprinted by permission of Scott Foresman/ Addison Wesley.

Back cover photo of Bonnie Jo courtesy Jerry Jacka.

Mad Bear Press
Albuquerque, New Mexico

Catherine Cornwall DeMoss, author, original manuscript

"LAND WITHOUT A COUNTRY has been written with the hope
that it may, in a measure, preserve for posterity an awareness of
the courage and unfaltering faith of the men and women who
endured much to bequeath to us our great Pacific Northwest."

Catherine Cornwall DeMoss
(from original manuscript, 1954)

This book is dedicated to Catherine Cornwall DeMoss,
author, teacher, historian, beloved grandmother and
original creator of

LAND WITHOUT A COUNTRY

A special thank you to our fine editorial staff for their detailed and tireless efforts to make this book right. We especially are grateful to Betty and Vern Hunt for generously giving their time and talents to the Lone Wolf Clan series of books.

The authors wish to express their deepest appreciation to all who support ARTISTS OF INDIAN AMERICA, INC. (A.I.A.) in its work with Indian youth. All proceeds from sales of LAND WITHOUT A COUNTRY go to further the work of A.I.A. Contributions to A.I.A. are tax deductible and most gratefully received. For information concerning A.I.A. write Mad Bear Press 6636 Mossman Place NE -- Albuquerque, New Mexico 87110 Telephone and FAX (505) 881-4093.

The country was made without lines of demarcation,
and it is no man's business to divide it . . . .

Chief Joseph, Nez Perce

Foreword

We are indebted deeply to Catherine Cornwall DeMoss, 1882-1955 who fifty years ago wrote a manuscript entitled LAND WITHOUT A COUNTRY. Upon her death, she left me, her grandson, this manuscript along with her research notes that filled two apple crates. Out of this plethora of material emerged this, the fifth volume of the Lone Wolf Clan series of books. A number of pages in LAND WITHOUT A COUNTRY are almost identical to those in Grandmother's original manuscript.

As a teacher, Grandmother had a unique ability to make learning enjoyable, to leave students with the desire to learn more. Nearly fifty years after her death former students say Catherine Cornwall DeMoss was the best teacher they ever had. In her classroom subject matter, particularly history, came alive. No matter who we are, by our mere presence on Mother Earth we make history, she said. Grandmother's lessons left everyone with the feeling he or she played a role of importance in shaping social values and the future of our nation.

As an author Catherine Cornwall DeMoss employed her classroom technique. She added a plot and characters to a little known historical event, and it became meaningful and alive. After reading BLUE BUCKET NUGGETS, "A Tale of Oregon's Lost Immigration," the only book Grandmother published, United States Senate Minority Leader, Charles McNary, wrote "You have made a splendid contribution to the history of Oregon and I need not tell you that it is written in a most engaging style and covers a tragic bit of history that has been little explored."

As teacher, author and grandmother, Catherine Cornwall DeMoss left an impact that is hard to surpass. In the Lone Wolf Clan series we attempt to uphold the standards Grandmother established.

Lawrence J. Hunt

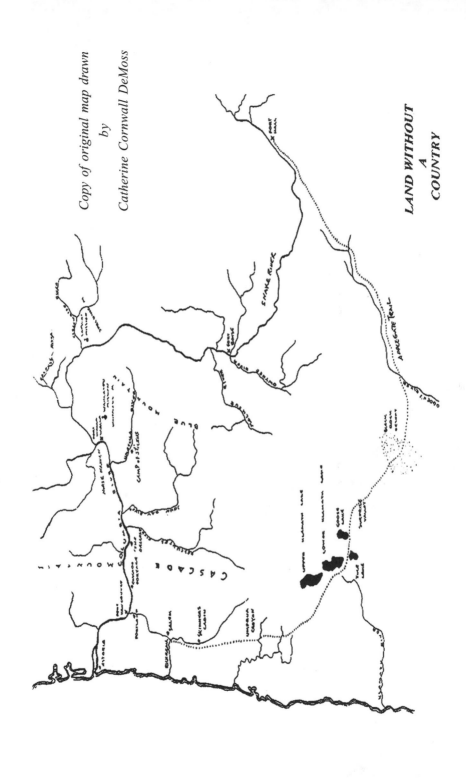

Copy of original map drawn
by
Catherine Cornwall DeMoss

LAND WITHOUT
A
COUNTRY

LAND WITHOUT A COUNTRY

I

The small town seemed to be literally overflowing with strangers of every grade of character and condition of life . . . civilized and uncivilized.
Edwin Bryant, 1846

From the very beginning, even at the frontier town of Independence, Missouri, the promise of a pleasant, uneventful journey was obviously wishful thinking. The Mexican War just had begun. The citizenry was in a quandary. How long would the conflict last? The nation's prestige and the people's safety were in the hands of General Zachary Taylor. Was he up to the task? A dozen or more American soldiers had been killed and fifty taken prisoner. Were Americans, so full of self-assurance, facing defeat?

These were among the agonizing questions people thronging the streets of Independence asked themselves. Many were about to journey across the plains to California or Oregon Territory. Others, who had arrived with the same intention, changed their minds but could not handle returning home to face friends and relatives. Like everyone else, they roamed the streets confused -- fearful of what fate had in store.

Further, the people were discomfited by the presence of numerous Indians. Sac, Fox, Shawnee and a few from the Kansas tribe, stood in groups on street corners or flowed in and out of already crowded shops. They gawked, pointed and chattered among themselves, saying nothing outsiders understood. Their little shaggy ponies lazed in the sun, jammed together like peas in a pod, blocking both sides of the street. Perspiring, red-faced officials, wearing shiny badges and swearing loudly, raced back and forth pushing and prodding the ponies to make room for a line of teamsters whose plodding oxen had come to a halt.

Suddenly, a terrifying shriek shattered the air. People stopped dead in their tracks. Indian ponies snorted and reared. In the effort to clear a path for the oxen drawn vehicles, a child had fallen among the shaggy Indian ponies' stomping hooves. An Indian man alertly pulled the screaming youngster to her feet. All anyone could see were the Indian's hands clutching the child. A roar of angry voices cut through the cacophony of street noises.

"String thet Injun up!" "Where's the law an' order in this jerkwater berg?" "A person ain't safe on the streets." The crowd surged forward. Horses yanked frantically on tether lines. Owners of shaggy ponies ran to quiet their mounts. A woman's shrill voice rang out, "Thet's me child. Thet savage's got me baby!" Her husband, a burly, bearded fellow, lunged for the Indian man. A red-faced official furiously ordered the crowd to disperse. No one paid him the least bit of attention.

For a heart-stopping moment it appeared mayhem could not be avoided. Then, a streak of brown hurtled over the hitching rail and onto the back of an Indian pony, the movement so swift the mob was stunned. Standing on the quivering animal's back, a slender six-foot young man clad in neat buckskins, glowered down like a vengeful angel.

"All right!" the buckskin clad figure shouted. His voice cut through street sounds sharp as the snap of a bull whip. "Stop right where you are. No damage has been done. Actually, this man pulled the child to safety. Leave him be." Only armed with a knife that remained in its sheath at his belt, the young man's commanding figure and implied reprimand hushed the crowd. Amongst the paunchy, bearded white men and scantily dressed natives, the graceful, slim form was a knight in shining armor.

The sobbing child pushed through the onlookers to her mother. The young man leapt from the horse and was lost in the throng. The Indian who had saved the child took his pony's halter line and led the animal away. Soon every Indian horseman followed.

"Who was thet young fella?" a red-faced official asked a

fellow officer. "He sure saved our bacon."

"Reckon he's one of those mountain men who hits town onct in awhile. I seen him hangin' 'round the hotel meetin' the St. Louie stage. Probably 'spectin' someun. He oughta be pleased with hisself. No doubt he saved thet Injun's hide."

Instead of being pleased, the young man was furious. He had drawn attention to himself, something he wished to avoid. But he couldn't help it, seeing the Indian falsely accused had made him see red. Nevertheless, he should have let the Indian fend for himself. He had no business on Main Street. Except for meeting the stagecoach, he normally kept to the freight yards where huge piles of materials covered with canvas lay stacked cheek to jowl.

Here he could lose himself in the hustle and bustle of freighters arriving at all hours and from all points with supplies and merchandise of every kind. It was unlikely anyone would look for him in this chaotic corner of town. All would be well when the stage carrying the family members arrived. Once on the trail he would be able to manage most any emergency that might arise. It was the waiting he couldn't stand. He felt as jumpy as a jack rabbit caught in the open with hawks circling overhead.

Unmindful of where his legs took him, the young man barely dodged the errant kick of a mule, collided with a man carrying a side of beef and slipped on a pile of fresh manure. He regained his balance only to encounter a big-bellied teamster walking beside a three span team of mules, one of the last persons he wanted to see. He turned away, but not quickly enough.

"Tarnation! Whoa there." The teamster pulled his team to a halt. He pushed back a dust-crusted, wide-brimmed hat and inspected the young man's fringed buckskins, artfully decorated with beads and porcupine quills. "I swan! Didn't recognize yuh, dressed like a prize pig at the county fair. Last we met yuh looked 'bout as grand as a pail of buffalo chips."

"How are you, Beamer?" the young man asked politely,

shaking the big man's hand. The teamster's eyes were tired and red-rimmed. The man's hair had grown gray and thinned. The signs of aging lcft the young man feeling depressed.

"Yuh sure must've done right smart fer yerself," Beamer exclaimed. "Yuh ain't card sharpin'er holdin' up stagecoaches, are yuh? Yuh sure never got rich trappin' an' skinnin' beaver."

"Git thet damn wagon movin', yer blockin' traffick an' smellin' up the place like a family of skunks," shouted a fidgety, irate man driving a two-wheeled mule-killer.

"Ah! Shet up," Beamer growled but gave his long whip a pop, making the mules jump. "Gotta load of hides. From the stink, they ain't too well cured. Let's do some jawin'-- camped half mile down Independence Road. Come this evenin', yuh hear? Like ta ketch up on what yuh've been doin'."

The young man held up his hand in silent farewell. He had no intention of visiting the teamster. Meeting him had been depressing enough without talk of rendezvous and Buck Stone's trapping brigade and the shoot out ending those glorious days.

Moodily, the young man wandered on. Six years had passed since he first met Beamer. In that time so much had happened -- so many people had come and gone. Perhaps that was why he felt older than he should. He was so deep in thought he nearly ran into a newly erected corral. Perched on the top rail, a bearded hawker shouted the merits of a motley collection of horses and mules. Their drooping heads and scruffy hides loosely draped over protruding ribs, made the animals look more like candidates for glue factories than for pulling wagons across the plains.

A prospective buyer appeared. The stockman leapt down to display a horse's teeth. The man shook his head. Undaunted, the hawker seized a mule by the muzzle and pried its mouth open. After the dental inspection, he slapped the animal's rump, making it jump. It was obvious the stockman held a sharp object in his hand. The young man had an overwhelming urge to seize the hawker and toss him into the nearby watering trough.

The young man started to walk on when a handsomely

dressed gentleman in a tailored broadcloth suit and fancy-frilled shirt, paused to inspect the livestock. A slight, black-skinned man equally smartly clothed, waited at his side. The strange pair caused the young mountain man to stare. "These creatures are a bit thin, but I suppose on the frontier one has little choice." He overheard the gentleman say. In spite of dandified clothes and manners, the man had the look and eye of an expert horseman.

"Couldn't help overhearing you, sir," the buckskin clad youth said, surprised by his own forwardness, but, like the incident on Main Street, he couldn't stand to witness injustice take place. The stranger appeared to know horses but these frontier hawkers were slick as greased eels. "You're right about this livestock. A good breeze would blow most of these critters away. The mules came up the Santa Fe Trail from Mexican scratch herds. Others are crowbait, local farmers trying to unload them on unsuspecting souls."

The gentleman's cool gray eyes appraised the buckskin clad figure. "I suppose we do appear a bit green. I'm Macon Laird and this is Pascoe." He spoke in a precise manner, his obvious British accent strange to the frontiersman's ears.

"Joe, Joe Jennings is the name." He shook the stranger's hand, impressed by the firmness of his grip. The man had fancy manners but underneath lay a steely quality like that of polished flint. This man was here for a purpose. What was it? Joe had an irresistible urge to find out.

"If you're planning to visit the country west of here perhaps I can give you a hand," Joe suddenly offered.

The gray eyes again studied the slender buckskined youth. "He looks too young to have much frontier experience," Macon Laird thought, but appearances often were deceiving . . . this colorfully dressed youth with the honest, open face might be just the person he needed . . . .

"We are planning on traveling to Oregon Territory," Laird answered.

It was Joe's turn to study the speaker. People went to

Oregon to take homesteads in the Willamette Valley. This pair certainly were not homesteaders.

"I know we look out of place," Macon Laird said as if reading Joe's mind. "We came up river by New Orleans stern-wheeler -- before that, Jamaica, where Pascoe joined me. As you may have guessed, Pascoe is a freed slave."

"No, I didn't guess," Joe answered, trying to place Jamaica on the map. "Even so, take care. Folks are skittish about Negroes and those duds." Joe looked hard at the embroidered waistcoat and solid gold-knobbed walking stick. "You'll surely be joshed if you travel in that garb."

"Of course we must dress appropriately. Perhaps you will be kind enough to direct us to a haberdashery."

"Sure. Sol's Outfitters is the place to go."

Before the day was over, Joe Jennings and the two men from Jamaica were on first name speaking terms. Joe had guided the newcomers through one shop after another. When Laird and Pascoe were clothed and provisioned, Joe suggested they be armed properly. At the gun rack Laird threw a rifle to his shoulder and took bead on the barber pole across the street. "Feels comfortable and sights well," he said.

"Good!" Joe grunted. When it came to firearms Laird certainly was no greenhorn. "That's a Hawken," Joe explained. "Frontiersmen swear by them, powerful enough to knock a buffalo down, yet uncomplicated and never fail."

Laird purchased an ample supply of ammunition and a Barlow knife with a blade that folded into the handle. As he had for the clothes and provisions, Laird paid for the lot with newly minted five dollar gold pieces. Joe stored this information away -- another indication these were not average plains travelers.

When the storekeeper asked where to deliver the purchases, again Joe surprised himself. He always had made it a point not to get involved in other people's affairs, yet, here he was, inviting these strangers to stay at his camp. "Until you get squared away you're free to use my facilities, nothing fancy, mind you. Anyway, with all these people pouring in, you won't find a rooming house in town that'll take you, especially the two of you." Joe added, inwardly shuddering at the scornful remarks hostel keepers would make when they saw Pascoe's black face.

"Stay with your gear. I'll fetch a buckboard before you know it, and we'll be away to my camp." Yet, as Joe strode for the buckboard a tremor of apprehension gnawed at him. Why was he getting involved with these people he didn't know from Adam's off-ox?

After collecting Pascoe and Macon and their purchases, Joe made his way quickly out of town. He had set up camp in a small grove a few miles west on Independence Road. A stream, swollen by recent rains, ran through the trees and on to cross the roadway. A group of men at the creek crossing helplessly stared at the wheels of a wagon mired in mud. "These people who've never harnessed an ox or plowed a furrow are worse than school-boys," Joe observed. "If this trickle stops them, what'll they do when they hit the Big Blue?"

Joe unhitched and reined the team of horses in front of the stalled wagon. The owners gratefully watched as he hooked onto the bogged-down wagon. Pascoe held the horses steady while Joe calmed the travelers' oxen. Joe urged the oxen forward. Pascoe snapped the reins of the horses. The wagon wheels began to turn. Through the mud they rolled and onto firm ground.

"Good work!" Joe said approvingly to Pascoe.

The Black's ready smile grew wider.

The quartet of travelers were profuse in their thanks. Each in turn introduced himself: Edwin Bryant, George Curry and two names Joe promptly forgot. "Bound for Oregon?" he asked.

"No, California," said Bryant in a soft voice that marked him as a man of education.

Joe nodded. They looked like good solid folks, the kind of men one could count on in a scrape. Too bad they weren't off to Oregon. With Pascoe's help he hitched the team to the buck-board and drove across the creek toward his own campsite.

The camp consisted of a tent set between two covered wagons. The livestock were corralled in a grove. Blaze, the bay Joe inherited from his dead partner, Hawk Beak, thrust its head across the fence and neighed.

"Nice animal," Macon said approvingly. "Must have Arabian blood -- easy to ride and fast afoot."

"Yeah," Joe agreed, impressed by the man's observations, but said no more. He should get rid of the horse but couldn't bring himself to do it. It would be like selling an old friend.

Hardly did Joe start unharnessing the buckboard team when Pascoe announced, "I'll be gettin' suppa." He dug into the provisions Macon had purchased and rattled among the pots and pans kept in a box cupboard nailed to the trunk of an oak.

Joe, prepared to be skeptical of the black man's worth, covertly watched Pascoe set about his work. The way he built a fire, handled the skillet and his deft, quick manner, made it clear the man knew what he was about. The big grin, readiness to volunteer and tasty meal, changed Joe's thinking about Negroes.

"Sure good vittles," he approved. "I haven't eaten grub like this since I left home."

"Yassuh, boss. I knowed yuh'd 'preciate good cookin'. I sure enuff knows a hungry man when I sees one."

Joe gave Macon Laird a glance of respect. The man was unaccustomed to the ways of the west, but he had horse sense and anyone who recruited a handyman like Pascoe also had people sense. A promising thought began to form in Joe's mind. With Pascoe along, life on the trail almost would be pleasant.

"What are your travel plans?" Joe bluntly asked. Macon remained silent so long Joe wondered if he had heard. He said he was traveling to Oregon Territory but why? Foreigners appeared on the frontier for a number of reasons. Some came to hunt. Others collected specimens, painted or wrote tales on frontier life. Some merely wanted to rub elbows with rough-and-ready men who made their living in the wilderness. Laird didn't appear to fit any of these categories. He was mannerly and good looking. Perhaps he was fleeing from a broken romance. If that was the case he could well sympathize with him. Joe's thoughts momentarily flitted to Bithiah Abernathy. How foolish he had been, leaving her like he did . . . . "Ah! Quit thinking nonsense," he ordered himself.

"If you'd like, you can travel with my sister, granddad and me," Joe said, finally breaking the silence. "I could use a driver and I'd welcome Pascoe as camp cook and roustabout."

"Sister? Grandfather?" Macon glanced around camp.

"They haven't arrived. I expect them any day."

Laird poked thoughtfully at the fire. Traveling with a wagon train was perfect . . . but he shouldn't appear too eager. "What's it like on the Oregon Trail?" he asked. "I've heard lurid tales of hostile Indians and other hazards of travel."

"I don't doubt it. This is a great land for sucker stories, some guy trying to lead people astray. Last year a mountain man, Greenwood by name, came to meet westbound wagon trains. The old geezer, hard and weather-beaten as a rock, preached the glories of California and knocked Oregon. To hear him tell it, danger lurks behind every tree and boulder on the trail to Oregon. Travelers will drown in the River Snake. If they survive, they'll for certain not get across the Blue Mountains. If they manage these hazards, they still have to chance a God awful fight with the Cayuse and Walla Walla. If the hostiles don't get them, the falls on the Columbia will certainly sweep them to their deaths. His stories would discourage the devil, himself. Truth is, it's a hard road whichever way you go, California or Oregon."

"Are Indians as warlike as I've heard?"

"Like everybody else, there are good and bad Indians. From here to Fort Laramie they're nuisances but harmless. From Fort Laramie to Fort Hall tribes usually go about their business. Some northern plains Indians are upset. Can't say I blame them. White hunters slaughter their buffalo just for the sport of killing. Wagon trains carve ruts in their grasslands and leave campsites in a mess.

"'Tween Fort Hall and Fort Boise tribes are tolerable. Beyond Fort Boise they're sometimes fractious. They see no end to wagon trains that grow larger and larger each year. Through the lands of the Bannock, Cayuse and Walla Walla, travelers should proceed with caution. There's no telling what'll be their mood. It can change from one day to the next."

"You seem to have good knowledge of the west."

"I should. I've traveled one end of it to the other: trapped beaver, hunted buffalo, fought Indians, prospected for gold . . ." Joe fell silent. He was blathering like a village idiot.

"Actually, the thought of traveling with you appeals to me," Macon said. "When in strange lands it seems wise to place one's self in experienced hands."

"Settled," Joe exclaimed. "We'll stow much of your stuff in the second wagon. A pack mule can manage the rest. For now, take over the tent. I'm accustomed to sleeping in the open."

The arrangement delighted Joe. In Pascoe he acquired a cook and helper who would be the envy of the wagon train. Sister, Tildy, would not have to slave over pots and pans and the other chores that made travel on the trail so tiresome. Macon, with his knowledge of horses, would make a reliable second driver. Everything was working out perfectly. He couldn't wait for Tildy and Granddad to arrive.

Yet, there remained the formidable task he never had been able to face. When Tildy and Granddad did arrive he would have to come grips with it. How could he tell them of their Indian brother and grandson who awaited them at Whitman's mission in the homeland of the fractious Cayuse?

II

Long ago the Arapahos had a fine country of their own. Then white man came to see them . . . and told them the country was big enough for the white man and the Arapahos, too.
Little Raven, Arapaho

Actually, the spring of 1846 found the homeland of the Cayuse quiet and serene. Fruit trees that were beginning to flower were a delight to see. The cloying perfume of locust blooms was so sweet and heady it almost was hard to breathe. The tipi lodges of the Waiilatpu Cayuse village resembled a cluster of oversized conical shaped mushrooms with tendrils of smoke rising above each one like a filament of silk. From the hilltop beyond the village one could see that the distant Horse Heaven Hills, where aged Cayuse horses were sent to live out their last years, were beginning to green. The Season of First Grass had arrived.

Doctor Marcus Whitman walked from the whitewashed adobe mission house with a spring in his step. He paused to breathe the clear aromatic air. For the first time in a long while, he felt well. No major problem faced him or threatened the mission. That was good. There was much work ahead. But for the moment he took pleasure in what he had accomplished.

When he arrived the mission site had been thick with high, coarse grass and brush. Now, with whitewashed buildings, cultivated garden plots and neat pasture fields, it had the look of the estate of an established country squire. It was hard to believe the change that had taken place in the space of ten years.

He strolled by the blacksmith shop that he had designed and equipped. From these forges poured tools and equipment of every kind: hoes, plowshares, harrows, horseshoes, scythes, bolts, latches . . . everything made of steel needed to maintain farm and household. He paused by the millpond that was full and overflowing. He inspected the gristmill that had been burned. It was now rebuilt and back in operation. He made a mental note to commend Josiah Osborne whose hard work had made this possible.

He came to the pasture fields. The livestock had weathered the winter well. They had started to lose their thick, hairy coats and were beginning to fill out. He quickly passed the noisy, smelly pigpens, then slowed to lean against the top rail of a fence. In the area beyond a hundred ewes were near the end of their carrying period and soon would drop their lambs. He smiled. Here was a fortune on the hoof. With the proper equipment he could start the first woolen spinning mill in the Northwest.

A yearling ewe broke away from the flock and came bleating toward him. He recognized her at once. She had been the lamb whose mother had been slain by a pack of coyotes. He had hand fed her for weeks. She always remembered him and came running when he appeared. For a moment he allowed her to nibble on the straps of his boots, then pushed her away.

"You are worse than a spoiled child," he chided, but nevertheless was pleased. On the edge of the wilderness any creature that offered love and affection was a friend indeed. He watched her crop on the grassy pasture. She was nearing breeding age. He made another mental note. To keep his stock up he must place an order with Hudson's Bay for one Merino ram and one Leicester ram. He also had to think of shearing time. The previously used shears had been made on the blacksmith forge and had not proven satisfactory. He had to bring factory made ones in from the east. In his next report to the Mission Board he would add them to his special request for tools.

The clang of the triangle gong announced the call to breakfast. Marcus Whitman hurriedly retraced his steps. "Ah!" he upbraided himself. He had intended merely to get a breath of fresh air. Instead, he had wandered around taking pride in all he had accomplished. He stopped to bow his head. "Pride goeth before destruction, and an haughty spirit before a fall," he quoted from Proverbs. "Forgive me, oh Lord, for my transgressions."

Through the open mission house windows came the chatter and clamor of youthful voices. The eleven children the Whitmans had adopted were reciting the morning prayer -- two-year old Henrietta Namoi's piping voice rising above the others.

"Ah!" Marcus uttered again, feeling a sense of shame. One of the joys of his day was to lead family prayers. Instead of joining the family to give glory to God for all the wondrous gifts He had bestowed on the mission, Marcus Whitman, the mission leader, had been gloating over his own personal achievements.

As usual, the Whitman table was crowded to capacity. Twenty-two places were set and twenty-two bodies waited for the benediction. "May all of you receive the blessings of God this day and every day forward whether on earth or in heaven. Amen." Marcus glanced around the circle of faces. Perrin Whitman, his adopted nephew, sat next to him.

Then came the seven Sager orphans who had come to them in the fall of '44. Both parents had died while crossing the plains. The grief-stricken, nearly starved children, were deposited on their doorstep like driftwood after a spring flood. Neither he nor his wife, Narcissa, had the heart to turn them away. After eighteen months of good food and loving care, they were normal, healthy humans again.

He mentally ticked off the names of the girls sitting in a row: Catherine, Elizabeth, Matilda Jane, Hanna Louise and baby Henrietta Naomi. Next were the two brothers, John and Francis. Then came the three dark-faced half-bloods; Mary Ann was the daughter of the mountain man and scout, Jim Bridger. Beside her sat Helen Mar, the daughter of another mountain man, Joe Meek.

Last was David Malin. What a transformation. Two native women had brought him in, nearly naked and toothpick thin. His father had taken to the mountains; his Canadian Cree Indian mother had run off with another man, abandoning the child. A malicious person had shaved a strip of hair an inch or more wide from ear to ear and from his forehead to his neck. He had a bad burn on his foot where bullies had pushed him into a campfire. He was crawling with lice and crusted with dirt.

Narcissa had bathed him, oiled him, cleaned away the lice and bound up his wounds. The unfortunate child did not understand kindliness and the comforts of home. For weeks he kept running away. Only recently had he begun to relax, surprising everyone by his quick mind and mischievous nature.

At the end of the table was another half-blood, the son of the mountain man, Little Ned. His name was Michael Two Feathers, the handyman who had become a fixture around the mission compound. Next to Michael sat Andrew Rodgers, the schoolteacher and his sick friend who was dying of consumption, Joseph Finley. Josiah Osborne, the millwright, his wife and three children and William Marsh, who operated the gristmill, completed the complement of diners.

Little David Malin, his dark eyes as bright and merry as a chipmunk's, held up a hand. "What is it, David?" Whitman asked.

"Father, is today yesterday's tomorrow?"

Whitman chuckled. This youngster posed questions that would make thinkers like Socrates scratch their heads. "Yes, my son. Why do you ask?"

"You said yesterday we might go on a picnic tomorrow if the weather was good. Well, today is tomorrow."

"Yes! Yes! A picnic!" Henrietta's shrill voice piped up.

With the children absorbed in planning the picnic, the men diners turned their attention to politics. Trouble along the Mexican border was the topic of the day.

"They say the Mexicans are much annoyed over the boundary question," Marsh, the gristmill operator, commented. "Those Mexicans've been grumbling about something or another ever since congress annexed Texas. Shouldn't wonder if things don't heat up into war. Those Mexes should understand that land is rightly ours. Texas is a part of the USA."

"You suppose the trouble will spill over into California

and then into Oregon?" Andrew Rodgers, the schoolteacher, asked. "California and Oregon share the same border."

"If politicians did what was right they'd annex California. Those Mexicans have got to learn we Americans are here to stay," Osborne declared.

"We have the Russians to worry about, too. They've invested a lot in their base on the north coast, Sitka by-the-Sea -- claim it's the capital of the New World. You can bet your life they'll be looking south. From all reports they're getting rich trapping and fishing up and down the Pacific Coast. They must be giving Hudson's Bay fits," the schoolteacher observed.

"I don't agree," Osborne said. "It isn't Russkies we should worry about, it's those Redcoats of Hudson's Bay. The British want this land so badly they can taste it. With trading posts already in place, they're in a strong position to add the entire territory to their empire."

Marcus Whitman, who had remained quiet, finally spoke. "Everyone wants Oregon. You might say it's a land without a country. The first nation with the desire and determination to claim it and hold it, will have a prize beyond any politician's wildest dream. We must be the ones with that desire and determination. Our people in Washington have to wake up -- lay claim to this territory and then stand by their decision. If we are firm, the British will give way. They don't need a war halfway around the world."

The Nez Perce youth, Michael Two Feathers, who had been silent throughout the meal, pushed his plate aside. The chatter of the children and their picnic plans bored him. The adult conversation angered him. The talk of these people was always the same: boundaries, annexing lands, threats of foreign nations, acreages under cultivation -- bushels of wheat, corn and oats that could be realized and inroads of the Redcoats of Hudson's Bay.

They spoke of these things with a religious fervor, as if possession and power over land and what it produced were their gods. Didn't they know Mother Earth was given by the Creator for everyone to use and enjoy? It was not meant for this person or that country to possess. Had these missionaries forgotten why they were here?

According to what they said when they first arrived, they were messengers of God. They had come for the purpose of spreading Christianity, saving the souls of the natives. Instead, they concentrated on expanding their hold on the land and adding to their wealth. They raised surplus food to sell to the homesteaders who every fall poured down the Blue Mountain slopes. They brought great flocks of sheep to grow wool far in excess of their needs, and even greater flocks were foreseen. It was no secret Missionary Whitman envisioned a great wool milling industry with dust-raising, clanking machinery much like the one that turned the gristmill's grinding stones.

Missionary Whitman also had plans for a major educational center, an academy, he called it, that would be situated in the Walla Walla Valley to serve students from all over Oregon Territory. Here again, these people were thinking only of themselves. Few natives could attend the academy. They could not possibly qualify. During the past year not one Cayuse student was given a place in the local mission school.

Michael Two Feathers did the unpardonable. He started to get up from the table before the final prayer. Always restless, Francis Sager, also made to rise. Narcissa Whitman frowned. They both quickly sat down. They had no wish to offend this lady who they looked upon as Mother.

"Father! It is time to say the after-meal blessing," Narcissa reminded. Normally she never broke into Husband's conversation, but this morning she felt as restless as the boys. She had so many things that had to be done, and there was a letter she should write; no, several letters. She wanted desperately for her brother and his wife to come and help out, and Husband had messages he wanted copied. "Oh!" she inwardly groaned. She was so thronged by her family of orphans she did not know how long she could keep going.

Michael Two Feathers left the mission house upset. For nearly six years he had lived and worked at the Waiilatpu mission. By now he should be accustomed to the way white folks did things, but it was one of those mornings when the conversation sent his Nez Perce Indian blood surging through his veins like liquid fire.

Michael walked to his tipi lodge at the edge of the mission compound where he kept his meager possessions and where he slept. He had half a notion to tear the tipi down and leave. He had been at the mission far too long. But where would he go? Things were just as bad in his Nez Perce homeland. It was said Henry Spalding, who managed the mission at Lapwai, ruled with an iron hand. When people disobeyed him or broke one of the Ten Commandments he ordered them whipped, an unthinkable act.

Michael moodily watched the dark thread of smoke rise above the forge where Smithy and his helpers were already at work, banging out hoes and plowshares. The noise hurt his ears. Not even magpies and blue jays liked to be around. They had taken to nesting on the far side of the hill that jutted up behind the mission grounds.

The skeins of honkers on their way south and back to their homes in the north, still swooped down in the cultivated fields to feed on harvest leavings, but how long would it be before they found more comfortable resting and feeding grounds away from the bustling mission compound? Squirrels and chipmunks were fewer in number. He missed their chatter and flipping about. How he wished for the old days, before fences, wood and adobe lodges, the noisy, smoke-belching forge and the rumbling grumbling gristmill.

Michael aroused himself. He did not have time to mope like a sulking child. Mission laborers were harnessing the horses, preparing to work the fields. John and Francis Sager, with buckets in hand, were shooing the cows in to be milked. He also had chores to do. There was a lame colt that needed attention, fence railing that had to be replaced, pens that had to be prepared for soon lambs would appear, and a batch of pigs had broken loose and had to be corralled.

He started for the pasture, trying to shake the black mood that hung over him like a suffocating cloud. In the back of his mind he knew what troubled him most. His Boston brother had forsaken him. Two years ago Joe had promised that when the Season of First Grass arrived they would journey east to the country where their mountain man father was born -- meet their grandfather and sister who lived near the big village called Boston. But spring arrived and Joe did not appear.

The next spring came and went and still no Joe. At first the thought of meeting strangers and traveling through foreign lands, had frightened Michael. Then, as he had time to think about it, the thought excited him. He looked forward to meeting his half sister, Tildy, and Grandfather Jennings. He wanted to see where his father was born and reared. He wanted to see how this Boston side of his family lived.

Michael groaned. That was the trouble with white people. When they came to good hunting grounds or beaver streams they stopped until they shot, trapped and skinned every animal that would bring them a few dollars in trade. Joe and his partner, Hawk Beak, had left to go trapping two years ago. Last spring they had been seen with a wagon train near Fort Boise, then both of them disappeared.

For months Michael had wondered if he should go to Fort Boise -- attempt to trace the two trappers. He decided against it. A search like that could take a long while, leaving the mission shorthanded when help was needed most. Besides, lately, the unhappy thought came to him that his Boston brother did not speak straight. He made promises with no intention of carrying them out. He would not be pleased to be tracked down by one who white folks disdainfully labeled "half-breed."

As the days passed Michael was caught up in the rush of

spring season work. There was little time to think about his absent brother. Then one day an acquaintance of Joe's appeared. Two dusty riders entered the mission compound and tied their mounts to the hitching rail. One was Hare Lip Bruce who had accompanied Joe on a prospecting expedition into the Oregon desert. The other rider Michael did not know.

Michael never liked Hare Lip Bruce, partly because the man was contemptuous of anyone with Indian blood. The man's facial deformity also made Michael uncomfortable. Although Bruce attempted to hide the cleft in his lip with a bushy mustache, it only made it appear worse -- like a constant sneer. Michael avoided the two riders most of the day but at nightfall Hare Lip Bruce and his companion, a hard-bitten man with steely gray eyes and crooked nose, strode up to Michael's tipi lodge and, uninvited, hunkered down to talk.

"The mission man says yer half brother ta Joe Jennings." Bruce spoke with a pronounced lisp. Michael couldn't tell if the speech impediment was a result of his cleft lip or the huge bulge of tobacco clamped in his jaw. The repulsive man shifted the chaw and sent a sluice of juice through his tobacco stained beard. The dirty, amber liquid splattered against the tipi skirt. Hare Lip Bruce laughed. "Sorry 'bout thet. I ain't quite house broke."

Michael remained silent. These people had come to do mischief. Anything he might say would not deter them.

"We ain't only lookin' fer yer brother but also his side-kick, Hawk Beak. Know anythin' 'bout their whereabouts?"

"I know nothing."

"Yuh mean, yuh ain't heerd from yer own brother?" The sneer on Bruce's face became more pronounced. "Yuh ain't perzactly on the best of terms, is thet it?"

Michael did not reply.

"Injuns! Yuh might as well talk ta a post," Bruce's hard-bitten companion said in disgust. "Look, son, we got good reason ta believe yer Boston brother has been up ta no good, liftin' things thet ain't his'ns. Maybeso, doin' a bit of killin' while he was at it. What yuh say ta thet?"

For the first time Michael looked the man in the eye. "I would say it was a lie. My brother is neither a killer nor a thief."

"La-de-dah! The kid speaks the King's English better'n we'uns. Makes no matter. If we find he's lyin', pertectin' thet varmint brother . . ." The hard-bitten man left the threat unspoken. The two men got to their feet. Hare Lip Bruce cut loose another sluice of tobacco juice, this time aiming at Michael's moccasined-shod foot. He missed, but just barely.

The following morning the two men were gone. Mission workers said they rode east, toward the Blue Mountain passes.

"Must've been in a hurry," Osborne the millwright reported. "Didn't even fire up an' have a proper breakfast. They was arguin' somethin' fearful, lookin' mad an' mean enough to bite the heads off of snakes. Vocabulary! They must know every cuss word in the book. They cursed the horses, whipped the dogs an' skittered through the mission gates like scalded cats. Didn't say where they were bound for but did stop rantin' long enough to ask after your brother, Joe. Hope he knows they're comin'. They're indeed a nasty pair."

III

The emigrants . . . express generally much apprehension in regard to the designs of the Mormons. Many predict collisions with them and fatal results.
Edwin Bryant, 1846

Joe Jennings indeed was aware sooner or later someone was certain to be on his trail. "Where's yer sidekick, Hawk Beak?" was the first question they would ask, especially if they had the least inkling of the treasure he left behind. "Ain't seed him 'round fer a coon's age," they would add, giving him a suspicious glance.

On the sparsely populated frontier any man's sudden disappearance was news. Hawk Beak's unique features, slender as a scarecrow with hooked beak and thin lips, were remembered wherever he went. When details of Hawk Beak's passing emerged, he was certain to be counted among the legendary figures who played colorful roles in the history of the early west.

Only he, Joe Jennings, had witnessed his partner's strange demise. He would have reported the death to family members and close friends, but Hawk Beak had been a loner. In all the years they had trapped, traveled and camped together, Hawk Beak had not once mentioned a relative. He told no one of his origins, where he was born or where and how he was reared.

Nor did Hawk Beak unbend enough to anyone to have them regard him as a friend. Whether dead or alive, the lanky man was a mystery. He entered the frontier unheralded and departed the same way. Nevertheless, Joe was never free from the haunting thought that someone from Hawk Beak's mysterious past would appear demanding an accounting of the manner in which he died.

The time-consuming task of outfitting for the trek across the continent had pushed the nagging worry to one side. Joe's new traveling companions, Macon Laird and Pascoe helped bury it deeper into his subconscious. Now that their travel arrangements had been settled, Macon Laird particularly, wanted to learn all he could about the makeup of the wagon train.

"What kind of travelers are these wagon train people, anyway?" Macon Laird asked the first evening in camp.

"Let's take a turn around town -- meet some of the folks," Joe suggested. Later, as he prepared the buckboard, he scolded himself. "What's the matter with me? Appearing in town with these two foreigners will attract attention like a lighthouse on a foggy night."

Joe's disquiet was justified. Everyone they met immediately recognized him as the one who fearlessly had stemmed the near riot. The first to mention it were J. Quinn Thornton, a lawyer, and his wife traveling to Oregon for their health. Thornton took it upon himself to introduce the hero of the hour to the Newtons, owners of blooded horses they hoped would start Oregon's first breeding stable. Then came Colonel Russell, ex-Governor Boggs of Missouri and Tom Wall and his gangly sons. Instead of shaking hands with Pascoe, Tom Wall turned away. "Didn't count on a mixed lot like this," his voice twanged like an overtightened banjo string. "If Oregon's goin' ta mount ta anythin' yuh cain't mix the races." He shooed his gang of offspring away and stomped after them.

"Pay him no mind," Joe said. "Wall is so sanctimonious he believes it a sin to play a musical instrument on the Sabbath."

They met William Smith and a few of his nine youngsters. Then, to their surprise, they ran into Edwin Bryant, whose wagon they had pulled free from the mud at the creek crossing.

"Fancy seeing you again. I supposed you'd be well on your way by now," Joe said.

"Five thousand Mormons have been seen crossing the Kansas." Bryant delivered the information as though reading from an official report. "They march with field pieces and side arms. It is said they vow to halt every wagon train heading west."

"Bushwa!" Joe blurted. "Whoever told you that has been reading too many wild west yarns."

"I suppose I'm a bit nervy but one can't be too careful. There are some odd ones about." Bryant glanced at Macon. "You British? Thought so. Met a couple fellows with accents like yours. Didn't say much. Closemouthed types, didn't volunteer a word about themselves -- one a red-nosed chap with out-thrust jaw. Perhaps they're acquaintances of yours."

Macon shook his head, yet Joe noticed a glint of recognition flash across his face. Later, back at camp, a sudden thought occurred to him; was Macon a high stakes gambler? Jamaica, New Orleans river boat, ready gold pieces, suave, secretive manner . . . it fit together. The thought was disturbing. Seldom did big winners in gambling casinos get away to enjoy their winnings. If they did, they did not keep them long. River boat game dealers were especially vengeful creatures, never forgetting the faces of those who bested them.

The sound of hard galloping hooves pounding down the trail from the west interrupted Joe's somber thoughts. He picked up his rifle and stepped into the shadows. The horsemen splashed across the creek, then cantered to a stop outside the circle of campfire light. "You're welcome to sit a while, strangers," Joe called out. After some hesitation, two riders dismounted and approached -- the Wall youths. Pascoe held out the blackened coffeepot. "Cuppa coffee?"

"Yeah, thet would be right nice," the older of the two boys said.

"What's the big hurry?" Joe asked, putting away the rifle. "You came tearing down the trail like a war party was on your tail."

"We was spooked. Some people was tryin' ta jump us."

"What did they look like?"

"Couldn't say. They was on us, an' we took off." The second youth took a tin cup Pascoe offered, his face white in the dim light. "We been told Injuns're on the warpath, plannin' ta ambush westbound wagon trains."

Joe grunted in disgust. Instead of Mormons, now it was Indians who were out to do the train in. "It's a rumor. People who don't want to see wagons roll west spread ridiculous lies."

"These galoots was no rumor," the older lad said.

"Why don't you fellows bed down here for the night," Joe suggested. "I have plenty of blankets. No point in riding into trouble."

For a long while after everyone had turned in, Joe sat by the dying campfire. Except for the babble of the creek and the snuffling of the livestock, everything was still, yet an uneasy feeling kept him alert. He took the rifle and strolled around camp. The Wall boys looked so young and vulnerable in sleep. Pascoe snored softly at the entrance of the tent. Macon's new Hawken lay by the black man's side. Like a watchdog, he guarded his master. There was no doubt about it, these two men expected trouble. The grim thought brought his dead grandmother to Joe's mind. One of her favorite sayings was, "Trouble begets trouble."

IV

The emigrants . . . were in great confusion, holding meetings, passing resolutions, and drawing up regulations but unable to unite in the choice of leaders to conduct them across the prairie.

Frances Parkman Jr., 1846

The St. Louis stage carrying Tildy and Granddad Jennings finally arrived. As usual, Joe was waiting as it rattled to a stop alongside the boardwalk. At first Granddad and then Tildy stepped down. Joe, who had not seen them for over six years, felt a lump well up in his throat. He had no idea the sight of his loved ones would bring him near tears. To cover his emotions he seized Granddad and gave him a great bear hug, then picked up Tildy and swung her around until it made him dizzy. She was light as a feather and far prettier than he remembered. Bystanders who had collected, clapped and cheered.

Embarrassed, Joe quickly escorted the new arrivals through the swinging doors of the hotel that served as the stage station. He led the way across the lobby and into the dining room. Male heads nearly swiveled off, watching the new arrivals' progress. The lissome lady with the lilting voice and bright smile entranced everybody. As Joe drew a chair out for Tildy, a man at the next table dropped a buttered knife in his lap. "Watch yourself," the man's sharp-faced wife snapped.

"Sis, I'm not sure the west is ready for you," Joe said, unabashedly admiring his twin. "No wonder Sandy only has to think of you and he becomes a new man."

"Did Sandy say that?"

"Yep. He went on about you until I thought I'd take sick."

Tildy's lilting laugh stilled the room. Every eye was turned her way. "Oh! I'm making a spectacle of myself," she uttered. The blush that colored her face made her all the more attractive.

She modestly studied the flyspecked menu, her mind racing. She could not believe what was happening. It only seemed days ago when the bank draft arrived. It was such a surprise and the amount so large, she barely could hold her hands steady in the hurry to unfold the accompanying note. "Hope this will pay the bills and see you on your way west. A wagon train leaves Independence, Missouri for Oregon early in May . . . .   Love, Joe."

Her brother didn't say where the bonanza came from and didn't question whether or not she and Granddad would travel west. When shown the draft Granddad merely shook his head and clucked. "My! What are we waiting for? Let's pack."

Granddad's enthusiasm had delighted her. After making the marriage pact with Sandy her greatest worry was what effect it would have on Granddad -- quitting a comfortable home for a log cabin in the wilds of Oregon? Yet, when the time came to depart, she was the one who nearly backed out. Arriving in the Willamette Valley a year early sent her into confusion. Sandy would pounce on her like a famished bear. Was she ready for the marriage bed, pregnancies, tykes hanging on her skirts . . .?

Tildy glanced at Joe . . . handsome and romantic in his buckskins. How had he managed to remain single all these years? He had to have attracted many a maiden's eye.

Granddad winked at Tildy. "Our lad has become quite a man, hasn't he? Incidentally, how did you come by the riches, beaver trapping, buffalo hunting or was it a pot of gold at the end of a rainbow?"

"Pot of gold, sort of -- came by it in the Oregon desert."

"You must have kept the find quiet," Granddad observed. "News of a gold strike usually sweeps the country like wildfire."

"Yes . . ." Joe glanced around the dining room. Every eye appeared to be turned their way, especially those of the bearded fellow in the far corner. Ah! What was the matter with him? He had to quit looking over his shoulder like a man on the run.

"Joe! Where have you been? I have been speaking to you for minutes on end," Tildy scolded. "I want to know all about

Sandy, and what about the Abernathies?"

"Oh, they're doing fine -- expect us to be neighbors in the Willamette Valley."

"Could it be Bithiah Abernathy has your head up in the clouds?" Granddad mischievously inquired.

Joe blushed. Tildy's infectious, lilting laugh again had every diner glancing their way.

"Tell us about your father? The news of his passing was a terrible shock. I still can't believe he's gone," Granddad said, shaking his head.

Joe remained silent. Could he bring himself to relate the details of his mountain man father's death? No, but this was a good time to prepare them for their Indian brother and grandson. But if he spoke of him he would have to bring in his father whose death was caused by his Indian wife, Raven Wing.

Joe pushed away from the table. "It's time we collect your luggage," he said gruffly. Tildy and Granddad glanced at each other, stunned by the abrupt change in Joe's manner.

However, the mood was again bright as the new arrivals rode in the open buckboard toward camp. Families gathered in the frontier town to make the trek across the continent, waved and shouted. Tildy laughed and waved back. Granddad politely tipped his hat. "What friendly folk," Tildy enthused. "This will be a wonderful experience."

"I hope so," Joe said guardedly. His main concern now was getting Tildy and Granddad accustomed to the idea of having a couple of foreigners as traveling companions, one of them black, a race seldom seen around their New England home.

When they arrived at camp Macon and Pascoe, who were puttering near the tent, stopped to stare. Then, as if suddenly remembering his manners, Macon Laird doffed his hat and came quickly to help Tildy down. Pascoe made no attempt at good manners. He gazed at Tildy in open-mouthed admiration.

"These are friends from Jamaica, Mr. Laird and Mr. Pascoe," Joe said, introducing the men to Tildy and Granddad.

"I'm happy to meet any of Joe's friends," Granddad Jennings acknowledged them in his usual courtly manner.

Macon Laird went through the introduction formalities with good grace but Joe easily read his thoughts; how could this rough-and-ready frontiersman possess such a lovely lady for a sister and cultured gentleman for a grandfather?

For a while Joe's apprehensions faded into the background. Tildy's cheeriness was catching. Pascoe's grin split his face. When Laird learned Granddad was a retired schoolmaster, the two engaged in a jocular debate on the usefulness of Greek and Latin as required subjects in preparatory schools. Joe noticed from time to time the Englishman's gaze drifted in Tildy's direction. Tildy did not appear annoyed.

If Joe only had known what these glances of Macon Laird's would lead to he would not have slept that night, nor the next or the next. Instead, he happily walked with Tildy to see the cattle he had purchased to replace the losses Sandy had suffered while crossing the Oregon desert. It was a small but fine herd. "How good you are to us, Joe," Tildy exclaimed. "Sandy and I always will be in your debt."

Tildy's exuberance seemed to have no end. After the evening meal she donned a bonnet and cape. "At the hotel I saw an announcement the Masonic lodge is giving wagon train people a send-off," she said gayly. "Afterwards, there's a dance and tomorrow a wagon train election. I think we should take in the festivities and elect Joe wagon train captain tomorrow."

Joe had hoped to avoid going into town again and he certainly did not want to be elected an officer of the train, but he didn't have the heart to dampen his sister's enthusiasm.

A number of people Joe already knew had gathered in front of the Masonic building. The occasion was ostensibly to give fellow Masons a proper send-off on their treks to Santa Fe, California and Oregon, a traveler bound for Santa Fe informed them. The spokesman for the Masons delivered an address on the perils of western travel. A minister invoked a solemn blessing. Several women broke down and wept.

"You'd think we were consigned to perdition instead of starting a trip to a new homeland," Quinn Thornton, the lawyer on the way to Oregon, growled, embarrassed by his weeping wife.

"We should sing and shout for joy instead of shedding tears," Tildy exclaimed, linking arms with Joe and Granddad. "Let's go dancing?" she said, glancing at Pascoe and Macon.

"Yes, miss," Pascoe answered, delighted to be included.

The dance, held in a high lofted barn already had begun. A band of youngsters, who had been herded up loft ladders, looked down from above. On a platform at the far end of the building a bearded man with a violin tucked in his whiskers conducted a group of musicians. A pimply youth plucked a banjo, another young man squeezed a small hand organ and a second fiddler sawed away with fury. A spare man motioned to the newcomers.

"Come, yuh'all, dance - dance - dance," he exhorted. Couples flounced onto the straw-covered floor. Macon bowed before Tildy and gracefully swung her into the milling crowd.

"I must say your sister is surprisingly light on her feet," Granddad observed. "They do make a handsome pair."

"Yeah," Joe grunted. No one was going to get him out there. It would be like watching a clumsy bear. He wondered if Bithiah Abernathy, the young lady he had set his heart on, danced. Probably not. Her parents regarded dancing and card playing as tools of the devil.

Abruptly, the fiddlers launched into a rollicking hoedown. The pimply youth put the banjo aside and leapt down to kick and stomp around the room. The dancers followed his lead. Another banjo exploded into a staccato of sound. Spectators clapped, keeping time with the catchy rhythm. "I say," Granddad uttered. The banjo player was Pascoe. The dancers stopped to watch the black man display his wondrous talent. Pascoe ended with a flourish, bowing to spontaneous applause.

Wall, standing with his gangly sons and timid looking wife, scowled. "Yuh're to blame," he growled, looking straight

LAND WITHOUT A COUNTRY

at Joe. "No good can come of this."

The music struck up again. Still thumping the banjo, Pascoe shuffled up the dance floor, expertly executing a soft-shoe routine. His white teeth gleamed in a broad smile. The crowd clapped and cheered. This was too much for the Walls. They filed out the door. "We got ways of fixin' such things," Dad Wall muttered, pushing his reluctant sons in front of him.

The next morning the travelers gathered to organize the wagon train. As Joe had expected, those bound for California dominated the meeting. Edwin Bryant and his companion, George Curry, were chosen chairman and secretary of the meeting. The first item of business was a request by Mr. Harlan that the election of officers be postponed until after a few days travel.

A lengthy harangue followed, the request for delay finally argued down. After considerable more disagreement the assembly elected Colonel Russell, a large man with commanding manner, trail captain and Governor Boggs chairman responsible for governing the wagon train. As the meeting finally broke up, Tildy turned on Joe. "Why didn't you assert yourself? You know the west better than any of these newcomers."

"Don't concern yourself, Sis," Joe soothed. "A week on the trail will tell who should or should not be train leaders."

The wagon train made ready to depart. Last moment purchases were made, medicine chests inspected, axles greased, wagon wheel tires tightened; ammunition, food, water and other essentials weighed, counted and recorded. To make certain wagons were travel ready, an inspection committee made the rounds, checking on the adequacy of supplies, equipment, animals and the health of the people themselves.

When the inspectors arrived at the Jennings' camp, already 60 wagons, 300 people and 1,000 head of livestock had been logged. That many more were expected to join later. Compared to '45, it was a small train, yet still provided wagon masters with formidable challenges. They had to guide this motley group of people across 2,000 miles of wilderness track that would take upward of 200 days.

That evening, Tildy, excited by the thought of starting for Oregon in the morning, helped Pascoe prepare a special meal. Afterward, everyone sat around the campfire in silence. Thoughts of the unknown, combined with the whisper of the trees and murmur of the brook, gave the night an eerie feeling of excitement, fear, doubt and the humbling sensation of being alone and mortal on these great plains the Indians called "The Big Open." The realization they were embarking on a journey that would shape the remainder of their lives made travelers pensive. Finally, Tildy broke the spell.

"If I'm to be bright-eyed tomorrow, I'd better get some sleep," she said. She thanked Pascoe for his help with the delicious meal and bid them all good-night. Macon politely stood until she closed the canvas flap. The mannerly gesture irked Joe. One would think we had dined in a palace hall, instead of a cottonwood grove, he thought to himself.

Pascoe aroused himself and began to putter around, preparing for the morning meal. Joe watched the black man work, his thoughts on Macon Laird. What was his purpose in going to Oregon? He was no farmer and if he was a river boat gambler, he would be in constant danger the whole way.

From the west came the creak of saddles and splashes of horses at the creek crossing. The riders stopped some distance away to engage in what seemed a quarrel. Joe picked up his rifle. He stepped out of the circle of light and into the shadows. Shortly, the horsemen moved off toward Independence.

Joe sat again by the fire, still holding the rifle. "People are nervy about starting out tomorrow. Probably take a few days for everyone to settle down," he remarked in answer to Granddad's questioning glance.

"You can't blame them," Granddad said, getting to his feet. "Crossing the continent is a mighty big step, even for an old codger like me." He said good-night and disappeared into the second wagon. Macon also said good-night and ducked into the tent. As usual, Pascoe laid out his bedroll just inside the tent entrance. He checked the Hawken and laid it beside him. "To keep bad mens away," he explained to Joe.

Joe pulled off his boots and lay back in the blankets. The camp cloaked in quietness, his two wagons ready to roll and the herd of stock snuffling in the woods, gave him a feeling of relief. His worries had been for naught, he told himself. Everything would turn out all right. He had done his bit by Granddad, Tildy and Sandy. Soon he would see Bithiah Abernathy. If he played his cards right Dad Abernathy could hardly refuse to give his blessing. With this last pleasant thought, Joe fell asleep, but not for long. A harrowing howl of pain jerked him awake.

For a moment Joe thought it a nightmare, then realized something terrible was happening at the entrance of the tent. Pascoe's strong white teeth were clamped on a human hand! Like the death grip of a bulldog, his teeth held the intruder fast. Quick and bright as a flash of light, a knife blade descended.

Joe threw the blankets aside and seized his rifle. Without taking aim, he pulled the trigger. The attacker staggered. The tent crashed to the ground. Out of the darkness came a muffled curse. A horse and rider lunged across an open space. Joe snapped off another shot. It did not strike home. A thunder of galloping hooves made it clear the intruder had escaped.

Macon Laird emerged from the collapsed canvas holding a pistol in each hand. As though walking in his sleep, he stumbled forward and dropped to his knees beside Pascoe's still form. From the front of the white nightshirt welled a flow of blood. A froth of red stained the black man's beautiful teeth. Against the whiteness of the night garment the death weapon rose up like the head of a coiled snake. Uttering a cry of horror and disbelief, Macon plucked it from Pascoe's chest and turned it over in his hand. It was a short dagger, the kind gamblers concealed in the band of their trousers. With a savage curse, Macon hurled the deadly killing tool into the blackness of the night.

V

Do not ask us to give up the buffalo for the sheep.
Ten Bears, Comanche

In Cayuse country, preparations were underway for lambing season. To make certain the ewes would have easy deliveries, Whitman had them driven into a pole corral. Then, reading the instructions in his shepherd's guide book, he had each one sheared about the dock and udder. It was a job he scrupulously supervised. Great care had to be taken not to injure the teats, the book instructed. Cleaning around the dock also made the process of lambing more sanitary and made the shepherd's task easier if the ewe needed assistance in dropping the lamb.

The tedious, delicate work was conducted by the Sager brothers and Michael Two Feathers. Everything went reasonably well until Francis Sager became irked. A ewe's sharp pointed hoof gouged a hole in the toe of his shoe. In turn Francis gave the ewe an unnecessary clip of the shears, drawing blood. Marcus Whitman, closed the instruction book and pointed a finger toward the mission house, dismissing Francis without uttering a word. John Sager and Michael completed the task, although it was well after dark when they were done.

Shortly after lambing season came shearing time. A sheep grower's success or failure depended on the wool harvest. Marcus did not want to trust his precious ewes to the Sager brothers, especially Francis. Francis was likely as not to shear away teats and udders along with the wool.

Of all the young farm hands, Michael Two Feathers was the only one Marcus Whitman truly trusted. Michael cared for farm animals as though they were his own, except for pigs. These grunting, rooting, squealing creatures disgusted him. Whenever possible, he avoided the pig pens.

In desperation Whitman made a bargain with the Cayuse

village chief, who, in return for supplying labor, would share in the crop. The missionary considered it a good arrangement for both sides. He got the sheep sheared; the Cayuse received sufficient wool to weave into shawls, blankets, clothing and other items the people could use for themselves or exchange for goods.

In the back of his mind Marcus envisioned the joint effort as the first step in creating a wool spinning industry that ultimately would serve the entire Pacific Northwest. To oversee the workers, he chose dependable Michael Two Feathers. He spoke Cayuse, knew the natives' work habits and had experience with shears.

Michael accepted the task of sheep shearing boss with reluctance. The Cayuse were able to clip a horse's mane and tail, but that was about the limit of their skill with a pair of shears. To make matters worse, they did not like sheep. Until the missionaries brought them to the valley, many Cayuse had never seen one. They were foreign, dumb things that had no place in the Cayuse homeland. Their sharp little teeth clipped the pasture clean of grasses that were meant for their precious horses.

The first day Tiloukaikt, the Cayuse leader, sent workers who, because of some village misdemeanor, were in disfavor. The drafted men were sullen and resentful. In addition to disliking sheep, they did not care for Michael Two Feathers. Like the sheep, he was also foreign to the Cayuse homeland. He was the fatherless mission boy who had run away from his Nez Perce home -- worst of all, he was a half-blood with no standing, neither among the Indian nor the hairy faced ones.

Michael was equally dismayed. There were men and women in the village who were capable, willing workers. Not a one of them showed up that first day. But Michael accepted what he had. He began by instructing the workers in the way to catch and hold a sheep while shearing. He seized a nearby ewe by the thick wool coat that covered her shoulders. He picked her up and sat her on her rump, keeping her body upright by the pressure of his knees. Holding the ewe's right foreleg across the body to tighten the skin, he made the first stroke with the shears. He followed that with a second stroke parallel to the first, keeping the shearing blades clicking until all the belly wool was removed.

Then, turning the sheep on its right side, he continued to shear, letting the cuttings cascade onto a carpet of grass. Around the sheep he went until the poor animal looked half the size it did before the shearing. Giving a few missed spots a last clip, he turned the naked, bleating ewe loose. The watching Cayuse men shifted uncomfortably. This task was like asking them to skin a carcass, the work of women and children.

Michael glanced at Tiloukaikt's son, Edward, who had earned his father's displeasure, and handed him the shears. "You see how it is done. I am sure you can do the task even better," he challenged. If he was to get any work from this group the village leader's son had to set the example.

Edward hesitated. He was furious with his father for placing him among the village riffraff and under the direction of the mission handyman who was younger than he. They had attended mission school together. He had not liked Michael Two Feathers then, and liked him even less now. Why should he bow to the wishes of this lowly half-blood? He would have outright refused to take the shears, but his father had a hold on him. Unless he did as he was told there would be no bargaining for Little Fox, the maiden he had set his heart on for a mate.

Edward seized the shears and reached for a sheep. After a tribesman helped him get the woolly animal positioned, he gave the shears a vicious clip. The ewe uttered a beseeching bleat. A red stain began to spread across her belly. For a moment rage blinded Michael. He jerked the shears from Edward's hand and held the sharp points menacingly before the stunned youth's eyes -- so near Edward dared not move to release the ewe.

"You are shearing a sheep, not skinning a buffalo," Michael stormed.

The workers began to edge away. It was not good to make

the village leader's son look foolish. What were they to do? They were in disfavor at the village. They could not go whining back. Their only choice was rush to the defense of their leader's son.

Michael, still holding the shears, retreated until his back was against the corral rails. A pack of camp dogs, smelling the fresh blood, began to whine and bark. One leaped the corral fence and the others followed. A ram gave a dog a butt, knocking it to the ground. The dog snarled and lunged at the ram.

Another dog clamped its jaws on the neck of the wounded ewe. The workers stopped to watch, fascinated by the violent encounter. Michael dropped the shears, pushed through the workers and beat the dogs off. The terror-stricken corralled sheep, rushed from one side of the enclosure to the other. The fence, not strongly built, began to give away. A section fell. The flock raced through the opening, the barking dogs close on their heels. Without sheep to shear there was nothing for the workmen to do. They quickly departed leaving Michael holding the wounded ewe.

Marcus Whitman came running from the mission house. Little David Malin, his short legs flying, raced to keep up. Near the shearing corral they slowed to a walk. Whitman surveyed the scene and grimaced. David Malin pointed a finger at the one shorn ewe that stood alone in the far pasture, bleating pitifully.

"Father! The poor thing is crying. It's cold and naked. We must take it inside by the stove and keep it warm."

"No, no! It's all right," Whitman assured the boy. "By winter she'll have a new coat."

Marcus Whitman grimly sized up the situation. "I should have known Tiloukaikt made the agreement to supply workers with mischief in mind," he said to Michael. "He was entirely too agreeable. Let's repair the corral and get the sheep back inside."

While Michael and the Sager brothers worked on the corral, the older girls and David ran to chase off the dogs and round up the scattered flock. Whitman strode toward the Indian village. Tiloukaikt was not going to get away with his scurvy trick. One way or another the sheep had to be sheared.

All night Michael tossed and turned, dreading the day ahead. Awakening sleepy and depressed, he walked slowly toward the shearing corral where a group of Cayuse workers waited. He stopped, appalled at what he saw. The workers were all women. Recovering his aplomb, he walked forward to greet them as though they had been expected. As he glanced around the group of round shiny faces, he was astonished to see Little Fox, the maiden Edward Tiloukaikt fancied and hoped to make his mate. Her merry dark eyes seemed to send a message. "Unlike Edward, I will not make trouble but will do the best job I can."

Michael's heart gave a painful beat. She was much too delicate to shear sheep. The thought of her being forced into a lifetime of drudgery as Edward Tiloukaikt's mate made him physically ill. The first time he saw her was at the gristmill. When he took the bag of grain she held out, their hands touched. A tingling sensation shot through every nerve in his body. From that day on he thought of little else but lovely doe-eyed, Little Fox. How could he keep his mind on sheep shearing with her so near?

However, the sheep shearing went well. Accustomed to hard labor and performing unwholesome tasks, the women quickly caught on. One sheep after another was shorn until at nightfall only a handful of unclipped animals remained in the corral. Michael worked along with the womenfolk, shearing sheep for sheep with the best worker of the lot who turned out to be Little Fox. After every shorn sheep she turned free she gave him a grin. The day Michael had dreaded was one of pure joy.

Little Fox's industry spurred the other workers to do their best. As dusk fell and the bundles of wool were tied and placed in a neat pile, Michael thanked the workers one by one, the last, Little Fox. Much to his own astonishment, he reached out and clasped her hand. She smiled and quickly turned away. No one appeared to notice, but Michael knew that before the night was out everyone in the Cayuse village would know the mission boy's heart yearned for the maiden, Little Fox.

Late into the night Michael sat in front of his tipi lodge

reliving the day. Little Fox! Little Fox! The name kept running through his mind. He groaned. He had to stop thinking unthinkable thoughts. He had no way of gaining any mate. He had nothing to offer a maiden's parents except two horses, a black mare and a black and white patched pony, both of which he had to keep hidden from the eyes of the horseman, Buffalo Horn, who ruled the rich grasslands on the lower Umatilla. Even after a period of two years Buffalo Horn adamantly insisted they had been stolen from his herd. A Cayuse man, especially one like Buffalo Horn, never forgot an injury to his pride or the face of a horse that had once been part of his herd.

Michael heaved a sigh. He rolled up in his sleeping robe and closed his eyes. He had to be ready for another trying day. In the morning he had to finish the shearing and then begin harvesting the spring crop of grass. Missionary Whitman also had bargained with Tiloukaikt to supply a hay cutting crew. Surely the Cayuse leader would not send Little Fox and the women again.

The following day Tiloukaikt and the sub-leader, Feathercap, came to see to the division of the wool. The agreement was that one sheep pelt out of four was to go to the villagers. Tiloukaikt demanded more. Whitman would not bend.

"First let us get the hay harvest in," the missionary argued. He had envisioned trouble and was prepared. He had John Sager bring a scythe. He demonstrated how it worked, cutting a wide swath in the waist-high grass. Tiloukaikt scowled. He pointed at the long curved blade and uttered a string of unintelligible words. "What does he say?" Whitman asked Michael.

"He says his people clip the hair of the sheep. They are animals. That is all right. Now you ask them to clip the hair of Mother Earth. You make Mother Earth naked like the sheep. That is not good. You hurt Mother Earth."

What Michael did not tell Whitman was that Tiloukaikt ended by saying, "You kill grasses -- you kill horses. No more horses -- no more Cayuses. Cayuse people no let happen." The tone of voice made goose bumps rise on Michael's skin.

VI

***There is no death! The stars go down to rise upon some
other shore . . .***
John L. Mc Creery, 1835-1906

The crack of rifle shots and pounding hooves of the es-
caping killer's mount shattered the stillness of the night. Barking dogs, shouts of alarm, frightened hee-haws of mules had everyone within hearing distance bolting out of wagons and shelters, running with their fire arms toward the sounds of violence.

The first one to arrive at the Jennings' camp was a red-
headed, half-dressed man named Short, followed closely by his
skinny, sharp-faced wife. Short's flaming hair rose above his
head like a tent, his equally brilliant beard lay in a mat against
his face. He pulled up and looked wildly around.

"What the blinkety-blank is all the commotion about?"
he demanded. He saw the still, draped form of Pascoe and fell
silent.

Edward Bryant, who had camped across the creek, arrived on the run, carrying a rifle. He saw the body and stopped to
uncover his head. He glanced around the circle of pale faces and
grimaced. "How terrible, a tragedy coming this soon. Is it the
little black-skinned man?"

Joe grimly nodded.

"You suppose the Mormons . . . ?"

"I don't suppose a thing," Joe retorted. "Forget that Mor-
mon rumor. Why should they sneak in and select a black person
to kill? Doesn't make sense."

"I tol' yuh the mixin' of races was no good." Dad Wall,
pushing his two sleepy sons before him, came to peer down at
the corpse. The sight of Wall made Joe furious. "You and your
narrow-minded prejudices, maybe you had something to do with
this."

Wall fell back into the gathering crowd. "What's the matter with yuh, anyhow? I ain't killed nobody. I'se a church goin' citizen. I'm surprised anybody'd think I'd do murder. What 'bout him?" He jerked a thumb toward Macon Laird. "Who had a better chance ta murder this black fella? He even talks funny. Maybeso, he's a scoundrel on the run from the law."

"Get out of here, all of you," Joe shouted. "This is a matter for the law, not you buzzards."

Muttering to themselves, the gathering drifted away leaving Laird and the Jennings family to mourn by themselves over their lost member. The quiet that fell over camp was almost as unnerving as the clamor of the crowd. Everyone was too stunned to speak or seek the relief of sleep. Tildy finally suggested they take turns in keeping watch over the body. For a long while she sat with Laird. The handsome man's face was pale and lined with grief. In a way she was surprised the man was so bereft.

How could he have become so attached to the small black man who he only had known a few months? It did not diminish her sympathy, rather it made Laird more human. The British reserve he affected was only a pretence. Tildy had an overwhelming urge to throw her arms around him and comfort him like she would a heartbroken child. She placed a hand on his arm, then abruptly retreated to the wagon. "Get hold of yourself," she muttered beneath her breath. "Don't mother the man. He may misunderstand." She tied the wagon flap, blocking Laird from view.

At daybreak Joe saddled Blaze and cantered toward Independence for the marshal. He found the lawman still in bed. Grumbling about the early hour and the troubles wagon trains caused, the marshal slid into his trousers, pinned the badge of his office to his shirt, buckled on his gun belt and shouted for his horse. The ride to camp was made in silence. At the murder site he examined the corpse and gave the grounds a cursory inspection. "'Pears ta me it's jest one dead Nigra," he finally observed.

"What do you mean, just one dead Nigra?" Laird protested. "He was a human being, a talented, loyal friend and companion whose life was snuffed out for no reason."

The marshal sniffed. "Young fella, yuh should pick yer travelin' company with more care. Folks in these parts don't take ta Nigras. Thet's a plain fact." He spit a stream of tobacco juice and wiped his whiskers.

"You mean you don't give a damn about Negroes and won't lift a hand to find the murderer," Laird retorted.

"Don't get testy, young fella, I could haul yuh in fer suspicion. I see the body. It's sure enuff been stabbed. No murder weapon. Motive's anyone's guess. It's my 'pinion some folk in this wagon train has a dislike fer Nigras. Anyhow, I shouldn't even be talkin' to yuh. This here's outta my jurisdiction. Yer outside the city limits. It's a wagon train problem." He swung into the saddle and spurred his mount away.

The marshal's attitude did not surprise Joe. Unless border lawmen outright saw a crime committed or had sworn witnesses, they didn't get involved. "He's right. It's our problem. I'll notify the train captain; you can make arrangements for Pascoe's burial."

With Tildy's help, Macon prepared a makeshift shroud. Then he hitched a team to the buckboard and drove toward town in search of a coffin. When Macon returned, he and Joe dug a grave near the grove where Pascoe had spent his final hours. More than fifty people gathered at the burial site. Some came willingly, others reluctantly. A few felt it their duty to attend; most were simply curious.

The wagon train officers appeared. Although this had been the day the train was scheduled to leave, Colonel Russell and Governor Boggs delayed the departure. They decided it was necessary to show official respect for the first wagon train member to lose his life on the long trek west.

Reverend Josephus Cornwall made the burial impressive by conducting a proper graveside service. In ponderous tones befitting a cathedral, he committed Pascoe's soul to the great beyond. The reverend concluded with a beseeching prayer. Holding his hands aloft, he requested Supreme guidance for all those who were about to hit the trail into "this land filled with wild beasts, savages and violent storms."

Still incensed over Joe's inference he had something to do with Pascoe's murder, after the service Dad Wall insisted an inquest be held into Pascoe's mysterious death. Governor Boggs, as chairman responsible for establishing rules of conduct, conferred with Lawyer J. Quinn Thornton. After lengthy deliberation with Wall standing nearby protesting his innocence, Governor Boggs announced the man known as Pascoe died at the hand of person unknown."

The decision did not please everyone. Short, the man with flaming hair was incensed. "If this is the way we'er goin' ta look inta killin's on the trail, God help us. Thieves an' killers'll go 'bout business as if it was open season."

Dad Wall was irate also. "I say we git ta the bottom this," he screeched. "It ain't right not ta examine thet Nigra's pardner. What's he doin' here, anyways? Who knows but what he's a up ta no good. The British want Oregon Territory as bad as we'uns. Fer sure this galoot's British as kin be."

Short and Wall were shouted down. Overhead dark clouds threatened a storm. "The matter is settled," Governor Boggs declared. The onlookers cheered and ran for their campsites to escape the rain that came pelting down.

The Jennings party was even more pensive than the previous night. The fresh grave at the edge of the grove was a somber reminder of the perils that could strike unexpectedly. Tildy, her eyes dim with tears, put together a meager meal which was eaten in silence. Afterward, Granddad, weary from the day's tension, excused himself and disappeared into the covered wagon. Soon Tildy also said good-night to disappear in the second wagon.

For a long while Laird and Joe continued to sit by the dying campfire. Joe was sick at heart. The journey they looked forward to with joy and excitement had started with a horrendous nightmare. The futileness of the murder enraged him. Why was this innocent man the victim of such an unfeeling, needless crime? What possibly could have been the motive? Surely no one in the train hated Negroes so intensely they would kill? Perhaps it was not an intentional racial killing. Pascoe just happened to be in the way. The intruder could have been after Macon Laird's gold.

Or was the killer someone who knew of his own good fortune, someone intent on squaring the score for Hawk Beak? Before the arrival of Macon and Pascoe, he had occupied the tent. Was the killer unaware of the change of occupants and meant the knife for him? The thought sent a cold chill racing up Joe's spine.

He reviewed every detail of the previous night. In his mind's eye he saw Pascoe nestled in his blankets, the Hawken carefully laid beside him. It was obvious he was guarding the tent, but from whom? Only armed with a short-bladed knife, the intruder meant to make a silent killing. What happened to the murder weapon? "Ah!" Macon Laird had hurled it onto the grove. Why in the world did he do that?

Joe was jerked from the brooding thoughts by hoofbeats that announced riders on the road west. This time Laird took a rifle to step into the darkness, but there was no need for alarm. The gangly Wall youths cantered into the light and swung down.

"We came to say how troubled we are about the small black man," the older youth said. "He was such a cheerful dodger. Jest lookin' at him grin made a fella feel good."

"Thank you," Macon said. "He liked you chaps, too."

"Sit a while," Joe invited. "What handle do you boys go by?"

"I'm Robin and this's Roy. On a number of things we don't exactly see eye to eye with Pa -- Nigras fer instance."

They sat and talked aimlessly. Suddenly Robin blurted, "Yuh don't suppose those fellas that spooked us a couple of nights ago killed the black man?"

"Did you get a good look at them?" Macon asked.

"Nah! We was so fussed we wouldn't've recognized our own kin."

The two youths got up to leave. Robin turned to Joe. "If yuh need a hand to take the place of the Nigra, I'd be pleased to have work. I kin drive, take care of stock an' hep 'round camp. Pa has enough mouths to feed without mine, an' there's still Roy to manage the chores."

"Splendid!" Joe enthused "You can start first thing in the morning."

"That settles one problem," Macon said as the two boys galloped away.

"Yes, but you still have to figure out your problem, don't you?" Joe grimly asked.

"What do you mean?"

Joe seized Macon by the arm. "Governor Boggs was wrong, wasn't he? Pascoe's death did not come by the hand of person unknown. You know who did it. He was after your gold, wasn't he? Don't give me that innocent look. Your actions betrayed you. You recognized the murder weapon. You were afraid it would reveal what you are. Otherwise, why would you conceal incriminating evidence by throwing it away?"

Macon shook himself free. "Don't be absurd. You're talking complete nonsense."

VII

The scene of "catching up," as the yoking and attaching of the oxen to the wagons is called in emigrant phraseology, is one of great bustle and confusion.

Edwin Bryant, 1846

At first streak of dawn the train bugler blew wake-up call. "Hook up! Hook up!" Drugged with sleep, campers crawled from blankets to start campfires. Aroma of wood smoke, frying bacon and pan bread; crack of whips, bray of mules; bellow of cattle, shouts of teamsters and creak of rolling wagon wheels would become familiar smells and sounds in the months ahead.

Shortly after daybreak, Robin Wall appeared to help Tildy with breakfast while Macon and Joe corralled the livestock and harnessed the teams. Although Joe had planned well ahead, departure was delayed by overlooked details. The rented buckboard had to be returned to the local stable. One water barrel wasn't secure. A brake would not release. A cracked king pin needed replacing. It was after nine o'clock when the Jennings' wagons rolled away from the grove. Robin drove the four-span team of one wagon; Macon followed with the second. Joe, riding Blaze, trailed behind, herding the loose livestock.

It appeared all of Independence was on the move. According to rules framed by Governor Boggs' organizing committee, wagons would march in two parallel lines so if danger threatened they quickly could be formed into a square corral. The vigorously debated rules of the road were ignored.

Teamsters, inexperienced and flustered, guided teams and wagons willy-nilly onto the track, one following the other. The thick dust and confusion sent the little worked drayage animals rearing and snorting. Two wagons collided. A dog was run over. While limping away it narrowly missed getting run over again. A screaming child ran to rescue the injured pet. Startled by the commotion, the already skittish loose stock, bolted. Back and forth through the wagons they went, finally scattering in all directions. Riders frantically galloped in pursuit.

Gradually, a semblance of order took place. Like an elongated snake, the wagon train unraveled and took shape. In the distant morning haze, the lead wagons twisted and turned, marking the route some two miles away. The trailing wagons, undulating into the dips to rise again, cut a muddy track through the fresh spring prairie grass. As distant wagons turned broadside, Joe understood why they were called prairie schooners. They glided along, cutting through green ridges of landscape like sailing ships forging against the swells of a moderate sea.

Joe breathed a sigh. It was good to be on the trail. The long stay in civilization somehow had dulled his senses, made him feel inept. He was comfortable in the open prairies, the high mountains -- away from the hustle and bustle of the city where men committed heinous crimes like the killing of Pascoe. He was anxious to get to Oregon and see Bithiah. Perhaps Sandy and Tildy would join with them in a double wedding.

Ah! Tildy! The death of Pascoe had given the poor girl the shock of her life. He hoped it would not ruin the trip for her. And what of Macon Laird? He must feel terrible. For certain the killer had mistakenly killed Pascoe instead of him.

Other unsavory thoughts came to mind. Was he heading for a showdown over his recently acquired fortune? Anyone who knew Hawk Beak would know to whom the big bay had belonged. Then there was Michael Two Feathers. If his brother came riding up in buckskins and feathers on his colorful Appaloosa, train members would panic. Already they were scared half to death of encountering Indians. Some crazy like Dad Wall was apt as not to shoot him on sight.

Joe gave Blaze a frustrated kick and galloped ahead to turn a straying heifer back into the herd. He had not left his worries in Independence. They rode the trail with him every step of the way.

VIII

It was lonesome, the leaving . . . . You know how you feel
when you lose kindred and friends through sickness — death.
You do not care if you die.

Wetatonmi, Nez Perce

Death also had come to the mission in far-off Waiilatpu.
Joseph Finley died holding the hand of his close friend, Andrew
Rodgers, whose blonde hair prompted the Cayuse to call him
Hushus Muk Muk -- Yellow Head. For a long moment after the
man's spirit departed, his friends stood by the still figure. He
looked so peaceful they almost could hear him say, "Thou shalt
be gathered into thy grave in peace," for near the end he frequently quoted the Scriptures.

In a voice that quavered and nearly broke, Narcissa
Whitman softly began to sing, "Ah! Lovely Appearance of
Death!" Andrew Rodgers joined in. The touching refrain carried to the gathering of Cayuse outside. An elder, holding his
hands up to Father Sky, said a prayer. The Great Mysterious had
taken Hushus Muk Muk's friend to the other side.

Reverend Spalding, who was on a visit from his Lapwai
Nez Perce mission, preached the funeral sermon. Afterward the
body was carried to the grave dug at the foot of the hill behind
the mission. Finley was laid to rest not far from the grave of
Alice Clarissa, the Whitmans' little daughter who seven years
previously had drowned in the Walla Walla River. Joseph Finley
was the first white male to be interred in the mission cemetery.

Soon after the burial service, Andrew Rodgers told the
Whitmans he was leaving Waiilatpu. "The torturous ordeal of
watching my friend and companion die has left me physically
and spiritually drained," he said, his voice hoarse with grief.

Michael Two Feathers sat in front of his tipi lodge moodily watching the schoolteacher leave, his thoughts as dark as the

evening shadows that cloaked the mission grounds. The sadness of the day and the departure of his friend made his heart ache. He also had a sudden urge to get away, but where could he go? He was trapped like a fly in a spider web. He had become so involved with mission affairs the missionary family considered him one of their own.

As the Whitmans gained confidence in him and the burden of their responsibilities increased, they turned more and more to him for help, especially where Cayuse villagers were concerned. He even had been asked to be present when Joseph Finley took his last breath, probably because in his latter days Joseph often spoke for the need of brotherhood. "Behold, how pleasant it is for brethren to dwell together in unity," he liked to quote the Psalm at the dinner table.

It was gratifying to have the confidence and affection of the Whitmans, but it was also a strain. He did not wish to be beholden to them or anyone else. He had hopes and dreams of his own. He once had attempted to express himself to the Whitmans, but words failed him. They kindly nodded and made appropriate remarks, but there was a lack of understanding.

They did not know the Indian mind. He could see this from the way Narcissa Whitman reared her adopted children. She scrupulously kept them away from the local village youngsters. Never once had she entered the Cayuse camp. It was her firm belief Indian lodges were filled with infectious vermin.

"Bringing children up in a heathen land, where every influence tends to degrade rather than elevate, requires no small measure of faith and patience, as well as great care and watchfulness," she wrote to her folks in the east.

One evening after prayers, Marcus Whitman surprised Michael by motioning for him to wait -- he would walk with him to his tipi lodge. On the way the missionary explained his plans for an academy that would serve all peoples of the Northwest. "To make this possible, we need teachers who understand the students," he told Michael. "This is where you come in. There isn't an Indian student on the plateau more qualified than you. Before he left I discussed this with Andrew Rodgers and he agrees. You've learned all you can at the mission school. To keep you here any longer would be a waste of your time.

"The next step is an academy," Marcus Whitman continued. "If you are willing to continue your education, we will send you east. A missionary group is leaving soon. They gladly will take you and introduce you to the Mission Board. The Mission Board wants young men like you to develop their talents. They are certain to place you in a good preparatory school."

The missionary did not press Michael for an answer and if he had, Michael would have been too stunned to respond. The idea of traveling alone or with a missionary group beyond the River of Many Canoes, frightened him -- to live and go to school among white strangers was beyond his comprehension. Several weeks passed before Whitman mentioned the matter again. "The missionaries I spoke of are leaving for the east next week. If you like the idea I expressed, I'll ask them to take you along."

Michael still had no answer. He could not envision living far from his homeland. He had become accustomed to the regime at the Waiilatpu mission -- the daily routine; morning prayers, breakfast, chores, field work, midday meal, more prayers, supper and nightly Bible study. Almost from one minute to the next one knew what was going to happen. If he chose to go east he would have to fend for himself. The thought of being alone in the unknown was almost more than he could contemplate.

Then there was his brother, Joe. Surely, he would come to Waiilatpu this spring. He would not disappoint him again. Going east with Joe would be a far better experience than traveling with a group of long-faced preachers. Joe would guide him, show him how he should act and what he should do. He just had to turn Missionary Whitman down.

In the evening as he sat in front of his tipi lodge, Michael again worried over the torturing problem. Swallows began their nightly sweep across the compound. The lights of the mission

house came on, one by one. He thought of the orphaned children
the missionary couple had taken in and given a home. They were
probably settling down to the assignments given by Mother and
Father Whitman: sewing, reading, memorizing Scriptures -- comfortable and protected from the outside world.

Michael groaned. There was no point in feeling sorry for
himself. He had to make up his mind -- should he go east with
the missionary men or should he not? He wished someone he
trusted would give him advice. The next morning Michael saddled
the horse he had borrowed from Grandfather Lone Wolf and rode
toward his former Nez Perce home in Lapwai. There was one
person he trusted above everyone, Uncle Vision Seeker, a mysti-
cal, wise man who was viewed with awe and respect by everyone in the Nez Perce homeland.

Except for a tint of gray in his hair and a few more crin-
kly lines at the corners of his eyes, Vision Seeker appeared little
changed. As usual, he listened attentively to what Michael had
to say. For a long while he remained silent, trying to imagine
living in the land the hairy faces called New England. For once
his mind was a void. He never had the desire to go to this land so
he never had given it much thought. That did not mean this youth
whose blood was half white also should avoid it. Perhaps it would
be good for the young man to see how Boston people lived. There
were many good people there. Look at the boy's father. Yes, it
probably was wise the son of Little Ned should learn of his Boston ancestors, but Michael, himself, should be the one to make
the choice.

"Missionary Whitman's tongue is straight," Vision Seeker
finally said. "But it is you who must decide if what you do is
right. What does your heart say when you tell it you are leaving
your homeland for this country of the hairy faces? Does your
heart tell you to go or stay? If your heart says go, ask a second
question. What will you do with what you will learn? Will this
knowledge make you a better person? Will it help you do good
for your people? Perhaps you go because it makes you proud --

puffs you with importance like a bullfrog. Knowledge matters little if not wisely used."

Vision Seeker paused to study his nephew. There were many seeds of value within this boy just waiting to flourish. If only he could help make them take root and spring into life. This young man had the potential to become a great leader, a leader who could guide his people through the troubled times they were certain to face.

Vision Seeker thought back to the day the lad caught his first glimpse of Mother Earth. It was in Buffalo Country. Snow was on the ground. He was taking his sister, Raven Wing, to Lone Wolf's hunting camp on Sun River. Raven Wing's pain became so great they were forced to stop. Under a canopy of blue without a cloud marring Father Sky, the miracle took place. A pink head appeared, and then the tadpole-like body. He cut the umbilical cord with his skinning knife and held the protesting child up for the mother to see -- the only witnesses to the miracle were Raven Wing, himself and two shaggy Nimapu ponies.

The baby had grown to manhood. He was considering entering another world as strange and frightening as the one he faced when he first drew breath. At birth parents were there to guide and comfort him. This new world he would face alone, no loved ones to watch over him. He had to turn to a greater power. Suddenly, Vision Seeker knew what counsel to give.

"Son, The Great Mysterious placed us on Mother Earth. He expects us to do the best we can with what we have. Whether you stay in your homeland or travel far away, remember the wishes of The Great Mysterious. Every day make time to clear your mind of all thoughts, somewhere quiet and peaceful. Humbly seek the advice of The Great Mysterious. Listen well. He will tell you the path to follow." Vision Seeker fell silent. From the vague look on Michael's face he knew he had been of little help.

Vision Seeker was right. Michael's brain was in a whirl. He didn't know what advice his uncle had given and was reluctant to ask him to explain. He had received years of mission school instruction, yet felt unlearned and inept before this man who spoke words that seemed to come from some invisible power.

He thanked Vision Seeker and numbly wandered about the valley, mulling over every word his uncle had said. First, he went to the pasture to see his black and white patched pony that had to be kept hidden from Buffalo Horn, the acquisitive horseman who reigned on the lower Umatilla. Michael wrapped his arms around the silken neck and scratched between the velvety ears, acts the animal loved. How he wished he could forget everything -- get on the Appaloosa pony he called Magpie and ride beyond the horizon, leaving his troubles behind.

The thought was so strong he leapt on the pony's back. Riding like the wind, he went up the valley and on into the hills. A flock of blackbirds flew out of a patch of bulrushes and a jackrabbit dashed across the trail. High above a hawk circled in and out of the clouds. Otherwise, he was alone in a place as quiet and peaceful as Mother Earth's living things would allow.

Michael pulled Magpie to a halt. Now was the time to put Uncle Vision Seeker's advice into effect. He dropped the bridle reins, slid down from the pony and walked over to sit under a pine. He attempted to clear his mind of every single thought. As hard as he tried he could not make his mind obey. Distracting sounds came from everywhere: the beat of his heart, a grasshopper scraping its wings, Magpie's tail swishing at a fly, a breeze rustling through the brush and grasses . . . . Why don't I give up and leave -- go back to Waiilatpu, he thought. I'm wasting my time.

Not until he returned to the valley and was turning Magpie out to pasture did he realize The Great Mysterious had spoken. "Return to Waiilatpu!" The message had been strong and clear. Did it also mean he should take the path of the white man -- make the trip east with the missionaries? He sought the answer but his mind remained blank.

IX

*On Friday last, we caught up to the main caravan . . . We find
ourselves under the vigorous captaincy of Colonel William H.
"Owl" Russell . . .*

Tamsen Donner, near the Kansas River, 1846

The wagon train's first day's journey was short. Early in
the afternoon Train Master Colonel Russell ordered teamsters to
circle for night encampment. Upon hearing the order Edwin
Bryant, who rode out front, whipped his horse around to gallop
furiously back. "Why stop here?" he shouted. "We've barely
covered six miles! At this rate the crossing'll take forever."

In spite of protests, Russell had the wagons corralled. The
livestock were turned out to graze. Campfires began to flare up
and preparations were made for the evening meal. Russell walked
back and forth, slapping his boot top with a riding crop. It was
obvious he was unsure of himself; undoubtedly this was his first
command of a convoy of civilian wagons.

That evening Russell announced the wagon train was too
unwieldy. After lengthy discussions, it was decided to divide the
column into four sections; each section was to have its own captain, assistants to the captain and helpers with varied duties. Joe
Jennings was among those chosen train captain.

Initially, the breakup of the wagon train produced good
results. The following day the column traveled sixteen miles.
The flush of success did not last. Two days later the heavy ground,
saturated with rain water, held the wagon train to one mile. The
next few days also were slow -- twelve miles and ten miles. On
May 18th the caravan remained encamped in order that Alphonso
Boone, a grandson of Daniel Boone, and his family, who wished
to join the train, could catch up. To everyone's disgust, they
never appeared. Instead, a party of nine wagons from Illinois

rolled into camp. They belonged to James Reed and George and Jacob Donner. Each family had three heavily loaded wagons. George Donner, Jacob's older brother, led the small column driving a double team of oxen. In his retinue were five saddle horses, a herd of milk and beef cows, a dog and countless youngsters.

With a free day on the trail, almost everyone was on hand to greet the newcomers. Poorer members of the wagon train were overwhelmed by the display of riches. "Kin yuh 'magine? The Reeds hev built-in beds, a built-in stove an' cabinets in what they call their live-in wagon!" an awed onlooker exclaimed. "'Twouldn't surprise me if'n they hev a built-in outhouse, too."

The travelers later learned the second Reed wagon contained almost nothing but fine foods and liquor which caused a good deal of head shaking and tongue wagging. These people had the riches of Midas. What possessed them to leave comfortable homes to make the long torturous journey across the continent? What did they have to gain?

A couple of old timers familiar with trekking through the wild terrain of the western plains, looked the wagons over and shook their heads. These folks had wealth but lacked good common sense. Heavy wagons, even without loads, were apt to sink into the sandy and boggy soils that were certain to be encountered on the trail.

These old timers' fears were well grounded. Seventy-four days later the Donner party would take leave of the proven Oregon/California Trail in favor of Hastings' Cutoff, an untested track. The teamsters encountered narrow passages which would not allow the heavy wagons to pass. They had to be winched to the top of steep canyon walls. Slowed by the difficult terrain, the Donner train party arrived at the Sierra Mountains to founder in the heavy early winter snow. Forty-five members of the party perished there, including George Donner and his wife Tamsen.

In the meantime, weather and terrain slowed travel on many sections of the trail. On May 20th eight miles were covered, on May 21st six miles. Progress was hindered that day by a treacherous stream crossing and the tardy arrival of the Boone party. The tortoise-like pace didn't bother some. After an early camp a group of men organized a target shoot. The winner, Brown from Lexington, Kentucky, was toasted with numerous rounds of whiskey that came from Reed's richly stocked live-in wagon.

The raucous hilarity was heard all over camp. Sober-sided families frowned on the merrymaking. The following morning thirteen wagons broke away to set out on their own. Friends attempted to dissuade the small company. The route now neared the land of the Pawnee who had an alarming reputation as raiders and thieves. Also, there was an Indian war of sorts taking place. The Pawnee had recently attacked a Kansas village in which a number of people were slain and their lodges burned.

Edwin Bryant became a familiar figure to the Jennings party. He never forgot the time Joe, with Pascoe's help, pulled his wagon from the mud. Frequently, he rode alongside and spoke with whomever was driving. He confessed he was an ex-news-paper man and was keeping a journal. "I'm really concerned about the tardiness of our travel," he said one day. "If we don't watch out winter will catch us in the high mountains. The way the people are consuming their provisions, they'll be lucky to get that far. Most of these folks act like they were on one big picnic. They eat and drink whatever takes their fancy. Already several are ill with fever and bilious complaints."

Joe listened to Bryant with concern. He especially was worried about Granddad. For days he had not looked well.

"I take an interest in medicine," Bryant continued. "I believe most of our ills can be cured by natural remedies, I mean herbs and such provided by nature. The sicknesses we are expe-riencing were contracted on the trail. A local disease means there should be a local cure. For instance, the inner bark of the alder is good for digestive problems. Choke cherry gives relief from cramps, sumac relieves dysentery . . ." Bryant went on to list a variety of plants and their medicinal properties.

Joe took a new look at his responsibilities as train captain. His main concerns had been to see that wagons and live-stock left on time, were safe on the trail and securely encamped at night. But that was not enough. He had to become more sensitive to the people's needs. The threat of sickness and depletion of provisions were making everyone uneasy and quarrelsome and they had not been a month on the road.

Macon Laird was also a constant worry. What if Pascoe's killer were on his trail? From the way the Britisher acted Joe was certain this was the case. Macon never left camp without his Hawken and slept with it by his side. Often he was up before the break of day, prowling around the outskirts of camp.

Then there was Tildy -- all of a sudden she seemed withdrawn. Her lilting laugh and cheery smile were less frequent. She did not linger around the campfire, slipping into her wagon as soon as supper things were cleaned up and put away. Were the strains of the trail getting her down? Perhaps she was worried over Granddad's health.

That evening, while they made camp, Joe studied each member of his party. Granddad sat on a blanket-padded log looking old and pale. Macon and Tildy went about their chores in silence. Only Robin Wall appeared himself. "How is the Wall camp making out?" Joe asked cheerfully, attempting to brighten the atmosphere.

"The folks're good enough," Robin replied. "They're tired of pokin' along, is the main complaint. Pa's downright nervous. He didn't bring near enough grub. Not the right kind, neither. The bacon's maggoty. The barrel of beans has got weevils. Don't know what we'd do if I didn't work for you folks."

"Well, we'll just have to do the best we can, won't we?" Joe said, disappointed in his effort to bring cheer to the camp.

#

On May 26th the caravan camped on the eastern bank of the Big Blue. Bryant wrote in his journal, "Big Blue is a stream about one hundred yards wide at this point. Recent rains have it swollen and fast of current. Much debris floats on its surface.

The advice of train leaders is that we wait several days for the waters to recede before attempting a crossing."

Early in the afternoon Tildy gathered up the dirty clothes and carried them to the water's edge. She dropped the bundle of clothes on the river bank and began to scrub. Joe was right. She started the trip with high spirits but now they were subdued. Neither the bumpy, dusty, tiresome travel nor Granddad's illness were to blame. A personal crisis she faced affected her whole being. Every waking hour thoughts she never before had possessed rose up to torment her. She knew Joe and perhaps Granddad, too, noticed her distress but it was something she had to work out by herself.

Soon, all along the river bank campfires flared up. Kettles, tubs and all other equipment necessary for washing soiled clothes and linens cluttered the edge of the stream. A stray dog, believing the women wanted to play, romped from one pile of clothes to the next, snatching up a garment, dragging it a ways, then dropping it when shouts threatening mayhem poured down on the playful animal. Running to the next washerwoman's bundle, it joyfully repeated its antics until a scattering of well-aimed rocks came hurtling its way. A youth ran to get a rifle to shoot the frolicsome creature but Joe interceded. "Save your ammunition for more worthy targets," he ordered.

While the women washed, the men gathered in a meeting to decide what punishment should be meted out to those who broke wagon train rules. Speeches, wrangling and voting carried on until the assembly proceedings recessed at nightfall.

The next morning the meeting resumed with a motion to make the officers responsible for the safety and welfare of the train. Under this motion they could be charged with tyranny or neglect of duty by any individual who wished to register a complaint. The motion was voted on and carried. At this point all officers resigned. Bryant alertly called for a new vote. After much arguing, a second vote was taken and the motion defeated. The officers were reelected by acclamation.

After the matter was settled, there were those who still weren't satisfied. To hide his disgust, Joe saddled Blaze and rode out of camp. He came upon an old Indian trail. Fresh hoof prints signaled that horsemen had passed recently. Blaze confirmed this. The horse's ears pointed straight up the trail. At the top of the ridge, outlined against the sky, three Indian men sat their horses, impassively watching the approach of horse and rider.

Joe pulled the rifle from the boot then quickly pushed it back. It was no time to act warlike. He clasped his hands together in the sign of peace. The nearest rider held his hand up to sweep his index finger across his forehead to signify the brim of a hat.

"Hello, white man," the signal said. The three horsemen turned to disappear behind the ridge. Thoughtfully, Joe reined Blaze toward camp. He had gotten careless. If the Indians had been on the warpath he well could be dead.

X

The crescent moon sheds her pale rays over the dim landscape; the whippoorwill is chanting its lamentations in the neighboring grove; the low and mournful hooting of an owl is heard . . .

Edwin Bryant, 1846

"Watch out!" a youngster screamed. The horse bucked, jumping stiff-legged to the right and then to the left, then pitched over the edge into the river. The swift current pulled horse and rider beneath the surface and swept them away. A dozen men raced to the rescue. Just when it appeared the man and his mount were lost, they bobbed to the surface, the rider clinging to the tail of the horse for dear life.

The lad who had screamed tossed out a length of rope. The drowning man seized it; with spectators urging him to hang on, he was pulled to shore. Downstream the wild-eyed horse struck a bank cluttered with driftwood and frantically clawed its way to safety. A witness wrote down the near tragedy in his journal, the date, May, 28th, 1846.

The following day two members of the California party died: a child of Judge Bowlin and Sarah Keyes, a lady of seventy and mother-in-law to James Reed of the Donner wagons. At the elderly lady's graveside, her daughter Margaret, and granddaughter, Virginia, sobbed as though their hearts would break.

The display of grief and the solemn service conducted by Reverend Josephus Cornwall left Joe indifferent. He studied the bowed heads. Most of these people had yet to understand the difficulties and heartaches incurred in crossing the plains. No matter how well the train was managed, the trail would still take its toll.

The swollen waters of the Big Blue did not recede as the travelers had hoped. Colonel Russell called the wagon train captains together. "We can't wait any longer," he said, snapping his quirt against a boot top. "We've got to chance it. Who'll take the first wagon across?"

"Are yuh crazy?" Short asked, his red hair standing on end. "Yuh saw how the water picked up thet guy an' the horse nearly sendin' them ta kingdom come."

"Yeah! Well, we have to do something. We just can't sit here like bumps on a log," Russell retorted.

"Maybeso, we kin ferry 'em across," a voice in the crowd suggested. "I seen it done afore. I'll tell yuh how it's done."

The idea was seized upon. A party of workers, armed with axes, adzes and a variety of mauls, chisels and other tools, fashioned two large dugouts from thick cottonwood tree trunks. They were fastened side by side, just wide enough to accommodate the wheels of the wagons. Two cables were then attached to the raft, one on either end, to pull it back and forth across the stream. On May 30th the workmen launched the primitive craft they christened *Blue Rover*. By evening nine wagons were safely on the far bank.

The next morning ferry operations came to a complete halt. On edge from their labors, two teamsters began to shout, then pummeled each other with fists and finally drew knives. Robin Wall and Joe seized one combatant and a bystander named Kirkendall, grabbed the other.

"The trials of the trail test the temper and endurance of everyone," Edwin Bryant observed that night in writing up his journal. "Distance covered -- one mile! What is worse, the Big Blue crossing has frittered away four days traveling time."

That evening a quarrel between two families erupted. Passions became aroused nearly to the point of violence. People came from all parts of the camp to harangue. A committee was formed to settle the dispute, but the squabblers refused to submit to arbitration. Shouted curses and threats kept the exhausted travelers awake late into the night.

The next day the Oregon-bound settlers decided to separate from those bound for California. Twenty wagons pulled away to proceed on their own. Robin Wall, driving the Jennings' second wagon, was beside himself.

"What'll we do?" he asked Joe, almost in tears.

The ridiculous situation infuriated Joe. For safety's sake it was wise to remain together, but his obligation was to the Oregon people. "I guess we'll have to pull out, too."

The breakup did nothing to soothe tempers, improve wagon train discipline or speed up travel. After lurching over a particularly hard stretch of track, family heads decided they would remain camped the following day. Disgusted by the delay, Joe mounted Blaze. "Take charge of the wagons for awhile," he ordered Macon Laird. "If I don't get away I'm apt to string a few of these crazies up by their ears."

With alarm, Tildy watched him gallop out of sight. Indian signs had been seen -- one of the main reasons everyone was in such a state. She turned to see Macon Laird's watchful eyes upon her. "I don't like to see him go like this," she said. "What will we do if something should happen?"

"I shouldn't worry. He wouldn't have left if he thought there was danger," Macon assured. He took a protective step toward her, then stopped to pick up an ax and vigorously began to chop firewood, a task usually left for Robin Wall.

"I suppose you're right," Tildy said between chops. "Actually, I don't blame Joe for taking off. Some of these people are impossible. Maybe it's our fault. We have been so tied up with our own problems we haven't attempted to make friends. Will you watch over Granddad for a while?" Tildy asked. "Perhaps by visiting with people I can calm their fears." She hurried away feeling a sense of shame. She had lied to Macon. She couldn't face being alone with him. She had fought against it, but every part of her being yearned for his touch. Along with worries of the trail, this terrible torture had her nerves ready to snap.

As soon as Tildy was out of sight, Macon tossed the ax aside. He knew Tildy had left to avoid being alone with him.

There was an indescribable force pulling on them, drawing them together. Maidens like Tildy, who had led sheltered lives and suddenly found themselves thrust into a man's world, were vulnerable. The only honorable way out was for him to leave -- remove this temptation that sooner or later only could end in disaster. Yes, that is what he would do, but he couldn't slip away. Joe had left him in charge of the wagons. Until he returned it was up to him to keep the camp secure.

Macon picked up his Hawken. It won't help to moon around like a sick calf, he told himself and took a turn around the wagons. He pulled aside the canvas cover to peer in at sleeping Granddad Jennings. He liked the old man. He once had a schoolmaster just like him, a strict but jolly, good-hearted fellow who took students' problems as seriously as if they were his own.

Macon came to the canvas jacket Tildy tossed aside before taking her walk. He carefully folded it and laid it in the wagon where she slept. He glanced in at the bed covers ready to receive her body that night, her soft cotton flannel sleeping garments neatly placed on top. He quickly closed the flap. What was the matter with him? He had no business invading her privacy. As he turned away, a sharp cracking sound shattered the air -- a rifle report. A swarm of blackbirds, in the tulles at the edge of the creek where the travelers had camped, swept overhead.

"Injuns!" a wild voice yelled. A roar of alarm surged through the wagon train. The people's worst fear had come to pass, red savages had surrounded them, prepared to kill and plunder. Men ran to save the stock. Mothers frantically called for their children. Screaming tots raced to hide behind their mother's skirts. A flimsy barricade of boxes and barrels was hastily put together. The assistant train master scurried by. "Take cover!" he shouted needlessly. Macon Laird ran in search of Tildy.

#

An hour's ride from camp an inviting flock of turkeys gobbled in the underbrush. Joe ignored them. He didn't want to bother with them. If he brought meat into camp he wanted it to be large game. Near noon he spotted a band of antelope. He circled behind a ridge to approach from downwind. When he came within rifle range Joe dismounted. He selected a likely looking animal and took aim.

Without warning, the band of antelope darted away, only to wheel about and run directly toward him. He caught the leader in his sights and squeezed the trigger. A series of gunshots rang out. For a moment Joe thought they were echoes of his own rifle's report, but his animal fell and so did three others. Something behind him moved. He swung around. Like a three-eyed monster, three black rifle muzzles stared at him from the underbrush.

#

After leaving Macon, Tildy strolled from one wagon to the next, forcing herself to greet everyone with a smile and a cheery hello, asking them how their day had gone. Most fellow travelers were happy to exchange friendly words. Others voiced their fears, grumbling about the dust, heat, sore feet and threat of Indians. Short, the redhead, was downright rude. "What business is it of yours how our day went?"

His skinny sharp-faced wife piped up. "Tell her ta take her fancy smiles an' la-de-dah ways somewheres else. They hev no place amongst folk thet's tryin' ta follow the path of Grace. Thet thar English feller's her style of folk. Why don't they quit tartin' 'round an' git Reverend Cornwall ta make honest peoples outta therselves? It ain't fittin' ta carry on like they do amongst God fearin' folk."

Tildy gasped. Like a fire doused with a bucket of water, all the bright spirits she had willed herself, turned black. She felt so faint her feet failed her. She stumbled forward to lean against the side of the next wagon.

"Ah! Miss, forgive them for they do not know what they say." Buell, the wagon owner, attempted to soothe the sting. "Good cheer is not always appreciated by all folk, especially when things're not goin' their way."

"Hmph!" Short's skinny wife snorted.

The wagoner's well meant words added fuel to Tildy's smoldering anger. "Nasty minds contain nasty thoughts," she retorted, quoting from Granny Jennings long list of homilies.

Buell chuckled, returning to his work. "That's the stuff, give as good as you got."

Tildy left the Buell wagon feeling somewhat better, but still the Short woman's insidious remarks left their poisonous sting. Thus far she had faced afflictions of the trail well but this . . . She never dreamed something like this would happen. If the Short woman was saying these things who else had the same thoughts?

Tildy's ears burned with indignation. It was so unfair. She gritted her teeth. This scurrilous gossip must never reach Sandy. Hardly had this terrible thought entered her mind when the shot went off. Short, the evil-minded woman's husband, came running from the pasture grounds, waving a smoking rifle. "Injuns! The blasted devils hev stolen my oxen," he shouted.

It was the signal that sent everyone scurrying for cover. The stock was brought in and corralled. The barricades were erected and strengthened. The men primed their weapons and counted their ammunition. When all precautions to protect the camp were taken, the people sat back and waited. One hour went by, two hours -- three hours passed. The sun reached its zenith and started on its way down. "I wish those bloody Injuns'd attack an' git it over with," Short grumbled. "Ho! There're the villainous savages! Cock yer guns an' let 'em hev it."

People who had relaxed, dove back into their hiding places. The clicking of cocking rifles was like a band of crickets suddenly coming to life. A baby cried and was hushed to silence. "Aw! Shucks!" someone uttered in disgust. Down the trail rode Joe Jennings accompanied by a trio of horsemen: a bushy-bearded man and two Indians leading a string of burros loaded with gutted carcasses, their heads and antlers nearly scraping the ground.

"What's the matter?" Joe asked, glancing around at the ranks of armed men. "Stow your guns. These folks are friendly." He dismounted by the Jennings' wagons. With a wave of his arm, he invited his odd companions to step down and make themselves at home. The wagon train members were stunned. Here was their leader consorting with the "red savages" who had stolen Short's oxen and had them surrounded, looking as pleased as can be. A child broke the tension. "Mama! Look! Ain't they funny lookin' people?" she said, pointing at the two Indians.

Joe and the newcomers ignored the commotion they had created. When introduced to Tildy, the bushy-bearded white man doffed his cap, revealing a head as hairless as a freshly laid egg. "'Pon my word, yer sister! She's purty as a newborn fawn," he said, his voice squeaking like a rusty hinge.

"Deacon Walton's the moniker. Knowed yer brother since he was a pup. Innocent as green grass, he was when we first met. Knowed yer father, Little Ned, too. Me an' him stretched many a beaver pelt. The big galoot was the best friend a body could hev. These're me Cheyenne friends, Buffalo Nose an' Walkin' Eagle." Deacon nodded toward the two Indian men.

The solemn-faced Cheyenne lifted their hands in a respectful salute. "We come from Bear Claw's camp on Porcupine Creek, doin' a leetle huntin' an' fishin'," Deacon continued. "Brung yuh some fresh meat, antelope. Best we could do on short notice. I 'spect yuh've hed yer fill of beans an' biscuits an're hankerin' fer a change."

The crowd uttered a grateful murmur, all except Short. "These red devils ran off my oxen. I want 'em back, an' damned quick." He shook his rifle menacingly at the two Cheyenne.

Deacon slapped his cap on. "Oxen're no use ta the Injun," he snapped, his hand dropping to the ax at his belt. "Now, if'n yuh wanta make certain yuh kin come to Bear Claw's village an' look fer yerself. I'll betcha yer critters strayed. Hev yuh looked aroun' yon hill? Beyond is a mighty invitin' patch of high grass.

If yuh need help trackin', perlitely ask Buffalo Nose. He sniffs out buffalo like a bird dog goin' fer a shot down goose."

"I ain't countin' on Injun findin' me oxen," Short growled.

"It's up to you," Joe said. "You better hustle. It'll soon be dark. Robin, please divide the fresh meat among the wagons."

Anxious to get their share, the people dispersed. Short, his flaming mustache twitching, motioned to his wife and went in search of his oxen. He found the animals exactly where the rotund mountain man said to look.

Joe spread blankets on the ground and invited his three guests to sit and take their ease. From a fringed kit bag he withdrew a long-stemmed pipe and a beaded pouch. He filled the pipe with a mixture taken from the pouch. A flaming splinter of wood from the fire served as a match. He took two puffs, passed the pipe to the man called Deacon, who also took two puffs before passing it to the Cheyenne on his left. Only after the pipe was placed back in its buckskin bag did the men speak.

Tildy, who watched from the wagon opening, could not take her eyes off the circle of motley men who chatted back and forth like long lost friends, Joe the most animated of them all. Why was he not like that with her and Granddad? No wonder she understood Macon Laird better than she did her own brother. Macon and she thought much alike. They had been nurtured by a common European culture. After coming west Joe had shed eastern trappings and customs -- adopted the native way of life.

Tildy sighed. Bringing the family together had turned out far differently than she had expected, and what did the future hold? Would she forget all the niceties? Would all the good things they took for granted back east disappear? Look at him. Joe was as comfortable with the paunchy, uncouth lout and the two red men as if they had come from the same womb.

"Oh!" she groaned. Granddad was ill. Her brother was as communicative as a wooden post. Macon Laird was tearing her heart out by the roots . . . . For the first time on the journey Tildy wished she never had left home.

XI

*How smooth must be the language of the whites, when they
can make right look wrong, and wrong like right.*

Black Hawk, Sauk

The journey back to Waiilatpu did not start well for
Michael Two Feathers. As he left Lapwai to turn onto the
Clearwater Trail Tom Hill, the Delaware half-blood, hailed him.
He also was on his way to Waiilatpu. Michael raised his hand in
a brusque greeting. He wanted to be alone with his thoughts.
Besides, he did not like to be seen with Tom Hill.

Hill was a glib-tongued troublemaker. He hated the missionaries and did everything he could to undermine their influence on the Nez Perce. In turn the missionaries disliked him
intensely. Reverend Spalding called him a "debased infidel."
For months Tom Hill had kept Lapwai villagers upset. Now, his
sights were set on creating unrest among the Cayuse. For miles
they rode in silence. Tom Hill finally broke the spell.

"You don't like me, do you?"

"I don't even know you," Michael replied.

"Hmm!" Hill grunted. "But you know about me and do
not like what you hear, is that it?"

"I guess so," Michael mumbled. He did not know how to
answer. It was not like an Indian person to speak in this personal
manner. They continued on in silence. The only break in the
monotonous ride came when a cottontail dashed across the trail.
Hill lifted his rifle and shot the scurrying creature in mid-stride.
He swung down to pick up the bloodied fur and thrust it into a
saddlebag pocket.

Near evening a likely campsite caught Hill's eye. He
reined up. "Why not make camp here for the night?" he asked.
"Water, grass, firewood, everything needed is right here."

Tom skinned and roasted the cottontail, then carefully

sliced the carcass, giving Michael a generous share. Moved by the gesture of good will, Michael began to speak. "They say you do not believe in God, is that true?"

Hill picked his teeth with the point of his skinning knife. "You think I preach against God. It is not God I speak against, it is missionary people. They say their god is the only god. We must accept this god or go to the place they call hell. Do they know the things they preach are true? Did they see heaven or hell with their own eyes? How do they know what they are and what happens there?

"The preaching of the missionaries makes our people troubled. They wonder if they and their ancestors were wrong all these many years. They worshipped those gods who give everything needed to live. Mother Earth always provides food to eat, water to drink, shelter and clothes to wear. Father Sun is always there to give warmth and make the seasons change. The breezes from the four directions clear the air and bring the rains. What more do people need to make life good?

"Think back and see if what I say does not make sense," Hill continued. "Before missionaries came our people were happy and lived together in peace. When the first white men appeared our people became unhappy. They thought these men with white skin had a power greater than they had ever known. They desired this power. In the struggle to get this power our people humbled themselves. They did things their ancestors never would have done.

"They gave away land, women and their freedom. They replaced old gods with the white man's god. They did these shameful things because they wanted to rise in the white man's eyes. Why should we care what white men think? All the hairy faces worry about is themselves. They take what they want and leave what they do not want to the Indian. The white men despise us. They feel Mother Earth would be better with us gone. That is what they intend to do, push us off our lands and take them for themselves."

In spite of the man's unsavory reputation, Michael was deeply affected by what Tom Hill said. He spoke with such intensity and eloquence naive listeners had to be impressed.

"To these people the Indian is no more than an annoying sand flea or mosquito that should be swept away," Tom Hill bitterly continued. "Does Missionary Spalding ask what we want or what we believe? No! Even to the missionary we are without feelings or minds of our own." He viciously poked at the fire with the roasting stick, sending embers shooting skyward like fireflies. "I speak with true tongue, peace now, but only for a while. Soon a man comes bringing death and . . ." Tom Hill fell silent, as if he already had said more than he should.

Although the evening was warm, Michael Two Feathers shivered. He reached for his sleeping robe but it did not help. He inwardly groaned. Why did The Great Mysterious tell him to return to Waiilatpu only to place him in the path of troublemaker, Tom Hill?

When they arrived at the mission compound the next afternoon, little David Malin saw them coming and ran as fast as his short legs could move. "Come quick. Peoples wait for you!" he shouted to Michael, his voice as shrill as the cry of a killdeer.

# # #

Before daybreak Macon Laird made ready to leave. He had argued with himself all night. Was it the right thing to do or was it not? His mind said yes; his heart said no. He hadn't slept a wink. He would be leaving the Jennings short-handed. Joe would have to find someone else to deal with the horses and drive the second wagon.

It was Tildy that made him hesitate. She needed his presence more than did Joe. She had to care for a sick grandfather. He could tell by her wan expression that she feared for his life. Her brother, busy with wagon train affairs, almost totally ignored her. If he left she would have no one to turn to, but it also was too dangerous to stay. Sooner or later the fine thread holding them apart would weaken, then break. He must leave. He packed

LAND WITHOUT A COUNTRY

and went to announce his departure to Joe. Tildy, who had awakened early to tend to Granddad, heard the two men's voices.

"What! You're leaving?" Joe's voice was harsh with weariness and irritation. "We count on you. Besides, this is a rotten time to . . . Pawnee . . ." Joe's words were lost in the morning breeze. Tildy hurriedly dressed, her heart beating in her ears. Macon leaving -- without saying anything to her! The thought made her ill. With Granddad sick abed and Joe acting so strangely, without Macon the trail ahead would be torture. "Aaah!" she moaned. She could not bear it.

Her hair was tangled and dusty but that didn't matter. Tildy clapped a hat on her head, swung down from the wagon and strode toward the men. She had kept quiet too long, accepting everything as meekly as a timid mouse. It was time she put her foot down, had a voice in wagon train affairs. She started to scold only to hold her tongue. The men had stopped arguing. Macon was unsaddling his horse. Somehow, Joe had talked Macon into remaining with the wagon train.

The bugle sounded, followed by the call, "Wake up! Roll out!" Macon put away the horse and went about the morning chores. After a hurried breakfast the column again began to plod along on the Oregon Trail. Clouds of dust swirled up, making it difficult to breathe. The creak, rattle and squeak of dry harnesses and wagon parts began the daily play on nerves. And for Tildy the grim visages of Joe, Macon, and even that of usually cheerful, bright-eyed Robin Wall gave her a mounting feeling of unease. There was something going on and, as usual, she was kept in the dark. Finally, Tildy could stand it no longer. When Joe rode near she leapt down from her perch on the wagon seat and seized Blaze by the reins, bringing the horse to a halt.

"What is it, Sis? Is something wrong" Joe asked, swinging down to face her.

"Yes, something is wrong. Why don't you ever tell me what is going on? Obviously there's trouble afoot and you haven't breathed a word of it."

Joe gave her a sharp glance. He led Blaze back away from the roiling trail dust, looking perplexed. "What has come over you? It's just another day on the trail. Maybe you should sit in the wagon with Granddad and get a little rest."

"I'll not sit in the wagon and stew," Tildy retorted. "I want to know why Macon nearly left this morning without a word. Did your potbellied friend warn of danger ahead? If he did, don't we have a right to know? I thought by being together we would be family again, but we're as far apart as though Granddad and I never left home. Perhaps we should have stayed there and waited for Sandy."

Joe grimly stared at the distant horizon. That was the trouble with women. You tried to protect them from needless worry, and they worried all the more. He tenderly took Tildy by the arm. "Sis, everything is fine. Macon is not leaving. We did have a few words. I guess he thought I didn't want him around, but it's all straightened out now."

Tildy was not satisfied. It was just like men to leave questions half answered. "What took place on your hunt? You're gone all day and the next morning Macon is packed and ready to ride away. What happened that made him do that? He's an honorable person. He would not desert his friends unless there was good reason. The thought that he would, makes me feel awful."

Joe put an arm around Tildy but remained silent. He, too, wondered what had possessed Macon to depart abruptly for no apparent reason. Was there something about the hunt that gave him cause? He carefully went over the previous day's events, minute by minute.

# # #

It was near noon when he had aimed at the lead antelope and shot. His antelope and three others dropped. He swung around. Three rifle muzzles stared him. He was paralyzed. There was no escape. What he feared would happen had occurred. These people were after Hawk Beak's gold. They didn't want him dead. If they killed him it would be after a long, hard grilling. They would persist until he told where to find the gold. The bushes parted. Three men emerged -- two tall and bronze, the other short, bearded and nearly round. Joe raised his right hand in the sign of peace. He would buy as much time as he could.

"I'll be switched," the bearded, rotund man exclaimed. "If it ain't thet rascal, Joe Jennings. What'n thunder're yuh doin' out heya, ridin' Hawk Beak's Blaze?"

Joe's heart dropped into its proper place. How stupid to think he had been about to draw his last breath. The rotund man was his old trapping partner, Deacon Walton. The man had a Cheyenne wife and family. The Indian men were his wife's brothers. They often came here from the Sweetwater to fish and hunt.

"I'll be switched," the bearded white man repeated. "Joe Jennings. I swear we took yuh fer a rascal, thought yuh a hoss thief, ridin' Hawk's nag. Where's the ol' galoot, anyways? Last time I saw Hawk, he an' Hare Lip Bruce was off prospectin' in the Oregon desert. As I recollect, yuh was thinkin' on goin' along."

Joe breathed a sigh. Finally, he could unburden himself. Deacon was an old cob but honest as the day was long. "We went gold hunting all right -- didn't find a penny's worth -- came back worse off than when we started. After mooching all winter off Red Craig in Lapwai, we took up with Steph Meek's train that crossed the Oregon desert. On the way one of the emigrants picked up strange pebbles laying on a stream bank like kernels of corn. No one knew what they were until we were days down the trail. Then a fellow lays one against a wagon wheel and gives it a rap with a hammer. It flattens out; it's shiny.

"Sure enough, the pebbles were nuggets of gold. At the end of the journey Hawk takes it upon himself to go back and find them. Soon as I can manage, I go back, too. Hawk found the stream and picked up a fortune in gold nuggets. He packed them in little sacks and loaded them on his mules. I don't know why, but he was expecting me. I guess he thought I intended to rob him or demand a share. Whatever his thoughts, he took a bead on me -- sends a bullet sizzling my way, probably trying to scare me; when he aimed at something he didn't miss. Maybe he slipped. There had been a heavy wet snow and then a thaw. The ground was soaked -- thick with mud and slippery as grease.

"Anyway, when Hawk fires there's a terrible rumble. I was flat on the ground thinking he'd shoot again. The earth began to tremble like a dog with the shakes. When I stuck my head up to take a peek, the cliff behind Hawk was gone. It had thundered down on top of him -- swallowed him slick as a whistle. He didn't even have time to holler for help."

"Yuh don't say, buried alive by a landslide!" Deacon exclaimed. "Tarnation! Shot at yuh! The crazy coot, all thet gold must've gone ta his head. Served him right fer bein' so infernally hoggish. What happened ta the hee-haws an' sacks of gold?"

"The mules and Blaze were hobbled downstream, not a hair on them was disturbed."

"So yuh fell heir ta Hawk's fortune? No wonder yuh're dressed like a prize pig at the Middlesex fair. What a lucky cuss . . . didn't even hev ta dig Hawk's grave. The creek bank jest give way, buried him neat an' clean. An' there was all the gold nuggets he collected, bagged an' strapped ta the mules ready ta carry away. I'll be tarred an' feathered, jest goes ta show the Lord works in mysterious ways."

While Deacon was speaking his Cheyenne companions came alongside leading three pack mules loaded with antelope carcasses. "I say," Deacon said apologetically. "I plumb fergot me manners. Yuh 'member me wife's brothers, Buffalo Nose an' Walkin' Eagle."

Joe nodded to the two Indian men and tried to think of what he had on him that would make appropriate gifts. All he could think of were a couple of gold pieces he had been carrying around in his pocket. He gave one to each man.

"Your heart is good," they said in signs. Joe nodded, holding two fingers up in the sign of friendship. After what he considered a polite period of conversation, Joe glanced at the position of the sun. It had been hours since he left the wagon train. He had left Macon in charge but if trouble broke out could he manage? "I'd best get back. Folks will be wondering where I have gone."

"Yuh cain't leave without meetin' the family. They'd be sorely distressed. Come!" Deacon motioned to Buffalo Nose and Walking Eagle. "Bear Claw's village ain't but a step away."

Although he had seen many Indian encampments, Joe was still moved by the sight of the Cheyenne village. His thoughts went back to his first winter with Buck Stone's trapping brigade. They had stopped at a village like this to trade. That was where he met the dark-eyed maiden with raven black hair who captured his heart. He never learned her name but her lovely face remained imprinted in his brain.

More than a dozen lodges sat pitched along the banks of a clear flowing stream. In the background a herd of horses grazed in a meadow. On surrounding ridges herders stood guard. Otherwise, the scene was so peaceful and calm it had the appearance of a landscape painting. Two dark-headed youths bounded up to take Deacon by the hand. A slender teenage girl followed to greet them with a shy smile.

"These're me younguns," Deacon said proudly. "This's Left Hand an' his brother, Small Hawk. The young lady's Mornin' Star. Our regular home's on the Sweetwater. At times, such as this, we mosey down here fer a bit of huntin' an' tradin'. We don't come often. It's Pawnee country. They're terribly touchy people. They steal horses, women -- anythin' thet takes ther fancy." He put a protective arm around his daughter. "We don't stand still fer thet, do we, Sister?"

The contrast between the rough-and-ready mountain man and the quiet dignity of his daughter enchanted Joe. Discreetly, he scrutinized Morning Star. Her lightly tanned skin had the bloom of health and glow of contentment. She was not beautiful but possessed the classic features of the noble red men eastern painters liked to portray. Aware of his attention, Morning Star looked away, her long lashes hiding limpid brown eyes.

Embarrassed, Joe turned to study his surroundings. Along one side of the camp layers of meat hung on makeshift racks. Nearby, an old woman scraped a hide stretched taut on a frame of poles. Farther on five men sat in a circle. They tossed strange objects in the air, uttering shouts when they struck the ground. Joe guessed they were gambling with buffalo dice.

Youngsters and dogs ran among the tipis playing tag. Everything was inviting and homey; for a brief moment Joe had the urge to cast his wagon train responsibilities to the winds and stay. Morning Star's shy glance gave the thought additional appeal.

"Come! Sit!" Deacon invited. "Yuh can't travel on an empty belly."

As was the custom, while the male folks ate the women stood in the background, ready to serve them. From time to time Joe glanced up to see the eyes of Morning Star watching. Had Deacon whispered he was a potential mate? He wouldn't put it past the old codger. For years he had hinted he should get hitched and settle down. Well, it wouldn't be long now. In another couple of months he would see Bithiah Abernathy. Hurriedly, he finished eating and politely belched his appreciation.

"Keep yer powder dry," Deacon said as Joe got up to leave. "Maybeso, there's trouble waitin' down the line."

"What makes you say that?" Joe asked.

"Could be Pawnee on the prod. They've been gettin' mighty nervous 'bout wagons ploughin' through their huntin' grounds. Buffalo Nose sniffed the air an' came up with a smell he doesn't like, ain't thet so?" Deacon made a sign to his Cheyenne relative who sat motionless near a makeshift corral. For a moment they carried on a dialogue Joe couldn't understand. The Cheyenne then turned to Joe. He pointed to the west. Holding a clenched fist over his heart, he thrust it away, opening his fingers as he did -- the sign of evil.

"Don't perzactly know what danger Buffalo Nose sees, but when it comes ta sensin' trouble he's mighty accurate.

Maybeso its Pawnee, maybeso someun else. A couple of hard-bitten galoots come through yestiday. Yuh know the type, like they'd been raised on rusty nails an' fish hooks. They was tryin' ta stir up Bear Claw, offered him a handful of gold pieces ta run off stock, plunder wagons an' sech -- ain't sure what they planned ta git out of it, but they was sure enuff itchin' ta take part'."

"When was this?"

"Yestiday. We was on the way ta give the warnin', then ran inta the antelope. 'Course didn't know yuh was part an' parcel of the train."

"What did they look like?"

"Like I say, meaner'n rabid skunks. One of 'em, with a red nose an' hatchet jaw, was hurtin', had a rag wrapped 'round a paw an' his arm in a sling."

"Hmm!" Joe murmured. "Bandaged hand, arm in a sling, you say?" The bullet from his Hawken could have damaged the arm and Pascoe's big teeth . . .   "I must get back. If hostiles attack, hardly a soul knows what to do."

#

Joe's thoughts returned to the present. He glanced at Tildy and shook his head. "I don't know, Sis, why Macon should suddenly take it into his head to leave."

There was no point in alarming her over speculations, but somehow he must have let it slip about the shenanigans of Red Nose with the bandaged hand and his companion. Macon recognized Pascoe's killers. He hadn't wanted to draw more trouble to the camp so decided to take off. What other reason could there be? He certainly would not run away because of the threat from the Pawnee.

XII

"See that ye fall not out by the way," was Joseph's advice to his brethren. And it would be well if it were written on every Christian's wagon.

Narcissa Whitman, 1846

Michael Two Feathers sat at the mission house kitchen table silently observing the black-coated newcomers who Marcus Whitman introduced as the men who would accompany him east.

"You will be in good hands," Whitman had assured. "These brothers in Christ will see you to your destination and help you enroll in the academy. Should you do well, as I am sure you will, the seminary will follow. How good it would be to have you ordained. My greatest wish would be fulfilled if you came back to carry on our work among the Cayuse."

Michael's expression did not change but inwardly he quaked. He had made the decision to follow the path of his white ancestors. Now was his heart telling him he had made a mistake? Michael Two Feathers, a half-blood, preaching the Gospel, giving communion, telling people how they should live, baptizing, conducting prayer meetings and burial services . . . the mere thought was too overwhelming to consider.

As usual, when outsiders visited, the conversation turned to politics and mission affairs. The two men from the Willamette Valley, Mr. Coleman and Mr. Taylor, spoke of the efforts to get the Oregon Territory boundary question settled.

"Certainly the British can't procrastinate much longer," Taylor said. "Oregon's Provisional Government is confirmed; we have a newspaper, *Oregon Spectator* . . ."

"That's very well and good but we've got to do a better job with what we have," Coleman interrupted. "People are bitter about the treatment they receive when they get here. The folks who crossed the Oregon desert in '45 were treated so miserably at Wascopum mission they wanted to burn the place down. The survivors of that ill-fated journey were sick and starving, yet those who could have eased their pain and saved them, did not. Twenty of the wagon train died right there at Wascopum Mission."

Coleman seemed to enjoy being the bearer of bad news. "Archibald McKinlay, Chief Trader at Fort Walla Walla, who did his best to keep the Cayuse peaceful, has been replaced by a scruffy half-breed named McBean," he continued. "People say McBean doesn't have the strong character of McKinlay and will do little to appease the Cayuse. Also, he's Catholic and favors building a Catholic mission near the fort. We stopped to confirm these rumors but getting anything out of McBean is like trying to unscramble an egg."

"He probably has good reason to beat around the bush. He may not be on very solid ground," Taylor said, suddenly coming to life. "His longtime boss, John McLoughlin, is no longer chief factor. A committee has been formed to take over management of Fort Vancouver and Hudson's Bay's Northwest empire. As some wit once put it, 'a committee is a group of the incompetent, chosen by the unwilling to do the unnecessary.' One thing we can be assured of, this committee will not have the ability to get things done like Dr. McLoughlin."

Marcus Whitman nodded. "We'll miss Dr. McLoughlin, that's for certain. Most of us in the territory are in debt to him. I fear you are right; a committee won't have the influence over the Indians that Dr. McLoughlin did. More than once he kept the region from getting a bath in blood."

The news the two men brought had little effect on Michael Two Feathers. The white man could squabble over the territory as much as they pleased. Whoever was in charge would make little difference to the natives. As Tom Hill so eloquently stated, Indian people were ignored -- they were merely obstacles in the way. He rose from the table and picked up the bag of corn the Whitmans insisted be ground into meal and taken on the journey.

As usual there was a line of Cayuse waiting at the

gristmill. Michael started to turn away. He did not want to wait and did not want to make trouble by breaking in at the head of the line. Then he spied Little Fox. The sight of her made his heart leap. She was near the front of the line, only three women before her. The urge to be near her was too great to resist. He walked quietly along the line until he was by her side. She glanced up in surprise.

"Oh! Do you work the gristmill?" she asked, her dancing dark eyes sending an exciting chill up Michael's spine. He took her bag of grain, lifting it to his shoulder as easily as if it were a feather. "Let me do this," he said, striding up to place the bags so they were the next ones to be ground.

The women at the head of the line nudged each other. The buoyant youth's romantic gesture brightened what otherwise had been an ordinary day. They couldn't wait to return to the village and spread the news. The implications of the love affair would be the topic of the night among the Cayuse.

Early the next morning Michael took down the tipi lodge that had been his home for the past six years. He stacked the tipi poles neatly behind the blacksmith shop and rolled up the buffalo skin tipi covering which he stowed in the rear of the shop where bags and boxes of supplies were stored. The few pieces of clothing and other items he possessed, he rolled up in his blankets and tied behind his saddle.

Michael mounted up and rode to the mission house only to find his missionary companions still were dawdling over their breakfast coffee. He could sense they were not pleased with the idea of being caretakers of an Indian youth who never had been east of the Mississippi. Unaware of his fellow missionary brethren's reluctance, Marcus Whitman was instructing them on items to be aired before the Mission Board.

"The Cayuse are quiet now but for how long? Who can tell?" Whitman said. "The invasion of the Catholics is certain to be upsetting. As you have heard, it's rumored McBean plans to help the Catholics establish a mission on the Umatilla and another in the Walla Walla Valley. If we are to hold our own, we must have more help. You know how the Catholics operate. Their approach to the Scriptures is haphazard at best. They baptize almost anyone who joins them in worship. Their openhanded manner is certain to get results. Protecting our flock will be difficult. The Mission Board should be aware of this. Urge them to send as many dedicated mission workers as can be spared."

Finally, good-byes were said. The family gathered around to see the travelers off. Michael pressed the hands of each one. His heart brimmed with love. They all had been so kind to him. How he would miss them. Helen Mar Meek threw her arms around him and kissed him on the cheek. Mary Ann Bridger squeezed his hand extra hard. Both of these half-blood girls knew how he felt -- realized the frightening challenge he faced.

Then Missionary Coleman led them away, down the trail east toward the Blue Mountains. Little David Malin trotted along beside Michael's black and white pony, Magpie, the one friend he would not leave behind. "Good-bye! Good-bye!" David panted. "Come in spring an' give sheeps haircuts," he finally called out, then ran toward the mission house fiercely rubbing his eyes.

Michael watched until the mission house door opened and the boy disappeared inside. As he turned back a movement on the hill behind the mission compound caught his eye. A lone slender figure was waving a piece of white buckskin. Little Fox!

A lump rose in his throat. His heart beat painfully. While he was gone she was certain to be forced into leaving her parents' lodge for that of Edward Tiloukaikt. Had he acted wisely? Was he turning away from a life he should have lived? Far down the trail uneasy thoughts tortured him. If he had foreseen the awesome events soon to occur his thoughts would have been even more tormented.

XIII

A death and funeral, a wedding and a birth, had occurred in this wilderness, within the diameter of two miles, and within two hours time . . .

Edwin Bryant, 1846

The Pawnee threat was a constant dread for members of the wagon train. From early morning to late at night Joe scouted ahead. He barely took time to eat or sleep. One evening it was well after dark by the time he returned to camp. Before he could locate the Jennings' wagons, snatches of angry conversation drifted to his ears. Tildy, Robin and Macon were arguing among themselves. Before he could dismount, Tildy turned on him.

"We've been worried sick. Granddad is half out of his head. He insists on seeing you before he will take to his bed."

Since the day Tildy had accused him of brotherly neglect they had maintained an uneasy truce. Now the truce appeared at an end. Joe glanced at Macon who pointedly turned away.

"All right, Sis. Let's tuck Granddad in." Joe took Tildy by the arm and walked her to the wagon.

Fear of an Indian attack frayed everyone's nerves. Petty disputes flared up over the most trivial things. A few evenings later Joe returned from inspecting the livestock to find Short stomping after Macon, waving his fists.

"Negra lover!" Short shouted. "Why don'tcha go back where yuh belong? Eurup's yer home. Git, an' stay there!"

"All right! Enough of that talk." Joe dismounted and glared at them both. Patches of red flushed Macon's face, his eyes were hard as steel. He hadn't seen him this agitated since Pascoe was killed.

"What's this ruckus all about?" Joe asked.

"A little difference of opinion," Macon gruffly replied and went about his chores. Joe turned on Short. The man had a sneer on his face.

"Never turn yer back on a Negra lover," he spit out. "They're jest as apt as not ta knife yuh when yuh ain't lookin'."

Short's skinny wife, standing behind him, vigorously nodded her sharp featured face. "Amen! Husband. Amen!"

"Keep your thoughts to yourself. Look to your oxen; maybe they've been stolen again," Joe said sarcastically. If there was any man in the wagon train he disliked, it was Short. He was the first to complain and find fault. His wife was the most scurrilous gossip in the entire train. Anyone who met with her disfavor was in for a stream of invective that could be heard from one end of the train to the other.

Joe strode toward the Jennings' wagons pondering the disturbance. For some reason the thought clung to his mind that Macon and Tildy had been the focus of the quarrel. The Short woman had probably uttered a piece of vindictive gossip and Macon had taken exception. Short had stepped in to add his two cents worth . . . Joe shook his head. Keeping a motley group of people under control was a task King Solomon, with all of his wisdom, would be hard pressed to manage.

Joe's thoughts were interrupted by the arrival of Edwin Bryant. "I'm glad you dropped by," Joe said in greeting. "I'd like you to look in on Granddad. He's had a relapse."

Bryant clambered into the wagon where Granddad lay. He was gone so long Joe began to pace back and forth. If something should happen to Granddad . . . he could not bear to think about it. Tildy was right. It would have been best to have left them in their Middlesex County home.

Bryant did little to cheer him. He came out of the wagon looking grave. "I fear your grandfather is in much the same condition as the sick in our camp -- chills, fever, diarrhea . . . . Some wagons haven't one fit person to drive. At this rate we'll never reach Fort Laramie, let alone cross the Rockies."

"What can we do?" The specter of deaths that had occurred on Meek's crossing of the Oregon desert flooded into Joe's mind, a series of tragedies he never would forget.

"One of the main things is to get these people to take better care of themselves. They're scared, ill-fed and wonder why in God's name they left comfortable homes to rough it on this fever-ridden trail."

Joe nodded. He debated whether or not to say anything to Bryant about the Pawnee rumor. He decided he would. Bryant was levelheaded and would not create alarm.

"I thought something like this was in the wind," Bryant said. "A band of Shawnee notified the California train captains three hundred or more Pawnee are encamped five or six days' travel hence. Why should they tell us if they didn't believe them hostile?"

"Yeah!" Joe said. "Of course, they merely may be gathering for a big hunt. Most Indian people avoid trouble. The main thing our people should do is keep calm, not do anything stupid. If we mind our own business the Indians will mind their's."

Bryant nodded but Joe could tell he was not reassured.

The next morning Tildy was all smiles. "Granddad's better," she joyfully reported. "He opened his eyes, asked where we were and promptly went back to sleep. Surely, the crisis is over."

Joe left Macon in charge of the wagons and rode back along the trail to tell Bryant the good news. He found the Californians camped in a clump of cottonwoods near the bank of a stream that emptied into the Platte. Bryant explained they had stopped to take advantage of the presence of wood to shim up loose wagon wheels.

"I'm delighted Granddad Jennings is better. Gives me a lift to know my healing attempts are working. I'm going on the rounds of our sick. Why not come along?" Bryant invited.

"I would like that," Joe said. Soon the trail would split; the Californians would be going one way and the Oregonians another. Bryant's medical skills no longer would be available. It was essential someone with rudimentary medical knowledge be able to take over Bryant's good work. Joe was delighted for the opportunity to learn everything his friend could pass on to him. Keeping his eyes fixed on Bryant, the healer, Joe made a mental note of his every move and what he prescribed.

Bryant quietly listened to a patient's symptoms, examined the patient's eyes and sometimes poked around the afflicted area. He ladled out herbs of various types: powdered black root to ease aches and pains, dried borage leaves to relieve itching and swelling, willow bark to boil for fever, fat root for stomach disorders and a concoction of molasses and ground wild onion to relieve coughs. Bryant's confident manner made the most down-in-the-mouth patients believe his medications would heal.

When they completed the rounds, a cheery call came from the Reed wagon of the Donner party to take tea. Bryant readily accepted. The Reeds and Donners intrigued everyone, probably because of their affluence. Their wagons were sturdier, oxen better kept and their provisions more sumptuous than any party in either the California or Oregon train.

The Reed wagon was of particular interest. Margaret Reed called it The Palace car. The wagon's side steps, built-in bunks, built-in stove, hidden recesses for storing food and a private inner compartment, made it truly a palace on wheels.

Joe silently watched Margaret pour tea into flowered porcelain cups that were far too delicate to entrust to the paws of a mountain man. The last time he had seen her was at her mother's graveside. She appeared recovered, but he sensed her pleasant, sad countenance concealed many grievous wrongs. James Reed had a reputation for arrogance and ruthlessness. It was said his violent temper turned into meanness at the slightest offense.

Tamsen, George Donner's youthful wife, joined them. Joe secretly admired her. No matter how dark the outlook, she took it in stride. Daily disasters did not upset her. She continually was busy seeing to her elderly husband's welfare and that of five active daughters.

While they were sipping tea, three riders on sweaty horses thundered into camp. For a sickening moment Joe thought they had come to report an Indian attack or that Granddad had taken a turn for the worse. Instead, a boy had fallen into the path of a wagon wheel which had crushed his leg. The accident victim lay prostrate in a camp twenty miles ahead. The stricken family knew of Bryant's medical expertise and pleaded for him to come to their aid.

"I guess my reputation precedes me," Bryant said rue- fully. "Why not ride with me and we'll see what we can do."

They arrived at the camp in late evening. Since the horse- men had not given details of the accident, Bryant and Joe as- sumed it had occurred that day. At the entrance of the victim's tent, immediately they knew otherwise. The stench of putrefied flesh assailed their nostrils. The accident had taken place nine days previously. A lad of eight or nine, lay on a makeshift bench of planks patiently waiting; his leg lay in a trough-like enclosure covered over with a cloth.

Bryant pulled away the covering. The sight made Joe gag. Knee to foot was a mass of gangrenous flesh, crawling with maggots. Bryant motioned Joe outside. "That lad's too far gone even for amputation," Bryant said, gulping the fresh air.

They reentered the tent. The mother waited expectantly, her eyes bright with hope. Bryant shook his head and quietly told her he only could try and ease the boy's pain. "Please! Oh, please! Take the leg. Save me son," she implored.

"It is too late," Bryant insisted, but the mother would not accept the verdict. She prevailed upon a French Canadian mem- ber of the train who had served as an assistant army surgeon to amputate the limb. Armed with a butcher knife and carpenter's saw, the surgeon made an incision below the knee. Bryant and Joe watched in horror as the Canadian began to saw. Suddenly, the surgeon changed his mind. "Not good. Better above the knee," he said. He tied a cord above the new incision so tightly it cut into the skin. Again he began to saw. Before he finished the boy expired.

Shattered by the tragedy, Bryant and Joe went to the next

tent where the dead boy's father lay prostrate with rheumatism, his joints so painful and swollen he could not walk or sit. "One wonders why anyone ventures to make the crossing," Bryant said, blowing his nose fiercely as they left the tent.

The news of Bryant's presence spread like wildfire. A feverish woman, a young man with chest pains and others with sundry complaints, demanded attention. Patiently and methodically, Bryant dealt with their ills. Although weary and sleepy, Joe remained attentive, amazed at how much he was learning. As they mounted their horses to leave, Lawyer Quinn Thornton hailed them. He was with a section of the Oregon train camped less than a mile away.

"Come join us," he invited. "We're having a wedding."

"What a welcome change," Bryant exclaimed.

As they walked away from the bridal tent where Reverend Josephus Cornwall had joined the nuptial pair, a man rushed up and breathlessly announced the arrival of a baby and wanted Bryant to see mother and child.

"Another happy event," Bryant said delightedly. They left the tent of the newborn to see a procession of torches and lanterns, the funeral entourage taking the dead boy to the grave.

"A death, a funeral, a wedding and a birth within two hours time and within a diameter of two miles. Where could a series of events happen like this except on the Oregon Trail," Bryant marveled.

Just as the eastern sky was beginning to lighten, announcing a new day, Joe arrived back at the Jennings' camp. Like a squirrel peeking out from its hole, Robin Wall's bright eyes greeted him from his bedroll, but Macon was not in his usual place. Alarmed by his absence, Joe strode for the wagon where Granddad slept. When he left Macon and Tildy were tending the sick man.

Joe carefully opened the canvas flap. The sick man appeared to breathe normally. Relieved, Joe backed away, then noticed his sister's sleeping form. He stared. Asleep beside her was Macon Laird.

XIV

Great Spirit! Bless our children, friends, and visitors through a happy life. May our trails lie straight and level before us.

Prayer, Great Plains Indians

It was the second day on the trail. The missionary party was deep in the Blue Mountains. The travelers topped a ridge and reined their mounts to a halt. Before them lay the bluest lake Michael Two Feathers ever had seen. Nestled in a circle of deeply forested mountains, it was shaped in the form of a half moon.

The sparkling blue surface of the water, glistening in the bright sunlight, gave the lake the appearance of a polished precious jewel. The brightness almost hurt the eyes. Only once before had he been privileged to view this wondrous scene. It was here the Wellamotkin band of the Nez Perce lived. Their leader, Tuekakas, was one of the first natives to be baptized by Missionary Spalding who gave him the baptismal name, Joseph.

Although Michael's mind had been elsewhere -- back in Waiilatpu saying a proper good-bye to Little Fox -- the thoughts of romance were overcome by the beauty Mother Earth lay before him. The missionary men were similarly affected. Awestruck by the sight, they dismounted.

"If I were Catholic, I would make the sign of the cross," Coleman said, his voice choked with emotion. "Only an all-knowing Supreme Being could create a vista like this. Look! There's a village. Heavens! The people have seen us."

On the near shoreline stood a cluster of tipi lodges. People were scurrying from one lodge to another. From that distance the hurrying, stick-like figures resembled a frantic swarm of ants, yet the air was so light and pure the excited shouts of children and barking of dogs drifted to the travelers' ears.

Michael smiled to himself. He could imagine what was taking place. Lookouts had sent word travelers approached on the trail from the west. Like a prairie fire, the news swept through the village sending the people into a frenzy of activity. To house the visitors extra lodges were being erected; pasture land set aside for their mounts; workers were digging a huge fire pit and gathering great quantities of firewood. Hunters were racing into the mountains in search of game and fishermen scrambling to empty fish traps for a gigantic welcoming feast.

Drums were dusted off, inspected and drum skins tightened to celebrate the occasion; ceremonial clothes were being laid out and personal ornaments polished and otherwise brought up to perfection. Never should it be said the southern band of Nez Perce did not properly honor those who visited their beautiful Wallowa homeland.

Michael knew from the way the missionary men spoke of the Indian and their correct politeness to him, they did not have a high opinion of the red man, but the magnificent setting and picturesque village sent them into raptures. They suddenly were as excited as the people awaiting their arrival. "Think of spending a lifetime surrounded by all this beauty," Coleman exclaimed.

When they approached the village the turnout was no less than royalty might receive. Except for two sentinels on distant hilltops, every member of the band in residence was on hand, including babes in arms and a blind old man who had to be led.

"Why all the fuss?" Taylor asked Michael. "After all we are not the wise men bearing gifts of gold, frankincense and myrrh. We have nothing to offer but the word of God."

"This is their way. Not many white men travel this trail. They feel honored by anyone who takes the time and trouble to seek out their village. Men of God are extra special. Hidden in the mountains, these people have a great need to know that the white man's god they worship does not forget them."

Teukakas, leader of the band was away. This did not dampen the welcome. It was obvious the people did their utmost to make the missionaries feel at home. Tuekakas would be displeased if they did not tender the guests every possible courtesy.

After greeting Coleman and Taylor, the most senior elder held a hand up for quiet. With great solemnity, he presented each missionary with a gift, a beautiful bleached elk skin rifle scabbard. Even Michael was surprised by the openhearted generosity. Fringed and intricately decorated with beads and porcupine quills, it had taken hours and hours of painstaking toil to make these items they gave away so freely.

Dumbfounded by the lavish gifts, the two missionaries were at a loss on how to respond. For a moment they talked among themselves. "What are we to do?" Coleman asked. "We don't possess a thing worthy enough to give in return."

Taylor was equally perplexed. "We could give them our rifles. That would be a gift about equal to theirs."

"That's ridiculous," Coleman said. "We need our rifles. Besides, if we give them away, we won't need these scabbards."

Michael, always alert to the feelings of others, could tell the head elder understood every word spoken. His expression was impassive but his eyes twinkled as the white men wrestled with the problem.

"I agree, it's a foolish thing to do, but as the Bible says, Corinthians 1:27, 'God hath chosen the foolish things of the world to confound the wise,'" Taylor quoted. "Let's do it. I'll give up my rifle if you will. Remember! We are men of God. Didn't Apostle Paul set out on the long journey from the Holy Land to Rome without any weapons at all?"

Both of the missionaries presented their rifles with good grace, hiding their trepidations as best they could. Now it was the turn for the villagers to gasp. To give up the fire sticks, the only protection the two men had, was a gesture only a true believer in the Great Spirit could afford to do. For a moment there was confusion, then the elders held a short counsel and began to bark orders. Youths ran to stake the visitors' horses where they could graze. The missionaries were quickly seated in places of honor before the fire, a log draped with a cushion padded with buffalo hair. The women scurried to serve the guests with carvings of roasted elk meat and wooden platters heaped with wild rice. When the food was placed before the guests the elder issued a command. Everyone fell silent. The leading elder turned to the missionaries, raised his hands and made a sign the missionaries did not understand.

"He asks you to bless the food," Michael translated.

Coleman complied with an eloquent prayer that at the request of the elder, Michael carefully interpreted. The meal was eaten with a show of great fellowship and gusto. When the platters were scraped clean and dogs had picked up every fallen morsel, the elder again rose to his feet and made signs for a prayer of thanksgiving. Again Coleman dutifully complied.

"We were strangers and these good people took us in. We were hungry and these good people gave us food. As Jesus said 'on earth peace and good will toward all men.' Here we have peace and good will. May this always be true between our peoples. Amen."

Afterwards, the people circled the fire. In the background came the thump of a drum. Members who had attended Reverend Spalding's Lapwai mission school stood to lead the gathering in song. The opening hymn of Presbyterian services burst forth. Coleman and Taylor gaped in astonishment. The faces glowing with reverence, the earnest voices trying to master the tune and words, the backdrop of dark shiny water, aroma of pungent evergreens and towering mountains made a scene that brought tears to the missionaries' eyes.

Not even the Twelve Apostles could have enjoyed a more heartwarming experience, Coleman thought.

When the song was finished there was a hush. A loon on the lake sounded its mournful call. A breeze rustled the aspen leaves making them dance. Swallows darted out of the shadows to skim over the darkened waters. The moment was so overpowering and emotion filled, Michael would not have been surprised to see God descend from the heavens on a stairway of gold.

The spell was broken by the lead elder who stepped forward. "Now, Bible talk," he said to the visitors. Coleman responded with a sermon he afterward thought was the best he'd ever delivered.

The following morning the two men of God were given a royal send-off. An honor guard of horsemen escorted them the length of the lake and into the pass beyond. When the escort finally pulled to a stop, the elder held up his hand in the sign of peace; again he spoke English. "God good. Bible talk good. Make people happy." With that he raised his hand in farewell and, along with his men, galloped away.

"Wonders never cease to happen," Coleman said, as they watched the escort of horsemen disappear around a bend in the trail. "I wonder what surprises we'll encounter next?"

More surprises indeed did await the travelers. Late in the evening another delegation of Nez Perce appeared, this time led by Teukakas. He apologized for his absence the previous night and insisted the missionaries return for a lengthy visit. The people were so inspired by their presence they wanted the men of God to remain in the land of the Welamotkins permanently. Coleman thanked the noted leader but said they must press on. They had a long way to go and important business to do.

Tuekakas understood. "God's work will be done," he said. He motioned to a rider who came forward carrying two rifles, the ones Coleman and Taylor had presented as gifts. The Indian leader handed each missionary his rifle. "In Wellamotkin land God give protection. In Bannock land fire sticks needed."

When they arrived at Fort Boise Michael was glad they were armed. The first ones they saw were Hare Lip Bruce and his hard-bitten companion who went by the name of Smith.

# # #

On June 21st members of the wagon train sighted Chimney Rock. The excited travelers compared the rock formation to the capitol building in Washington. Others thought it resembled the remains of an ancient Egyptian temple. A few insisted it compared favorably to the ruins of the Athenian Acropolis. At an encampment some three miles from the "Rock," Joe, riding ahead of his Oregon group of wagons, came upon Bryant and his companions.

"Thirty-five miles today," Bryant chortled. "We forsook the wagon. For the rest of the way it's horseback and pack mule. That's the only way for people without family to travel."

The next day rain came down in torrents. Vainly, the bedraggled travelers attempted to keep warm and dry in the cold wet camp. Even the usually reliable buffalo chips were too drenched to ignite. The inclement weather caused new worry about the sick. Joe went to look in on Granddad. Inside the wagon Tildy spooned him broth. She gave Joe a tired smile. Joe avoided her eyes. The memory of her and Macon asleep alongside each other made him uncomfortable in her presence.

The following day the caravaners sighted Fort Laramie. Train officers rode back and forth ordering the drivers to close up. The teamsters quickly complied when they came near enough to see hundreds of tipi lodges clustered near the fort.

"What're all these blisterin' Injuns doin' here?" Short demanded, his flaming mustache twitching.

Joe eyed the camp uneasily. It was one of the largest gathering of Indians he had ever seen. Were they waiting for the wagon train? "It's a tribe of Sioux," an employee of the fort informed him. "Don't perzactly know why they're here. They ain't done much tradin'. 'Peers they're waitin' fer somethin' ta happen. I wish they'd move on. They're keepin' folks upset."

After corralling the wagons a safe distance from the Indian village, yet still near the fort, the nervous travelers began to set up camp. A big worry was the livestock. Although here in buffalo country Indians did not need to steal animals for meat, young braves anxious to show off and garner coups might not be able to resist driving away a cow or two. Yet, keeping the livestock close to the fort forced the animals to nibble on stubble where Indian herds had cropped the grass clean. Joe and a group of herders spent a sleepless night standing guard. Only once were they disturbed. A mountain man stumbled from a fort cabin, shouting and waving a jug, causing Indian camp dogs to race out to bark. A mule hee-hawed in response. Two companions quickly shushed the drunk and hustled their friend inside.

The travelers awakened to find the Indian village on the move. Long columns of riders and pack animals trailing travois, threaded away to the northwest. A scout who visited with the Indians the previous night reported the Sioux were off to fight the Crow. Still wary, Joe rode to a rise above the fort and watched them until they disappeared into a fold in the distant hills.

Shortly after leaving Fort Laramie the wagon train encountered a company of men coming down the trail from the west driving a herd of horses. The riders hooked their legs over their saddle horns to palaver. They were on their way to collect families in the States, they said.

They spoke of rich farm land, the best locations to homestead and the high cost of living. Did the riders know the Morrises, Hansons and other people who had made earlier crossings? Dad Wall, impatient with the banal conversation, asked about the Indian situation. "What kin we expect from the red divils ahead?"

The riders glanced at each other. "Hard to say. Situation changes day by day. We skirted a bunch of Pawnee, big huntin' party, I guess. Farther west the Indians are feelin' a bit unhappy. They find the comin' of the white man not to their likin'. They've good reason. Poor critters're dyin' like flies from diseases brought by wagon trains."

There was a grim silence. Disease in their own wagon train had risen to alarming proportions. Did they carry death to the natives?

Several days after meeting the horse herders, a single rider from the west stopped to make camp with the wagon train. Mr. Bonney, who the previous year had emigrated to Oregon, gave out perfunctory reports on the trail ahead. He carried a letter from a Mr. Lansford Hastings addressed to all travelers bound for California. The message urged them to take a recently discovered shortcut. By traveling to Fort Bridger and along the south shore of the Great Salt Lake, Californian travelers could save more than three hundred miles, Hastings claimed. He was waiting in Fort Bridger to guide wagons over the new route.

On July 20th the wagon train made camp on the Little Sandy. Clumps of willows lined the stream banks and lupine spread over the campground floor like a blue carpet. The camp was a place no one ever would forget. Twenty wagons, including those of the Donners and Reeds, turned here to take the Hastings' Cutoff. James Reed had accepted Lansford Hastings' offer to guide the train over the new route, and no one in the party had the will to dispute his decision.

Before the group departed, Joe went to say good-bye. The first person he encountered was Tamsen Donner. She lacked her usual self-contained composure. "I don't feel good about this trail or Mr. Hastings," she confided. "James doesn't always use good judgment. This may be one of those times."

Most of the California party were in high spirits. James Reed toasted their departure with drinks from his bountiful liquor supply. His stepdaughter, Virginia, raced her pony through camp with gleeful shouts.

Many of the departing members were like the Donners and Reeds, well-equipped and of solid character. However, among them was Leslie Keesberg, the German who had earned the enmity of train members by robbing an Indian burial scaffold, taking a robe right off the corpse. As the Keesberg wagon drove past Joe had the terrible premonition it represented evil that would cause the Hastings' Cutoff caravan untold grief.

LAND WITHOUT A COUNTRY

XV

The ascent into South Pass, at the head of the Platte, is so grand that the traveler is not aware of it until he is through it.

Rev. J. A. Cornwall, 1846

The entrance to Fort Boise opened onto the Snake River. Even in the bright sunlight the fort's adobe walls and blockhouses that guarded the approaches looked dull, without life. The ground around it, beaten bare by the comings and goings of thousands of hooves and wagon wheels, had the same lifeless appearance. The late July heat beat down on disorderly rows of shriveled, wilted plants in the oblong patch of ground Trading Post Master Craig had tilled in hopes of raising a garden.

A pack of mangy dogs lying in a strip of shade, languidly scrambled to their feet as a dozen or more Indian horsemen rode up on bareback ponies with makeshift bridles. Carrying pitiful bundles of fur pelts, they walked into the trading post, firewater foremost on their minds. Almost immediately, out they came, their bundles of pelts following on their heels.

"Yuh ignorant apes, when we're doin' business it ain't perlite ta interrupt. Now scat! We'll let yuh know when yuh kin come back." Hare Lip Bruce, waving a half-empty bottle, nearly fell down as he came through the trading room door. Right behind him teetered Hard-Bitten Smith.

Michael Two Feathers, who had arrived the previous evening with the two missionaries, saw red. In two strides he was face to face with the two drunks. "Come back," he called to the departing Indians. "These white faces are just leaving."

"What the hell . . ." Bruce staggered against the trading post wall. He dropped the bottle and fumbled for the knife at his belt, but far too slowly. The Indian youth plucked the knife from its sheath and had the sharp pointed blade inches from the bulging waistline. "Hey! Yuh crazy coot, watch out! Thet thing's razor sharp. An' what yuh mean, buttin' in? Yuh've got yer gall. I've a notion ta take a horse whip ta yuh."

"Thet's it! Don't let thet Injun kid take advantage of yuh," Hard-Bitten Smith said, lurching forward. "Hey, yuh Injun rascal, give me thet knife afore yuh cut yerself."

Michael turned to Smith and held out the knife. Just as Hard-Bitten reached for it, Michael gave the knife a thrust and a quick twist. The sharp blade sliced in two the suspenders that held up the man's pants. Behind Michael's back, Hare Lip Bruce lunged his bulk toward him. Michael alertly dodged aside and thrust out a foot. The drunken man tripped and fell to his knees. Clutching at his drooping pants, with his free hand, Smith threw a roundhouse fist at Michael's jaw. The agile lad seized the extended arm and gave it a jerk. Smith stumbled over his fallen partner and went face down, sprawling in the dirt.

The Indian horsemen who watched, their mouths agape, looked at each other and tittered. Then, fear of the white men sent them scurrying for their ponies. They did not want to be involved in what was certain to become big trouble.

Craig, the trading post manager, stepped out of the door, followed by missionaries, Coleman and Taylor. "What's going on?" Craig demanded, looking at the fallen men and then at Michael. "What are you doing, trying to kill off my customers?" His voice had a sharp ring but his eyes betrayed him with a bemused twinkle.

"Well, now, let's put Humpty Dumpty back together again and have peace in the family. I'm sure these fellows meant no harm." He pulled the two drunks to their feet and waved the waiting Indians inside. "The trading post is open to all who wish to do business," he announced. Michael tossed the knife away and went to the pasture to see to his pony.

The incident was far from over. The two missionaries who witnessed the confrontation glanced at each other and shook their heads. The young man they were taking east to be educated was like an untamed cub.

"We had better think this business over," Coleman said. "Imagine what would happen if this lad cut loose in a classroom or in some Mission Board member's house. He'd frighten the people out of their wits."

"It's too late to turn back," Taylor replied. "We're duty bound to see he is safely delivered to the Mission Board."

"It's never too late to right a wrong," Coleman insisted.

"Yes, but we promised Brother Whitman . . . ."

"I can't help it. When you're faced with a scary situation, one has to take the bull by the horns. Think of it, this young heathen could cut our throats on the trail and think nothing of it. You saw how he took after those two with the knife, cold-blooded as a snake -- looked as though he enjoyed it. He isn't quite human. He may be mission trained but is still an uncivilized aborigine. I say we leave him right here. It's a lot better to prevent disaster than corral it after it gets started," Coleman persisted.

"Yes, but the young man helped us through the land of the Wellamotkins, you have to admit that. Besides, I don't like going back on our word. After all, this boy was with the Whitmans for years. And, quite frankly, these men had it coming, nasty drunk and uncouth as a couple of boar hogs. If I wasn't a man of the cloth I would've been tempted to take them on myself."

"I understand these men are not God's finest creations but they are white human beings -- for better or worse, one of us. I don't much like breaking our word either. But if we take this lad back east and he runs amuck the Mission Board will be furious. For certain they'll blame Brother Whitman, question his judgment -- perhaps recall him. As it is they are not pleased with the manner the Waiilatpu mission is managed. And then what'll the Board think of us, bringing this wild creature across country and dumping him in their laps?"

"All right! But who is going to tell the lad? For that matter who is going to tell Brother Whitman?" Taylor asked.

"Let's get this man, Craig, to do it," Coleman said after some moments. "He's accustomed to dealing with Indians and he probably sends regular messengers to the Hudson's Bay's fort in Walla Walla. We can send a letter. Setting the details on paper is the best way to handle this, anyhow. That way we are on record should anyone put up a fuss."

# # #

The column of canvas topped wagons threaded its way toward South Pass. In every direction, Mother Earth, the sculptress, had created out of sand, rock, plant and tree every art form imaginable. The travelers barely noticed the beauty. The bumpy, rock-strewn, dusty roadway made the going rough and demanding. From the west a hot wind raised gusts of dust that blew in their faces, making them sneeze and cough.

The lead wagons pulled up to the summit that had little to mark it but Pacific Springs that lay to the left of the track and an alkaline marsh on the right. For a short span of time a ripple of excitement stirred the travelers. They were standing on the backbone of the continent. From here on streams would flow west, instead of east and south. But when the teamsters pulled up to make camp they found both water and grass were scarce. There was talk of traveling farther but everyone, including animals, was bushed.

The following day the train made a similar passage over sandy, dusty terrain until near nightfall when they struck a nearly dry creek called the Big Sandy. The few sprigs of grass that grew along the creek bank made passable food for the animals and the pools of water, although bitter with alkali, were better than none. Several wagons that had gone ahead of the Jennings' train were already parked in the shade of a few trees. Joe motioned for his teamsters to join them. While he was helping Robin Wall and Macon unhitch and secure the livestock, a raucous shout came out of the twilight.

"Hey! Yuh lanky stuck-up son-of-a-gun. Yuh didn't look me up in thet Missouri town of Independence. Couldn't stand ta lissen ta me gab, is that it?"

"Why, hello," Joe said in surprise. It was Teamster

Beamer, the old acquaintance he had seen in Independence. "What're you doing here . . . after more skins?"

"Naw, I quit thet stinkin' business. Gotta a load of freight fer Factor Grant at Fort Hall. Should've delivered it afore now but one thing an' another slowed me down. I say, ain't thet yer ol' sidekick, Deacon. My! Looks like he's comin' bearin' gifts."

Out of the evening gloom Deacon Walton emerged, riding the old gray mule he called Lightening. Behind him trailed a string of pack animals laden with gear and sides of freshly slaughtered game. He slid off the gray mule and shook hands. A fur cap covered his bald pate. A heavy belt held in his girth. From the belt hung a holstered pistol, a hand ax and skinning knife. Under his arm he cradled a heavy barreled rifle made by the gunsmith, Hawken.

"I saw yuh galoots draggin' in too tuckered ta look beyond yer nose," Deacon greeted. "Tried ta holler yuh down but, oh no, yuh was much ta busy ta notice an ol' friend. An' here I was tryin' ta give yuh a leetle fresh meat." He waved a hand at the loaded mules. "Anyways, if yuh don't mind, thought I'd mosey with yuh fer a ways, ain't been out west fer a coon's age."

The evening meal was extra special. In addition to the fresh meat Deacon furnished, from his wagon of supplies Beamer produced a crock of sweet pickles and a jug of cider. With the help of Robin and Macon, Tildy laid out plates and cutlery on a blanket that served as a table cloth. Granddad, who dragged himself from the sick bed, said a short blessing. Then came a chatter of delight as the food was uncovered and passed around.

After eating their fill, coffee was poured and the diners sat back with a sigh. "Mighty fine vittles," Beamer said gratefully. "It ain't often a body eats this well on the trail. I 'member when . . . ." The teamster went into a rambling account of the last time he enjoyed such a munificent meal. The occasion was his first meeting with the young lady who became his wife.

"Tell me," Tildy asked suddenly, "how you first came to meet my brother, Joe." Some way or another she was determined to learn more about the way her twin had spent the past seven years.

"Let's see, ah, yes, how could I fergit. 'Twas the summer of '40, the last trip I had with me son, Clay. We was haulin' ta the Green River rendezvous. A broken wagon tongue had us fallin' behind the supply column. We was nervy as cats on a tin roof. Injuns was about. Any moment we reckoned we'd lose our scalps. It was dark, yuh see, spooky as all get out.

"Then, in the track ahead, Clay's sharp eyes spot a light. We cain't make up our minds ta pull up're keep travelin'. If'n 'twas an Injun camp we could've been in a nasty fix. Out of the dark comes a shout. 'Pull up! Pull up an' show yerself.' We sure enuff do as the man says. When we git near I see it's a young fella 'bout the age me son, Clay. 'Twas yer brother." Beamer fell quiet, picked up a stick and began poking at the fire.

Memory of that first meeting came flooding back to Joe. He knew why Beamer could not say more. He was thinking of his only son's unfortunate end. In a way Beamer blamed him for Clay's death. Clay had insisted on joining Buck Stone's trapping brigade. "If that Joe Jennings can be a mountain man, why can't I?" Clay argued. Reluctantly, Beamer gave him permission to join Buck Stone's gang. A few short months later Blackfeet raiders killed both Buck Stone and Clay Beamer. On that day the joy of living deserted the Beamer household.

Tildy, sensing she had touched a sore spot, began to clear the dinner things. Macon and Robin got up to help. The others sat quietly; Beamer's silence blotted out the desire to speak. Tildy could have kicked herself. Her effort to learn about Joe's life in the west had spoiled the night and she had gained absolutely nothing for her efforts. When everything was put away Tildy returned to the fire and said good night. She thanked Deacon for the meat and Beamer for the pickles and cider.

Beamer struggled upright to make a courteous bow. With his ponderous belly, it was an obvious effort. "Thet lass's pretty an' trim as a new buggy," he remarked as Tildy walked away.

"Yep, yuh don't see many maidens like thet," Deacon agreed. "Course I ain't been east fer quite a spell. Don't hanker ta go, neither. They say the cities back there're gettin' as cluttered an' smelly as untended chicken roosts."

"Things ain't perzactly what yuh'd call hunky-dory 'tween here an' St. Louie, neither," Beamer said. "Rider came by yestiday tellin' of a fuss with the Pawnee. Injuns took it upon theirselves ta run off a few head of wagon train stock."

"Few!" Deacon snorted. "Me Cheyenne brothers been keepin' an eye on the Pawnee, say t'were more'n a hundred."

"Yeah," Beamer agreed, "from the fuss it created I guess 'twas quite a few. Anyways, the people who went after 'em never found the animals -- in fact was bushwhacked. Trimble, I think's the name, ain't been seed since. Folks went ta find 'em but all they spotted was a pool of blood."

"So, someone is stirring up the Pawnee," Macon Laird stated, the first words he had spoken all evening.

"'Pears so," Beamer uttered.

For a while the men sat staring into the fire. Then Macon rose to his feet and said good night. Beamer and Deacon nodded. "We'll see yuh in the mornin'," they said in unison. Deacon stoked up a blackened short-stemmed pipe and Beamer took a chaw and spit. "Thet English fella, ain't he the one mixed up in the Independence killin' of the Negra?"

"It was his companion that was killed," Joe said.

"Maybeso yuh gotta Negra killer in the wagon train. Better sort it out afore yuh hit Oregon City. They don't take ta killers. Joe Meek got hisself elected sheriff. He'd hang his own mother fer two cents."

"Ah! Ol' Meek wouldn't do thet," Deacon protested. "Why he's been in fixes where he's had ta kill ta stay alive."

"Yuh'd be surprised how these mountain men kin turn inta God fearin' citizens thet wouldn't say damn on the Sabbath. Yep, ol' Meek got religion. It sure made a mess of a good mountain man, thet's fer certain."

Beamer fell quiet and took another chaw. "If'n I were a gamblin' man, which I ain't, I'd say thet English feller's got his cap set fer yer sister an' maybeso, she fer him."

"Nonsense!" Joe replied, amazed at the teamster's insight. "Tildy's spoken for. Her intended is making a home for her in the Willamette Valley."

"Good fer him. He's got a real womin." Beamer spit into the dying fire. "How 'bout yerself. Has a filly put a noose 'round yer neck yet? Seems I 'member a Cheyenne lass . . ."

"No! Nothing like that." Joe avoided looking at Deacon. If the old coot was thinking of his daughter, Morning Star, as the future Mrs. Joe Jennings, he would put a stop to it right here and now. "If you must know there's a young lady waiting for me in the Willamette Valley."

"I say, " Deacon said. "Yuh take after yer dad, keepin' family affairs quiet as a graveyard ghost. What's the dear maiden's name?"

"Bithiah . . . Bithiah Abernathy. We were next door neighbors in New England."

"Bithiah -- Bithiah," Deacon repeated, "a name outta the Old Testament. Yep! Bithiah was daughter of an Egyptian pharaoh and wife of Mered of the tribe of Judah."

Beamer stared at the bewiskered mountain man in open disbelief.

"Don't gawk like thet. I ain't always been a mountain rat. As the father of our country is claimed ta hev said, 'Do not be deceived thet fine clothes make fine men, any more'n fine feathers make fine birds.'"

"Yep, I learned long ago not to underestimate you," Joe said. "The way you've studied the Good Book you must know it word for word." How far is this old partner of mine traveling with us, Joe wondered. It would be just like the old codger to tag along all the way to the Willamette Valley for the mere joy of putting a spoke in his wedding plans.

XVI

*Fort Hall is situated in a large fertile valley; you will not
travel far, however, until the gloom of desolation
will spread around you . . . ."*
THE SHIVELY GUIDE, 1846

Michael Two Feathers awakened just as Father Sun peeked above Mother Earth's eastern horizon. He had chosen to sleep outside in the fresh air. The gnats and mosquitos that swarmed up from the river did not bother him but nearly drove the missionary men wild. To avoid the annoying insects they had made arrangements with Factor Craig to sleep in the dank rooms of the fort. So far there was no sign that they were up.

As taught by his grandfather, Michael stood to greet Father Sun with a silent prayer, thanking The Creator for bringing forth a new day. Next, he tended to the horses. Another act he had learned from his grandfather -- "See to the horses, that they're safe, watered and fed before satisfying your own needs," Grandfather Lone Wolf had instructed. The black and white pony was exactly where Michael had staked him the previous evening but the horses of the missionaries were gone.

Michael walked to where the missionaries' mounts had been tethered and examined the ground. For a moment he thought the Indians who had been at the fort the day before had run them off. After a careful examination of the tracks, he knew the Indians were not to blame. Men wearing boots had led Coleman's and Taylor's horses away. Michael's first thought was that Hare Lip Bruce and Hard-Bitten Smith were the culprits. But the footprints were too light and narrow for men of their stature. Besides, after last night's drunken spree it was unlikely they would be out before sunup.

Michael picked up the trail and traced it across the pasture field. It was not hard to follow; the crushed grass of the feet and hoof prints contained a film of dew, only slightly less than where the grass had not been disturbed. The trail of horses and men led toward the trading post gates. Michael suddenly realized the missionaries had been the ones who came for the horses. What were they doing up so early, bringing in the horses before the break of day?

A tremor of premonition flooded through Michael's mind. For some reason had the missionaries made an early start and left him behind? Every morning and evening on the trail he had been the one tending the animals. At day's end he was the one who watered them, rubbed them down and staked them out. In the mornings it was he who fetched the horses and prepared them for the trail. The thought was chilling, but true. The missionary men had abandoned him. They did not want him. That didn't bother him as much as the fact he had made a bad decision. He firmly believed The Great Mysterious had told him to choose the path of his Boston ancestors. Now, was the Great One telling him not to travel that path?

Craig came out the trading post door, snapping his suspenders in place, yawning like a dog with a bone in its throat. "Lookin' for the two men of cloth, are yuh? Well, they slunk away before the crack of dawn," Craig said, yawning again.

"You're well shet of them, I'd say -- 'bout as spineless as bowls of jelly. Didn't have guts enough to tell you straight out they didn't want you along. The way you handled those two drunken galoots put the wind up. They mumbled and argued half the night, talking about uncivilized savages and such.

"The man, Taylor, would have taken a chance on you, but the other fellow would have none of it. So here you are, alone. At least you have your horse and know your way back to Waiilatpu. Stick around and we'll tie on the nose bag. I'll be fixin' vittles soon. I expect those two other fellows will be rolling out of the hay. After downing every drop of firewater they could hold, they probably have heads as big as washtubs."

Growling at each other like angry bears, Hare Lip Bruce

and Hard-Bitten Smith finally wandered into the trading room.

"Tavern keeper!" Hare Lip yelled. "Whiskey! Whiskey! It's time ta open the bar." He noticed Michael silently watching.

"Keep yer distance, kid. Don'tcha git smart with me again. I hev half a notion ta slit yer gullet from belly button ta chin as 'tis."

"Yeah," Smith said. "Maybeso, the young feller out-smarted hisself yestiday." He drew his knife. "I've long had a hankerin' fer a Nez Perce scalp. Yuh folks always keep yer top-knots so nice an' clean an' free of lice."

Michael backed away but a barrel of meal blocked his path. Before he could slide around it, Smith thrust the knife forward. The cold prick of steel penetrated his buckskin shirt. Michael stumbled backward. Smith's free hand darted out, seizing him by the shirt front. He pulled him close until the stench of his breath nearly made Michael gag. The point of the knife blade inched up until it was level with his eyes.

"Thet's it!" Hare Lip crowed. "Carve 'em out, one eye at a time. Thet'll larn him ta mess with his betters."

Behind the two bullies came the sharp click of cocking firearms. Craig stood in the trading room entrance, a rifle in his hand and a second one on the trading counter by his side.

"We was only funnin'," Smith growled, slipping the knife into the sheath at his belt. "We'll be on our way peaceful-like."

"You're going nowhere until I say so," Craig snapped. "I don't cotton to people who make free with my friends. There's a little lockup out back that'll fit you right nice."

"Yuh cain't do this. We ain't done no harm. This is a free country. We demand our rights," Smith snarled.

"Of course it's a free country," Craig agreed cheerfully. "I'm free to put you in the jug any time you get out of hand."

# # #

The wagon train rolled down the slopes of Bear Valley and along the bumpy track that followed Bear River. The travelers took heart. Water and grass were good and willow tree wood for campfires abounded. Teamster Beamer claimed they would be in Fort Hall in a week, but not before journeying over another stretch of dusty, bumpy roadway.

For Joe the trip was somewhat pleasant. He was getting nearer and nearer to his love, Bithiah. He rode at the head of the column daydreaming of the home he would build for her. He made plans to patch up the family, too. They would take the trail through the Blue Mountains and stop at the mission in Waiilatpu. He would introduce Tildy and Granddad to their Nez Perce brother and grandson. It would be fitting to do so there. They had high regard for Marcus Whitman, whom they had met when the missionary went east in '43. With Marcus and Narcissa present everything was certain to go well.

Now that the Pawnee threat was behind them, he could send Macon Laird on his way. When they arrived in the Willamette Valley he would be able to present Tildy to Sandy with a free conscience. Separating Tildy and Macon could not come too quickly. The looks Macon and Tildy exchanged were no longer casual glances of friends. Their eyes spoke of something deeper . . . "Naw! It can't be," Joe said aloud. The thought was so disturbing he kicked Blaze in the ribs and gave him a swat, something he never, never did.

At Fort Hall the wagon train made camp near a grove of cottonwoods that lined the bank of the Snake. Campfire talk was of the trail ahead. The time was drawing near when another painful parting of the ways would take place. Governor Boggs' party and others bound for California who had refused to take the Hasting's Cutoff, would follow the Oregon Trail for a short distance west to the Raft River Crossing and then turn south into an arid rocky country of greasewood and sagebrush.

After a few day's drive the road would enter a desolate region, hot as Hades with little grass or water. Upon learning this, the California-bound travelers were aghast. The garrulous promoters had glossed over the hazards of the track that led to this supposed wonderland of milk and honey.

The disheartened Californians grimly geared themselves for the trek that reliable reporters had said tested the endurance of man, beast and equipment. In this region wagons broke down, harnesses cracked and oxen wearied, weakened and died. The dreams and lives of more than one traveler had come to an end in the heat and wastelands of a region called the Ogden sink.

Shortly after making camp, Deacon and Joe strolled into the Fort Hall trading room where years earlier they had entered the same door with Hawk Beak to engage in a showdown with the renegade Francois and the irascible mountain man, One-Eye Link. For a moment they relived the excitement of the near shoot out. Today the room was crowded with emigrants.

"Tain't room ta bend a elbow," Deacon complained. "Not thet I hanker ta buy a drink from skinflint Grant. 'Member the miserable sum he paid us'ns fer our prime pelts?"

As though he knew they were talking about him, Factor Grant appeared. "What can I do for you buckos?" he asked.

"Nuthin'. We jest came ta see if yuh was still in business," Deacon growled.

"Yep, still here. Say, some years back weren't you trading in pelts? Don't see much of your kind any more. Emigrants are the big business now. Some Indians and once in a while a party of riders come through. Rough lot dropped in yesterday. Looked like they'd cut your throat for a pinch of snuff."

"Is thet so? Headin' east or west?" Deacon queried.

"They were the kind you don't ask. The way they loaded up on red-eye and lead and powder, I'd say they were preparing for a big shindig of some kind."

"Wonder if those galoots was the ones thet sashayed inta Bear Claw's camp. If so, Grant sized 'em up right. They're cussed enuff ta bite the hind end out of a skunk," Deacon said as they walked away from the fort.

Joe heard Deacon with half an ear. In a clump of trees near the outskirts of camp Macon and Tildy were standing so close together they looked like one.

"Do yuh see what I see?" Deacon asked.

"Yes, I do and I'm going to put a stop to it." Joe strode for the trees. Just as he quickened his pace, Robin Wall ran up.

"There's a bunch of folks at camp waitin' ta see yuh," he breathlessly announced. "A party thet's rid all the way from Oregon's Willamette Valley."

Joe hesitated. Had Hawk Beak's friends arrived? He kicked himself for not bringing his Hawken. He knew better than to go anywhere unarmed. He turned and followed Robin toward camp. They rounded a clump of trees to see a dozen travel weary horses and pack mules bunched together outside the circled wagons. Joe seized Robin by the arm.

"Not so fast. You can't be too careful about strangers."

Robin looked perplexed but fell back to follow.

They circled around the travel-stained animals. Joe carefully inspected them. From their looks they had been ridden hard and far. They could stand a week in good pasture and still not be filled out. Joe snatched a rifle that had been left in a saddle boot. Cautiously, he led the way through an opening between two parked wagons and then stopped so short Robin Wall almost ran up his back. Before them was Granddad sitting on a blanket-padded log talking happily with Bithiah Abernathy's brother, Saul, a mountain man named Black Moses Harris and, Sandy Sanders!

"God!" Joe uttered irreverently. Sandy Sanders, Tildy's fiancee, was here and she was somewhere in the trees lollygagging with Macon Laird.

XVII

*The public mind has been happily put to rest . . . Captain
Jessie Applegate . . . succeeded in discovering a
most admirable road for the emigration . . .*
Oregon Spectator, 1846

At Fort Hall wagon train members, in spite of the alarming prospect of the trials that lay ahead, attempted to rest, visit and reprovision. The fort, although built in adobe much in the form of Fort Laramie, was looked on with interest. The walls that stood some twenty feet high, were broken by a heavy wooden door that guarded the entrance. The door was constructed in such a way it could be closed, barred and locked in an instant. To make the fortification safe from a prolonged siege, besides room after room of provisions, lead, powder and other necessities, an inside well supplied clear cold water.

The fortification was not nearly as interesting as the family who made it their home. The man in charge, Captain Richard Grant, a Scotsman straight from the old country, had an Indian wife who had borne him several children, two of whom were often seen during business hours in and around the trading room. A ten year old boy named Joe, raced about carrying out his father's orders. He always was courteous to visitors, answering their questions in surprisingly good English.

But it was a young lady about fifteen that fascinated visitors. Dressed in neat clean buckskin, with long dark hair falling to her shoulders, and moving with the gracefulness of a swan, she captured the hearts of everyone, old and young alike. "I have to pinch myself to make certain she is real," Chloe Boone, the daughter of Alphonso was heard to say.

In the Jennings' camp little thought was given inhabitants of the fort. The sudden appearance of Tildy's fiancee, Sandy Sanders, had Joe in such a turmoil he could not think straight.

On a log opposite him, Sandy Sanders, with his red hair and face as freckled as a turkey egg, sat looking perplexed. "Nice camp you have here," he said, glancing around.

Joe nodded. He felt too ill to speak. Tildy! How long had she and Macon Laird been carrying on . . . right under his eyes and he hadn't suspected. Wagon train captain! Bah! A turkey gobbler would make a better officer. He couldn't even keep his own family in hand.

"Why did you make the trip all the way to Fort Hall?" Joe finally asked Sandy, stalling for time. "Did you think we were in trouble?"

"No, we found a shortcut to the valley and wanted to let you know. Jessie Applegate, maybe you've met him; he's mapped a new route along the California Trail and north into the Siskiyous. It's shorter and we avoid the Columbia River rapids and the Cayuse and Walla Walla who are said to be out of sorts."

"Seems like I've heard that story before -- shorter, safer, plenty of grass and water . . ." Joe shook his head. "I hope you know what you're doing."

"That's what Steph Meek told us but I've just been over this road and it looks passable -- no Crooked River Canyon nor Deschutes to face. There are some dry stretches but water and pasture should be sufficient to see us through . . . . Where's Tildy, anyway? She's all right, isn't she?"

"Of course. Of course. She's probably picking berries and forgot the time." It was the only plausible excuse that came to mind. "I'll go and tell her you're here."

"I'll come with you," Sandy eagerly volunteered.

"No! Stay. She may show up anytime." Joe knew he spoke more sharply than he should, but if Sandy came upon Tildy in Macon Laird's arms . . . !

"Oh!" Joe inwardly groaned. "I must have been out of my head when I invited Laird to join us. Right from the start he was trouble." Joe went to the wagon for his Hawken, and strode for the trees where he last had seen Macon and Tildy. Granddad, who had regained his strength and enjoyed taking part in camp affairs, was watching. He started to call out but the look on Joe's face kept his mouth clamped shut. "Please, God! Don't let that temper of Joe's get out of hand," Granddad silently prayed.

Joe strode up to Tildy and Macon so unexpectedly, they barely had time to compose themselves. Joe planted his feet, holding the rifle before him. He gave the Hawken a menacing wave toward Macon. "In other words, your presence is not needed. Tildy and I have something serious to sort out."

"Oh! Joe! Don't be like that. It isn't Macon's fault, it's mine," Tildy tearfully pleaded. "I know Sandy is here. It's wrong but I just can't face him, not just yet."

For a moment Joe was taken aback. How did she know Sandy had arrived, and why had she immediately run to Macon? Tildy had to do the right thing by Sandy. There was no other way. He took her hand and nearly jerked her off her feet. "You're a big girl. You made a commitment, now you have to stand by it. Dry your eyes and greet Sandy as if nothing has happened. And don't you dare come around to spoil things," he said, brandishing the rifle at Macon. "I'll shoot you like I would a sheep killing dog."

Quickly Tildy dried her eyes, gave Macon a quivering smile and turned to leave. Her heart beat so wildly and loudly, she wondered if it would give her away. She had wronged Sandy, not by falling in love with Macon Laird but by making the wedding promise in the first place. It had been an act of desperation. She had been sick from taking care of, and burying poor Granny. Then there was the loss of the farm and Granddad turning into a zombie. Yes, and there was the fact she did not want to turn into an old maid. It was all too much with Sandy pestering her day after day to get married.

Tildy put a hand to her mouth to stifle a sob. Then, in Independence, Missouri emerged this man in shining armor. Right from the first day she lost her heart to him. "Oh!" she uttered a silent moan. When love strikes reason goes out the window, but she would do her best to hide her true feelings from Sandy. How long could she keep up the pretence . . . ?

She stopped for a moment to give a last swipe to her teary eyes. Joe glanced at her. "Come on, Sis. It isn't the end of the world," he said not unkindly. Tildy nodded. She ran into the circle of wagons. Uttering a squeak, she ran up to Sandy and kissed him full on the lips, then began to sob as if her heart would break. Embarrassed, everyone but Sandy, turned away. Joe found himself facing Saul Abernathy, Bithiah's brother.

"How is the family?" Joe asked, attempting to ignore the scene he had just created.

"Fit as a fiddle. They've put up a house an're fixin' ta raise a barn."

"And how is Bithiah? Is she all right?"

"Well, she's ailin' a bit. Can't seem ta git enuff sleep."

"Oh, stays awake at night does she?" Joe spoke as though he were pleased -- she must be missing him a lot. "Well, she'll be able to sleep well soon. When we get there and are settled everything will be all right."

"Well, maybeso, the doc ain't sure when it's comin'."

"When what's coming?"

"Why the baby, of course. Yuh know how these things are?"

"Are you saying Bithiah is going to give birth?" Granddad, seeing the stunned look on Joe's face, interrupted. "We didn't even know she was married . . . did we, Joe?"

Joe looked at Bithiah's brother in disbelief. He could not believe his ears. Saul had to be joking, but the earnest look on his sunburned face told he spoke the truth. "Wh-what do you mean?" Joe finally managed to stammer. "Bithiah is hitched? She married some man . . . ?"

"Yeah, I figured yuh knew. Right after we hit the Willamette Valley she an' Luke Olafson got hitched. Yuh 'member, they was seein' a lot of each other."

"Yeah! Yeah!" Joe mumbled. There was a weight in his

stomach as large and heavy as a cannon ball. Why couldn't she have waited? He would have made her a far better husband than that dried up Luke Olafson. It wasn't fair. Luke already had had one wife who gave him two kids -- even though the wife was dead, it didn't matter. He should not have gone after sweet, innocent Bithiah just to have a mother for his kids. He turned away and sat down between his two mountain men friends, Deacon and Black Moses Harris, attempting to collect himself. Instead, he found himself near tears.

"They say bad luck often brings good luck," Deacon clucked sympathetically.

"Yuh ol' scoundrel, are yuh still lookin' fer a man fer yer daughter?" Black Moses Harris chimed in, unaware of the underlying drama. "Let me tell yuh a story 'bout a father lookin' fer a son-in-law. Well, yuh see, he was particular. The guy he was lookin' fer had ta hev good looks, money an' manners. The fella searched high an' low, went ta Eurup an' inta the Middle East. From there ta Singapore an' the southseas." Black Moses paused to spit.

"Well, yuh see, the guy was in a real fix. The people with money was ol' an' crotchety. The good lookin' uns was poor as church mice an' unmannerly's boar pigs. So he comes home with no luck at all. He bellies up ta a bar an' orders what yuh call a highball. The bartender says, 'What kinda highball?' 'Well, what yuh got?' the fella asks. 'Well there's whisky, gin, rum, brandy, vodka an' a thing called Red-Eye Dick. The last one's so powerful we only kin serve one ta a customer.'" Black Moses again had to take time to spit.

"Yuh kin tell this guy ain't whach'd call a sophisticated drinker," Black Moses continued. "Anyway, he looks the bartender in the eye an' says, 'I been all over the world lookin' fer a galoot ta marry me daughter an' didn't see a one thet fit the bill. Now yuh befuddle me with this choice of drinks. Give me one of each, maybeso me stomach will tell me which is best.' Well, after swiggin' these highballs the poor feller falls off the bar stool, cracks his head on a spittoon an' kicks the bucket . . . . The postman brings the news to his daughter an' she up an' marries the man, though he ain't got a bean in his pocket."

"Maybeso, there's a moral ta the story, but I ain't gettin' it," Deacon said after a short pause.

"Yuh dumb ox, it means yuh kin be so particular it kin kill yuh."

"Hmm!" Deacon grunted. "Yuh ol' varmint, yuh know 'bout as much 'bout marryin' off a daughter as a bloomin' jackass . . . ." Deacon's jaw dropped open. "I say, ain't thet yer brother? Tarnation! He's brought an army of Injuns with him."

Joe glanced where Deacon pointed, his troubles with Bithiah momentarily forgotten. Approaching the circle of wagons was Michael Two Feathers on the Appaloosa pony he called Magpie. Close behind him were a dozen or more Indian horsemen. Following them was a crowd of women and children and a string of pack animals pulling travois.

"What the devil!" Joe uttered. What in the world could possibly happen next?

XVIII

The advantage gained by the emigrant of this new route is . . .
the distance is considerably shortened, the grass and water
plenty, the sterile regions and dangerous crossings
of the Snake and Columbia avoided, as well
as the Cascade Mountains . . . .

Jessie Applegate, 1846

The unexpected meeting at Fort Hall stunned Michael
Two Feathers as greatly as it did Joe Jennings. Michael had agreed
to accompany his Indian friends on their annual journey to the
upper Snake River where hunting and fishing during the Season
of Falling Leaves was at its best. The trek took them by Fort Hall
where they normally stocked up on needed items to see them
through the winter. They had been searching for a satisfactory
place to camp when they ran into the circle of wagons bound for
Oregon's Willamette Valley.

At first the two brothers stared at each other in amaze-
ment, marveling at the change that had taken place in the two
years they had been apart. Joe could not believe the confident,
broad-shouldered man with piercing blue eyes was the same
Michael Two Feathers he had parted with in Waiilatpu. He had
self-assurance and dignity, yet retained the boyish, retiring manner that made him so likable. Michael was astounded that his
mountain man brother, who, the last time he had seen him had
been poverty-stricken, now appeared so affluent. Much to the
astonishment of the people who eyed the Indian contingent with
a mixture of curiosity and fear, Joe went up and threw his arms
around the young Indian man.

Tildy gasped, momentarily forgetting her catastrophic pre-
dicament. Joe's friendship with the bearded, baldheaded mountain man who she doubted ever had taken a bath, and the two

Cheyenne was bad enough, but here he was, hugging an aborigine. The young man looked like he had come in from the wilds . . . shoulder length hair from which hung two feathers -- one glistening white, the other white with a tip of red that resembled a splash of blood. To make matters worse, with his arm around the man's shoulder, Joe pulled the wild creature toward her.

She pressed back against Sandy, thankful for his stolid protective body. She could not believe what was happening. The farther west they traveled the more strange Joe became. He was standing before her with this creature with two feathers in his hair, looking at him with admiration. Why didn't the wild thing go back to his own people, that scraggly horde who came in dragging their possessions behind their horses on crazy contraptions made of poles? Bad mannered -- they had stopped and were staring as if they never had seen a civilized person before. No, their eyes were on this Indian man Joe had led up to stand before her. They were waiting for him as though he were important.

"Sis, I want you to meet a very special person, our brother, Michael," Joe announced. "He's been living at Whitman's mission in Waiilatpu and now has come to join us."

Tildy could not believe her ears. Surely, this was all a joke. Then it came to her . . . out here when a white man and a red man became friendly, they called each other brother. This had to be a good friend of Joe's. Uncertainly, she put out her hand. The brown flesh had a warm, comfortable feel. She glanced into the eyes and was shaken. They were the shade of stormy blue that one saw when wind ruffled the waters of Nantucket Sound. For a moment she felt as shivery as the day she watched Granny's casket lowered into the ground. She quickly withdrew her hand and backed up against the comforting stolidness of Sandy Sanders.

Neither Joe nor the strange newcomer seemed to notice her discomfort. With his arm still around the Indian man, Joe took him over to his grandfather. "Your grandson," he announced. Unsteadily, the elderly man rose to his feet. "It is always good to meet a member of the family," he said, shaking hands.

Always respectful of his elders, Michael inclined his head with a slight bow and waited for his grandfather to say more but the elderly man was too confused to speak. He glanced at Joe. Had he heard right? Was this really a grandson? Had his son, Nathaniel, adopted a redskin orphan? Nathaniel always had been a strange one, much like his own seafaring father who sailed away one day and never returned. Granddad suddenly felt terribly old and weak. He sat down again on the padded log.

Michael turned away. "I must see to my people. We have to make camp for the night."

"Of course . . . I'll go with you," Joe said.

"Whew!" Deacon uttered more to himself than anyone else. He knew this was the first ever meeting of the Nez Perce lad with his eastern relatives. He doubted the couple from Boston country even knew the existence of their Indian relative until this very moment. He glanced at Granddad and then toward Tildy. Tildy's face was white as new fallen snow. The old man sat staring into space. What could they be thinking? Young Joe had really made a mess of things. He should have known better than drop the Indian brother on the poor innocents like he did. "Maybe I should try and smooth things over," Deacon thought..

Deacon cleared his throat to speak, then decided it best he not get involved. This family was a strange one. Young Joe - - as rough and ready as any frontiersman -- the sister . . . she was beautiful but standoffish and the old gentleman . . . ? They didn't come any better than him. The Indian brother . . . how in the world was he going to fit in? Like the tightening of a banjo string, Deacon could feel tension building. He pulled out his pipe and began to fill it. Someone in camp had to act natural.

A dust cloud rose up to settle over the circle of wagons. The Indians had wheeled about, ready to follow Michael and Joe to a grassy patch near the river's edge. Deacon, watching the brothers lead the way, thought back to the morning the brothers' father, Little Ned, died -- a day that was etched in his memory forever. The air had been brisk, the sky filled with mares' tails and checkered clouds -- a sky sailors called a mackerel sky. It was a warning to trim sails and batten hatches as heavy weather was on the horizon.

"Ah!" Deacon thought. It had been a day that broke one's heart. Young Joe had come running into camp, tears streaming from his eyes. "Little Ned has been shot and scalped," he cried. After all these years, Deacon still had to choke back a tightness in his throat. The occasion was too tragic to think about. He tamped more tobacco in the pipe bowl and put the pouch away. How his old friend, Little Ned, would love to see his two sons now, he thought sadly. The handsome pair would make any father proud.

Deacon forced his mind away from memories of the past and lit his pipe. Through the smoke, he studied the column of Snake Indians that began to file by. A group of young maidens took his eye. What a fine bunch of fillies. A girl, more stately than the rest, graceful as a fawn, strode behind Michael's black and white pony. She had a look of contentment as though she already had received what she wanted out of life. For certain Michael Two Feathers was the one who made her hold her head high and strut along the dusty track like she was the Queen of Mother Earth. Deacon turned to Granddad to comment on the Indian maiden but the old man had fallen asleep.

Before Deacon could get the attention of anyone, a rider came thundering alongside the circle of wagons. "Fust thin' in the mornin' Applegate's holdin' a meetin' on the shortcut ta the Willamette. Yuh'all should come an' hear what he hasta say -- good trail -- gettcha thar safe an' sound." With that announcement, the rider wheeled his mount about and galloped pell-mell for the next group of wagons.

The next morning all adult males and a scattering of females gathered to hear Jessie Applegate expound on the new shortcut route to the Willamette Valley. When the man of the hour stepped up to address the crowd, the people saw an unassuming person who had the appearance of a farmer that had just come from ploughing a field or cleaning a stable. Tildy, who had accompanied Sandy, was disillusioned. She expected a stalwart, forceful leader of men. Instead, she saw quite a homely person. His prominent ears stuck out like handles of a jug. His face was small but in the center was a great beak of a nose -- his expression was somber, as that of a person who found it difficult to smile. And probably for good reason, Tildy thought. It was said in the crossing of '43 he lost a son, nephew and a good friend in the treacherous rapids of the Columbia.

For a moment Jessie Applegate stood silently taking measure of the crowd. When he spoke he did so in a no-nonsense manner. His route was two hundred miles shorter than the present Oregon Trail and far less hazardous, he said. He had a party of laborers working on it now, smoothing out the rough spots. Actually, he needed more men. If anyone wished to apply he would hire them on the spot. The pay was $1.50 per day. The work: cutting down brush and trees; digging out boulders; filling up holes; locating camping spots with pasture, firewood and water.

Before Applegate finished speaking objections were voiced thick and fast. One of the first and loudest protesters was Dad Wall. "I ain't goin' ta tackle any newfangled road," he vowed. "Besides, it won't help me a whit. We'uns are goin' ta Doc Whitman's mission at Waiilatpu. We aim ta hep civilize those mean Cayuses."

Lawyer Quinn Thornton questioned the safety of the journey. "All of us are deadly tired and many sick," he stated. "Our animals and equipment aren't in good condition either. We can't afford to add to our burdens by uncertainties of an untried trail. We don't need another fiasco like the desert crossing led by Stephen Meek."

Applegate assured them the hazards of the southern route could not compare to Meek's Cutoff. "What do you say Jennings?" he asked Joe, whom he had met the previous evening.

"I agree with Mr. Thornton. We do not need another Meek

Cutoff. But I'm not the one to say. Sandy Sanders has been over both routes. Our family will abide by his decision."

Joe was too tired and despondent to give Applegate's shortcut to the Willamette Valley much thought. Although, in the back of his mind he remembered the year he and his trapping partners had wintered in the Siskiyous. It was rough country. There were the Rogue and Umpqua Rivers to cross. The Umpqua Canyon alone was enough to bring wagons to a halt. But if Sandy Sanders gave this route his approval, why should he object? He had his own troubles to worry about. What was he going to do now? The thought of traveling to the Willamette Valley and encountering pregnant Bithiah Abernathy Olafson made him shudder. Because of her he had made a complete fool of himself, insisting she was his love. How could he live where any day he might run into her -- see her tied down with Luke Olafson's two kids and another on the way. The thought made him ill.

At the edge of the crowd he caught a glimpse of Macon Laird. This was another problem his foolishness had caused. He had to put it right. This fellow had to be separated from Sandy and Tildy. If they traveled the same trail there was certain to be trouble. It had to be nipped in the bud right now, but how? Tildy had a mind of her own, and Macon was a man not easily cowed.

Robin distracted Joe by pulling on his sleeve. "What're we ta do, Cap'n? Pa hasta travel the old trail. He'll belt me good if I don't go with him. What yuh plannin' ta do? I sure enuff wanta keep me job."

"Hmm!" Joe grunted. He hadn't anticipated this problem. He had to get rid of Macon and if Robin also left, he, himself, would be saddled with the chore of driving the second wagon. For certain Sandy would drive the first one carrying his and Tildy's possessions. He glanced up. Sandy was standing by himself. Where did Tildy go? Was she with Macon Laird?

Joe gritted his teeth. "Blast it!" Macon Laird had also disappeared. Joe quickly elbowed his way out of the gathering leaving Robin staring blankly after him. He had to keep Tildy and Macon apart. He strode toward the circle of wagons. No one was there except Michael, who was sitting on the padded log where Granddad usually sat. He glanced up with a welcoming smile.

"I have been waiting to talk to you," Michael said.

"Not now," Joe said sharply. "There's something I have to do."

Michael got up and turned to leave. White people were all alike, he thought. Rude and always in a hurry. Everything had to be done right now.

"I'm sorry," Joe said. Michael had the hurt look of a friendly dog that had been slapped for getting in the way. "Please come back," he pleaded. "The chore can wait."

#

Joe had good reason to be concerned. The two lovers were at that moment together. Their rendezvous appeared innocent, but it was well planned. Macon had signaled with his eyes he would meet Tildy at the trading post entrance. Tildy replied with an imperceptible shake of the head -- it was impossible. Then she had a brilliant thought. Mrs. Alphonse Boone and her daughter, Chloe, were discussing whether they should go to the trading room to purchase a length of calico. "I'd like to go with you, if you don't mind," Tildy whispered.

"That decides it. We'll leave these men to wrangle over this new road by themselves. They may be at it all night," Mrs. Boone whispered back. Sandy Sanders frowned but remained silent. Now that he was finally with Tildy he would do anything to keep her happy.

Macon Laird, who had already slipped away, watched the three womenfolk make their way toward the trading post entrance. Nonchalantly, he strolled that way, too. He caught up with them at the trading room door. He tipped his hat to the Boone ladies and murmured his pleasure at the chance encounter. Tildy gave him a tentative smile.

"Please make your purchases," Tildy said to her companions. "I'll wait with Mr. Laird."

Mrs. Boone gave them a suspicious glance, then proceeded to pull her daughter, Chloe, into the trading room. For a moment Tildy and Macon stood looking at each other, their eyes filled with pain. Tildy broke the silence. "Oh, Macon! What's going to happen to us?" Her voice had a desperate ring. "We've been so happy these past few weeks. Now everything has suddenly become hopeless."

Macon cleared his throat to speak. For the first time he fully recognized Tildy's agonizing position. Why had he allowed things to go this far? It was not like him to act recklessly, but on this journey he had thrown caution to the winds, and those around him had paid for it. He let his guard down, and his loyal friend Pascoe was killed. He had made love to this innocent woman, and she was now faced with disgrace. It seemed everyone he came in contact with suffered. He glanced at Tildy, then quickly looked away. He couldn't stand to see the pain that marred the face he loved.

"How do you disclose heartbreaking news to an unsuspecting innocent party, especially one you loved and still respect?" Tildy cried out. "How can I face him every day after breaking his heart?"

Macon stood numbly watching her suffer. He could well understand how she felt. It had to be similar to the same terrible pain that clutched at his vitals like the claws of some ravaging beast. Why couldn't he think of some solution besides packing her up and carrying her away. He shouldn't even consider such a rash, irresponsible act. Her brother would track them down and likely murder them both.

"You must give me time," Tildy said finally. "I just can't disappoint Sandy so soon."

"When shall I see you again?" Macon hurriedly asked, noticing the Boone women approaching.

"Please, not for awhile. I just can't think straight. Maybe something will happen between now and Oregon. That's it! I'll lead up to it gradually, then it won't be such a shock. Perhaps Sandy will even be glad to see us part." The thought brought such a feeling of relief, Tildy laughed.

"They want an awful price for everything." Mrs. Boone said, coming up. All the way back to camp she continued to voice her complaints of the high-handed manner in which Hudson's Bay treated wagon train people. "It's because they're British. They don't want Americans around," she said, glaring at Macon. "They're still mad because we gained our independence."

Macon tipped his hat. "I guess that's a hint British folk are not exactly your cup of tea . . . I'll take my leave."

#

Tildy returned to camp to see her brother and the redskin youth, Two Feathers, sitting on the padded log. They stood to greet her, Joe giving her an especially sharp inspection. She cringed at the thought that he knew she had been with Macon Laird. What right did he have, disapproving of the company she kept? Look at him, as intimate with that redskin as if they were actually brothers. She entered the sleeping wagon and laid down. She suddenly felt so drained of strength she barely could hold her head up.

Tildy was right. Joe knew his sister had been with Macon Laird. But for once it did not jar him like it would have just an hour previously. Another problem had come up he never dreamed would happen. Michael would not be going with them. He was joining the band of Snakes. When he tried to argue against it, his brother remained steadfast.

"I am following the advice of the wisest man I know, my uncle, Vision Seeker," Michael explained. "I have to make a choice between two paths; the white path or the path of my native people. Uncle Vision Seeker said my heart would tell me which was the right path for me to take. I looked in my heart. At first it told me to take the path of the whites. It got me as far as Fort Boise. There I did what I thought was a good deed and the missionary people who rode with me, said I did bad. They abandoned me in the middle of the night, not even saying good-bye. The people for whom I believed I did good, took me into their hearts. They appreciated what I did and honored me by asking me to join their band. My heart now tells me that is what I should do. If you want to visit me, we winter in buffalo country near the Land of the Big Smokes. You always will be welcome as brother and friend."

XIX

Tomorrow I start homeward. The emigrants have almost annoyed me out of my senses.

Jessie Applegate, Fort Hall, 1846

Debate over the Applegate Road continued all day and well into the evening. The emigrants were not satisfied with Jessie Applegate's assurances. They raised questions, but the answers did not satisfy them. A group of disgusted men went to the trading room at the fort to interview fur traders familiar with the region. Their particular concern was the threat Indians presented. "Maybeso, the Injuns on the southern route're in better temper an' maybeso they ain't. It's like predictin' the weather. One day there's a storm abrewin'. The next day it's sunny and calm," a tobacco chewing bearded fellow observed.

Another seasoned veteran of the frontier was more forthright. "If I remember correctly, there's a right smart piece of desert inhabited by the Paiute. They'd steal the pennies off a corpse. Course the Modocs and Clamets' ain't much better, 'bout as trustworthy as sidewinders durin' moltin' season."

Joe, who knew the territory as well as anyone, did not take part in the discussions. Since the arrival of Michael and the band of Snake Indians, he was looked on askance. He was entirely too friendly with these "savages." The trust he placed in his Cheyenne friends was recalled and discussed. His mountain man companion, Deacon, now a fixture in the Jennings' camp, made no bones about having a Cheyenne family. If Indian trouble erupted he was certain to side with the natives. Then there was that doubtful British hanger-on, Laird. He played the role of a jolly good fellow well, but who knew where his loyalty lie. It was common knowledge the British would do most anything to add Oregon Territory to their empire.

Joe was quite aware that almost overnight his position as

train captain had deteriorated. He did not care. In fact he would like nothing better than to shuck the whole business. He never wanted to see these backbiting people again. The goodness he'd seen in them at the start had vanished. The trek across the plains and mountains he'd looked forward to with such eagerness had turned into a nightmare. His hopes and dreams had gone up in smoke. Hawk Beak's inheritance, which he thought would do so much good, had brought nothing but disappointment.

Joe stared across the open space that extended up the gradual incline to the fort. In the distance gleamed the campfires of the Snakes. He wanted to reach out to Michael -- tell him he was making a big mistake. He would have offered the world to him on a golden platter. But Michael rejected the offer before it was even made. As soon as he announced he was joining his Indian friends, he left and gave no sign he would return. What had happened at Fort Boise to turn him completely around? Joe had half a notion to invade the camp of the Snakes and find out. But that might be the worst thing he could do. Michael would lose face in the eyes of his new found friends.

Two horsemen leading pack mules and coming from the west, crossed the open space. In the dim moonlight they looked like black ghosts gliding along, leaving a low trail of silvery dust. They rode straight for the Indian camp, then veered toward the fort that loomed like an abandoned ruin guarding the roadway to some walled city in the hinterlands of medieval Europe.

"That's the way to travel," Joe said to himself. "Horses and pack mules -- average thirty to forty miles a day." Now that Sandy was on hand to take charge of the wagons, he could break away. He'd hire a second wagon driver so he didn't leave the family short of help. That was the smart thing to do -- buy himself a pack mule and wrap his personal belongings in a roll, strap them on the mule's back and be away -- leave the onerous wagon train responsibilities behind. Perhaps Deacon would like to go, too.

The more Joe thought over the idea the better he liked it.

He took a blanket from a wagon, selected a secluded spot a good distance from the campfire group who continued to debate which trail to take, and settled himself for the night. He closed his eyes but couldn't sleep. He had dreamed so long and hard about bringing the family together again, now he was abandoning them. How could he do that, especially leaving poor unsuspecting Sandy facing a showdown with Macon Laird?

Nevertheless, the following morning Joe and Deacon made their way to the fort to inspect the livestock Fort Factor Grant offered for trade or sale. It was Grant's policy to trade a good horse, mule or ox for two that were travel worn and could not carry on. He then doctored and fattened them until they were near normal again. The animals in the corral all looked like they had traveled as far as they could manage.

"Maybeso, thar's one thet might do," Deacon said, pointing to a mouse colored mule. "It's kinda puny but sometimes these critters surprise yuh. They put on like they're all done in but're still as tough as an ol' boot. Let's visit Cap' Grant an' make a deal."

Captain Grant, always ready to trade with anyone -- Indian, emigrant, trapper or another trader -- gave the mouse colored mule high praise. "Yep, got the critter off a fellow that knew horses but mules he couldn't tolerate; a red-nosed, big-jawed chap new to the west. It was one of those fellows I was telling you about, the two who loaded up on powder, lead and red-eye. I recognized right away they were straight from the old country."

"Yer old country, too, ain't yuh?" Deacon asked.

"I'm not a newcomer, by a long shot. Been in the service of Hudson's Bay for going on thirty-five years. I'm a Scotsman, not a blasted blimey like those blokes. Calling a Scotsman English is like throwing mud in his eye!"

"Well, you've been here long enough to be called an American by now," Deacon joked.

"Never, never! We've never outgrown our roots or loyalty to the crown! When I came across it was the policy of Hudson's Bay to employ men from the Shetland and Orkney Islands. Recruits agreed to work from three to five years at twenty-five pounds per annum, and that's what they had to live on. When the men arrived they were encouraged to take Indian wives. You can imagine on twenty-five pounds and saddled with families, these men quickly found themselves a bit short. Hudson's Bay was happy to lend them a bit here and there. Soon the poor fellows were up to their ears in debt. Many a good man slaved his life away to pay off his loans but it sure paid off for Hudson's Bay. The company gained an army of workers who stayed on the job. Yes, siree. I started . . ."

"Yer sad story's breakin' our hearts. We'll take thet mule afore it goes up another five dollars," Deacon said, cutting the fort factor off in mid-sentence.

"For no extra cost, I'll toss in a wee bit of information that might be of use," Grant said after he pocketed the mule money. "A couple of toughs rode in last night from Fort Boise. They inquired about the makeup of the train; particularly they asked if Joe Jennings was along. Didn't say who they were but one of them has a head like that of an oversized squirrel -- both surly as mad hatters. Seems Craig, our man at Fort Boise, threw them in the jug for a couple of days. You can be sure there isn't much charity in their hearts for anybody, so I'd be on guard."

"Who in the world could thet be?" Deacon asked as they went to the corral after the mouse colored mule. "Yuh expectin' company?"

"No, I'm not," Joe tersely answered. Grant's description of the men made his skin crawl. Came from the west, did they? Perhaps what he feared had finally happened. Hawk Beak's friends had arrived.

#

During his brief stay at Fort Hall, Applegate recruited over a hundred wagons for his new trail. His campaign completed, he and Black Moses Harris prepared to leave. "There still is work to be done," Applegate wrote in his diary. "Now that I have persuaded these people into taking my shortcut, I cannot let them down. Black Moses Harris and I must return to finish the trail before the first wagons arrive."

Upon taking their leave Applegate and Black Moses passed by the Jennings' wagons and drew Deacon aside.

"Since you're kind of an extra hand here, could you see your way clear to help us out? We're still not satisfied with the route through the Siskiyous," Jessie Applegate said.

"Tarnation!" Deacon exclaimed. "Yuh mean yer takin' these pilgrims over a trail yer not sure of?"

"It ain't so bad, 'cept a section through Umpqua Canyon. If rains come early it could git a bit rough," Black Moses Harris said. "We thought, maybeso, in yer trappin' days yuh came upon somethin' better."

"Hmm! I don't perzactly remember trails thet'll take wagons," Deacon said, scratching in his bushy beard. "Perhaps if we sashay 'round a bit we could hit on somethin'."

"We'd be obliged if you'd do what you can," Applegate said. "A lot's at stake."

"Suppose we should lend a hand?" Deacon asked Joe after Applegate and Black Moses had departed.

"I don't mind. First, I have to sort things out here," Joe answered.

"Yeah, yuh gotta problem, ain't yuh," Deacon said thoughtfully. "Maybe we should take Johnny Macon Redcoat along. He ain't doin' no good here."

Joe gave his old friend a sharp glance.

"Lissen! It don't take the smarts of a hen house fox ta see thet Macon fella is goggled-eyed over yer sister. If yuh don't separate those two men blood'll be spilled fer sure."

"Yeah," Joe grimly agreed. "Probably the blood of Sandy Sanders. He's no match for Macon Laird. I'm going to do something about it right now."

Hardly did Joe get to his feet before he was stopped by an

angry mob armed with rifles led by Short.

"Yuh an' yer Injun friends," Short stormed. "I knew right off they was no good. This time they've gone too far. They snuck right up an' took me prize heifer, the one I been countin' on ta start a blood herd. We'uns're fed up. We're goin' straight over there an' sort those damned redskins out. Are yuh goin' with us or are yuh not?"

Joe, intent on the encounter with Macon Laird, turned on Short. He twisted the rifle out of the redhead's hands and rammed the muzzle into his midriff. "No one is going anywhere, least of all you," he said heatedly.

"Easy!" Deacon cautioned. "Let's not go off half-cocked. Losin' a heifer ain't the end of the world."

"Short's right," someone in the crowd said. "Somebody cut the heifer's stake rope and led the critter away. The tracks lead straight toward the Injuns' camp."

"Well, now. If thet's the case, me an' me friend'll mosey over an' see what the other side hasta say. In the meantime why don'tcha cool off an' go 'bout yer work. Is thet agreeable ta yuh, Joe?" Deacon asked.

"Yes, it's the wise thing to do." Joe returned the rifle to Short who took it with an angry glare.

#

"Why is it that every time trouble comes Indian people are the first to be blamed?" Michael asked, when told of the stolen heifer. "Why don't you look up those two over there. This morning the smell of fresh meat cooking came from their camp."

Deacon and Joe glanced where Michael motioned. A bulky figure emerged from a lean-to shelter. It was the man Grant described as having the oversized head of a squirrel. "Tarnation!" Deacon exclaimed. "Thet's Hawk's friend, Hare Lip Bruce."

"That's him," Michael agreed. "He has a friend as worthless and ornery as he. For some reason they have a grudge against you, brother."

"Hmm!" Joe grunted. Hare Lip Bruce had been Hawk

Beak's friend, all right. There was no doubt about it, they were after the gold. He glanced at Deacon.

Deacon shook his head. "Fer sure thet's where the heifer went. An' we ain't goin' ta git it back 'less we wanta carve open ther bellies, an' I ain't much fer thet." They rode back to the wagons. Short was waiting, his face as red as his flaming beard.

"Well, what didja find out? Those redskins hev me heifer?"

"No, claim they've never seen it," Joe replied. "Near as we can tell it's those two hard lookers yonder who took your heifer, butchered her and are eating on her right now."

"I'll bet those savages're lyin'. They're the ones who stole her. I've a good mind ta go over an' see fer meself."

Joe dismounted and began to unsaddle his horse. His silence infuriated Short. "We sure enuff cain't depend on you," he said furiously. "Yuh've made a mess of things ever since yuh took over as captain, but this is the last straw. We need somebody who's not an Injun lover, someun who'll perteck our possessions an' keep us outta trouble. I demand yer resignation as train captain or the missus an' me'll move on by ourselves."

"Why don't you just do that. I'll see you on your way," came a voice accustomed to command.

Joe and Short both turned to face the speaker. Macon Laird, dressed in a riding outfit, entered the circle of wagons. Behind him trailed a horse and a loaded pack mule. "Come on! Hitch up! I'm leaving, too. I'll accompany you for a ways," Macon urged.

"Ah! Shet up!" Short snarled, stomping away. "Everyone of yuh's in cahoots."

"What's this all about?" Joe asked when Short was out of ear shot. He was so surprised he didn't know what else to say.

"Yes, I'm leaving," Macon said. "I shouldn't have traveled with you in the first place. You know the trouble I've caused."

Joe nodded. All of a sudden he felt sorry for the Englishman. Except for falling in love with Tildy he had been a first rate companion, and he really shouldn't be faulted for falling for Tildy. She was one in a million. "Be careful. Those birds who killed Pascoe are certain to be after you. Come to think of it Captain Grant mentioned two toughs. One with long red nose . . ."

Macon nodded. "Yes, not very friendly types."

"Why should they be so keen to run you down?"

Macon hesitated. Joe Jennings had been good to him, treated him far better than he deserved. He had every right to know the purpose of his mission but it was too early to tell anyone anything. People like Wall and Short, already suspicious of the British, were certain to jump to erroneous conclusions. No, it was better to keep quiet and hope for the best.

"What about Tildy?" Joe broke the silence.

"We've said our farewells and Saul Abernathy has agreed to help with the chores and drive the second wagon. Everything should go on as normal."

"Yeah!" Joe said skeptically, as if anything ever would be normal again.

Macon raised his hand in farewell and reined away, pulling the pack mule along behind. He glanced back only once toward the Jennings' sleeping wagon where the restraints that had held Tildy and he apart finally had been broken. A flood of passion had hurtled them together as violently as if they had been pitched over a waterfall. It was the wildest, yet most tender moment he had ever experienced.

"Ah!" Macon groaned. How had he scraped up enough will power to leave Tildy behind? The greatest urge seized him to ride back, tear open the wagon flaps, pull her from the blankets and carry her away. Instead, he spurred his mount ahead, jerked on the balky mule's lead line and hurried down the trail as fast as he could.

From the back opening of the Jennings' sleeping wagon a handkerchief fluttered and then was quickly withdrawn. Joe swallowed a lump in his throat. The pathway of ill-starred lovers was, indeed, lonely and hard.

XX

... as Applegate was personally acquainted with many of the emigrants, he succeeded very easily in persuading most of us to abandon the old route for the new ...

Rev. J. A. Cornwall, 1847

The travelers sat around campfires speaking in low tones, pondering the trials they faced before achieving their goal, a Willamette Valley homestead. The last evening in Fort Hall the mood of the camp was much the same as experienced by the train led by Colonel Russell upon leaving Independence. The travelers had a good idea of what to expect, yet doubt and fear of the unknown still beleaguered them. It did not matter which trail they had chosen, there were perils on either one. The twinkling gleam of the Snakes' campfires, a short rifle shot away, flashed like coastal beacons warning of dangerous shoals ahead. The threat the emigrants feared most was fractious Indians. Ominous rumors floating around Fort Hall were that tribes on both routes were on the warpath.

Joe Jennings sat alongside his grandfather, feeling a sense of relief. Early that afternoon the responsibilities of train captain had been lifted from his shoulders. He had spoken to Rice Dunbar, the captain of another group of wagons taking the Applegate Road, who had agreed to oversee the wagons Joe captained.

Joe felt good about the transfer as the Dunbar company included such reliable personages as J. Quinn Thornton, Alphonse Boone and Reverend Josephus Cornwall. He had a perfect excuse for leaving. He and Deacon were going ahead to search for a better roadway through the lands of the Rogue and Umpqua. Sandy Sanders and Saul Abernathy had agreed they could manage without him. Tildy approved. It was almost as if she was glad to be rid of him. He didn't blame her. The Laird episode would stand between them forever. All he had to do now was convince Granddad that travel and chores would continue as smoothly as before.

"Of course, everything will be all right," Granddad responded when told of Joe's plan to travel ahead. "Saul and Sandy are dependable young men. It's Tildy, I worry about. She should be happy as a clam, but I don't think she is. I trust there's nothing wrong between her and Sandy. She can't be pining for that Macon Laird fellow, can she?"

"Of course not. They were just good friends."

"Yes, she wouldn't hurt Sandy for the world," Granddad said. "If you'll excuse me, I think I'll turn in."

One by one, members of the Jennings' wagons took to their blankets until only Joe remained by the fire. Perhaps he should stay with the wagons. If Tildy broke with Sandy, what would happen then? Granddad was right, she did not look well -- it was that Britisher, Laird . . . .

Joe pounded a knee with his fist. He had wanted to do so much good with Hawk Beak's gold but he hadn't done one thing right, Joe grimly berated himself. Instead of a blessing, the gold had been a curse. If it hadn't fallen into his lap he would have gone to Waiilatpu, taken Michael east as he promised, and properly introduced him to the folks. Somehow, they would have scraped enough money together to make the journey to Oregon. There would have been no Macon Laird -- no Tildy-Macon love affair and if the sudden wealth hadn't blinded him, he would have given Bithiah more thought. Sending a few tender words might well have kept her from marrying that critter, "Olafson!"

Joe got up and stomped around the remains of the campfire. He was so filled with bitter self-incrimination he felt sick. He stared across the open area where the campfires of the Snakes gleamed brightly. The sight only made him feel worse. Not only had he made a mess of Tildy's life but he had lost his half brother as well. He didn't blame Michael for joining the Indian band. For certain the Snake people had treated Michael far better than had he and his eastern relatives.

Joe studied the line of Indian campfires. Why hadn't they moved on, he wondered. It was a long trek to the Land of Big Smokes, but of course Indians were never in a hurry. He had an urge to see Michael before he left, try and patch things up, but with his record he probably would make the situation worse. He had had his chance to do the right thing and bungled it. Perhaps an opportunity to make amends would show up in the months ahead. He hoped so. It would be impossible to live with himself if he didn't undo the harm he had done.

The next morning there was the usual bustle of breaking camp. Before dawn came the clang and shouts of night guards, "Hiya! Hiya! It's time to turn out." Hastily built campfires flared into life. A hurried breakfast was eaten and loose stock and draft animals were rounded up and brought in. Teamsters gee-hawed oxen around and hitched them in place, then waited impatiently for women and children to finish the chores and put the last utensil, blanket and food box in the wagons. A final search of the campsite and a count of heads were made to make certain no children or possessions were left behind. At last the wagons were ready to roll.

Joe saddled Blaze and packed his gear on the mouse colored mule. He glanced over at the camp of Snakes. They were hustling around, breaking down their shelters, fashioning travois, apparently also preparing to break camp and take to the trail. Again Joe had the urge to make a last plea with Michael to abandon his plan to go off with the Snakes. Since Michael had not come to say good-bye, he would swallow his pride and go to him.

Joe mounted up and reined away, then noticed the lean-to shelter of Hare Lip Bruce and his companion. Someone had reported seeing them on a sidehill, eyeing the circle of wagons. That was probably when they caught sight of Short's heifer. Of course their first thought was to make certain of his, Joe Jennings', presence so they could start hatching plans to take him by surprise. The foolish men weren't overly smart. They should have acted. Now he was forewarned.

Deacon came alongside packed, impatient to be away. They intended to travel as far as they could by nightfall . . . .

"Aagh!" From the first Jennings' wagon came a painful howl. Joe and Deacon quickly dismounted and ran to see what happened. Sandy was holding up his right hand, blood dripped down his wrist and into his shirt sleeve.

"Butter fingers," he said, his voice strained. "How awful to have this happen before we've even gotten underway. I hope it isn't a sign of things to come."

In hitching up, Sandy's finger got caught in the link of a singletree chain. Before he could pull free the team of mules started up and nearly snapped his finger in two.

"Here! Let's hev a look at it." Deacon, who had tended many a trapper's injuries and ills, jumped down to take charge. He quickly cleaned the wound and set the broken finger but Sandy was still in great pain and could not manage the reins. Deacon's and Joe's plans to ride ahead were dashed. Joe surrendered his horse and pack mule to Deacon and drove the first wagon.

Across the way, in the Snake encampment, sentries reported to their elders the emigrant wagons were on the move. Michael, who sat with the elders, acknowledged the report by motioning with his thumb and forefinger extended and thrust upward. He understood. "Keep watch on small camp of two men," he added with quick hand gestures.

Later the sentries returned to report the two white men who had harassed them at Fort Boise also were breaking camp, taking the trail west. "Now, we will have some fun," Michael said with satisfaction. "Let's go to the fort and do some trading."

Far into the night the fires in the Snake encampment glowed so brightly Captain Grant took his spy glass and studied the camp, lodge by lodge. "Those people are crazy," he said to his wife. "They traded for all of my wolf skins, took everyone, even a batch I was saving with skulls still attached. Why should they want them? For certain they're up to no good. If they're counting on causing trouble, they'd better think again. In the morning I'm going down there and send them on their way." But the following morning when Grant opened the fort gates, the band of Snake Indians was gone.

Three days' journey brought the emigrant wagon train to the crossing of the Raft River. Although not much of a river at this time of the year, it was a noteworthy landmark because here the trail split. Straight ahead lay the route through Fort Boise and the Blue Mountains to Oregon Territory. By turning left a traveler would go south on the trail to California.

The camp that night was just beyond the intersection of the Oregon/California trail. Water was good and pasture fair. A clump of willow and cottonwood trees provided wood for camp-fires. The mood among members of the Jennings party was more cheerful than it had been. So far no mishaps had occurred. Sandy's broken finger was on the mend.

Even Short briefly quit mourning over his lost prize heifer long enough to raise a cup of coffee in toast to the journey ahead. The only specter on the horizon was that they were still in the land of the unpredictable Bannocks. Before the night guards went out to take their posts, they were warned to be especially watchful; Indians liked to sneak up under the cover of darkness and drive away animals.

Though Tildy still protested, from here on Sandy would drive the lead wagon and be responsible for the Jennings' family. Sandy insisted it was more important for Deacon and Joe to proceed ahead and search for a better route than the present one that followed the Umpqua Canyon. The evening ended pleasantly with cheery talk of what they would do when they arrived in the Willamette Valley. Saul told of the Abernathy family's difficulties in raising their house and barn. It took them a fortnight to plane the floor of the house and still it was about as even as a plowed field.

"The barn was an even harder task," Saul said. "We hammered each wall together on the ground, then raised them in place. When we got the first wall halfway up, someone slipped, lost his hold an' it came crashing down. Poor old Luke Olafson had his foot in the way. He limped aroun' like a three-legged dog for days. On top of everthin' else, Bithiah had to do the chores."

"Served them both right," Joe said to himself. He took a blanket from the wagon, said good night and walked beyond the circle of campfire light. At the edge of the clump of cotton-woods and willows, he stretched out on the blanket. Gradually the drone of conversation and chorus of crickets made his eye-lids heavy. He dozed and found himself with Bithiah. She was doing the outdoor chores, scattering grain in the hen yard, pick-ing up eggs . . . Something suddenly came between them. A big hairy beast lumbered toward her. "Help! Help me, Joe!" she pleaded.

The dream was so real Joe attempted to scramble to his feet. He couldn't move. A heavy weight held him down. He tried again but still he could not move. The weight was holding him flat to the ground. It was the big hairy beast! It was sitting astride his midriff. In the dim moonlight the creature was a furry blur. It was no nightmare -- it was a big burly bear.

As his eyes focused Joe could see it was not a bear, but a man with a head shaped like that of a bear. He started to shout but a piercing pain stopped him. A knife blade pressed against his throat, breaking through the skin. Warm blood was trickling into his sleeping robe. He lay still, hardly daring to breathe. For a moment the pressure lessened. He gulped for air. A rank smell overpowered him. Not only was Bear Head soused with firewa-ter, but from his body came a smell as rank as that of a rutting billy goat. Behind him loomed a second man, also armed with a knife.

"All right!, we're goin' fer a little walk," Bear Head hissed, his breath so strong Joe nearly gagged. "Git up nice an' slow. Holler fer help an' I'll slice yer ears off." Bear Head seized Joe by the front of his buckskin shirt, jerked him to his feet, spun him around and half shoved and half dragged him away from the circle of wagons.

Unable to see where he was going, Joe stumbled and would have fallen if Bear Head hadn't held him upright. Everything was so unreal Joe again wondered if it were a nightmare -- he was walking in his sleep -- but the warm blood trickling down his neck and tree limbs slapping him in the face, made it clear the situation was real. Rudely, he was being thrust into the cottonwood grove.

"Now, we're goin' ta find out what happened ta Hawk Beak," Bear Head said, his voice so harsh and unyielding it made Joe flinch. He was furious with himself. He had known good and well Hare Lip Bruce and Hard-Bitten Smith would follow. He should have faced them back at Fort Hall and had a showdown. Now he was caught like a rat in a trap.

"Aeeyah!" A bloodcurdling cry, then another and another, came out of the darkness. Elongated, dancing shadows made the trees appear to writhe like coiled snakes. A brilliant light flared up. Joe, nearly blinded, could make out a hairy figure holding a flaming torch. It had the shocking appearance of an upright wolf with gleaming eyes as huge as fireflies -- firelight danced off ivory fangs that seemed to drip blood.

Like his captors, Joe was transfixed. Not so much with fear but with fascination. He was witnessing the reincarnation of a legend. Now that his eyes were accustomed to the bright light, he made out the pelts of wolves complete with heads and claws, draped over men. Before the coming of the horse, hunters camouflaged as wolves crept alongside buffalo herds, ready to spear or disable the beasts with knives. In those days youthful hunters went on practice hunts to perfect their skills. But this was no practice hunt. This was real -- the prey, him and the two burly men who held him captive.

The figure holding the torch glided forward, an awesome wolflike apparition. Heat from the torch was so intense Bear Head's beard began to shrivel. He uttered a scream and attempted to run. Claw-like hands reached out to hold him back. The wolf figure waved the torch in the face of Hard-Bitten Smith who dropped to his knees and moaned.

From the circle of wagons came a shout and then a rifle shot. The night guard beat on a triangle of iron, the signal the wagon train was under attack. Half-dressed men vaulted from wagons and scrambled from makeshift shelters to fire wildly into the trees. "Bloody Injun savages hev us surrounded," the voice of Short rang out. "See thet torch. They was goin' ta set fire ta the wagons -- murder us all in our sleep."

The wolf figures faded into the darkness, taking Bear Head and his companion with them. The leader of the wolf men doused the torch and removed the wolf skin . . . . For a long moment the brothers looked at each other. Joe grasped Michael's hand. The return grip was firm. His Nez Perce brother had watched over him -- rescued him. He probably owed his life to him.

"Good-bye until we meet again," Michael Two Feathers said. "We'll take good care of Hare Lip Bruce and his partner -- teach them proper manners." He gave Joe's hand another grip and was gone.

"It's all right! Go back to sleep," Joe said as he walked out of the bank of trees.

"What kinda monkey business is goin' on?" Short demanded, "scarin' womin an' children half ta death?"

"Some friends just came to say good-bye," Joe said. He went back to his bed roll, wrapped a piece of toweling around his wounded neck, laid down and pulled a blanket over him as if nothing unusual had occurred.

XXI

This desert is perfectly sterile, producing nothing
but greasewood and sage, and some of it perfectly barren
ground and the ground very salty.

Virgil Pringle, 1846

The route to California was well marked. Wagon ruts, discarded equipment, an occasional livestock skeleton and grave markers were sign posts pointing the way. As Joe and Deacon proceeded deeper into the region west of the Great Salt Lake, Digger Indians frequently appeared. They were as woebegone as the country that surrounded them. Impoverished, their clothing was poor, made mostly from ragged rabbit skins. Some wore practically nothing. They lived in fragile grass and willow branch covered huts looking much like oversized haycocks. The inhabitants popped out to stare at the travelers, their eyes covetously examining the packs and the mules.

"We'd best keep alert," Deacon commented. "Nuthin' these Diggers'd like better'n a roasted haunch of a mule."

Along the way they encountered wagons with weary teamsters urging on equally weary oxen traveling to California. It was imperative they reach the high mountain passes before early snows. Joe thought of the Donner party. Tamsen Donner had been so concerned about taking the Hasting's Cutoff, he wondered how they were getting along.

One evening Deacon and Joe unexpectedly camped with a group taking Applegate's new road to the Willamette Valley. They called themselves the Pringle-Brown party. It consisted of Virgil and Phrena Pringle and their five children; Tabiatha Brown, Phrena's sixty-eight year old mother, and her seventy-seven year old uncle, John Brown, a retired sea captain. Although travel weary as anybody, they were energetic and amazingly lighthearted.

"The road ain't much to brag about, but we're countin'

on gettin' there somehow," Tabiatha Brown cheerfully declared.

Leaving the Pringle-Brown party, the riders pushed on into the monotonous vegetation of sage and greasewood that stretched before them to distant purple mountains. The soil, so light and porous it resembled ashes, created a fine, suffocating dust that penetrated everything, coating animals and riders with shrouds of gray.

Each afternoon thick white clouds formed overhead, but never released a drop of moisture. A hot breeze blew into the riders' faces. It fanned dust into swirls and swept up sand and grit to clog eyes and nostrils. To add to the riders' discomfort, they came upon a series of hot pools, some nearly boiling. Beneath the surface the heated water gurgled and rumbled, frightening the horses and mules. Only after a careful search did they find water sufficiently cool to drink.

Deacon studied the sketchy map Applegate had given him. "I do believe we're on the edge of Black Rock Desert. From here we leave the California Trail ta travel thetaway." He pointed to the northwest. "If the passage gets any worse, God help those who follow."

Joe nodded grimly. The way was well marked but the terrain was even more formidable than that faced by Stephen Meek's unfortunate wagon train in crossing the Oregon desert. He thought of the dust filled wagons carrying Granddad and Tildy. If it was hard for him and Deacon with pack mules and horses, what would it be like behind teams of mules and oxen?

They took the track Deacon pointed out and wended their way across Black Rock Desert, an area so desolate even breezes seemed to avoid it. Beyond the desert the track passed through a narrow, high-walled ravine, so deep and narrow in some places the sun never penetrated to the canyon floor. When they finally broke into the open a sandy, gravel-strewn plain stretched before them. Along the distant horizon a low mountain range shimmered in the heat of the late August sun. Deacon pulled his white mule, affectionately called Lightening, to a stop. "Me thinks the wise thing is ta hold up here 'til nightfall. It looks a fer piece without grass or water an' our poor critters ain't in the best of shape."

After stripping the packs and saddles from the animals, Joe and Deacon sipped at their canteens and chewed on strips of jerky. "Every step we take I'm more afeerd fer yer folks an' the rest of the wagon train families," Deacon said. "There's miserable little water, not enuff grass to keep a jack rabbit an' it's hot as Hades. The trail ain't near as short as Applegate claims, neither."

The remainder of the day they rested, beating desert flies and sand fleas away. At dusk they started out again. The night travel brought welcome relief from the dazzling sunlight but the ground was still like an oven. Only toward midnight did it cool, and by early morning it even became chilly. Daylight found them on a barren dry lake bed. There was not a welcoming camping site in view, so they continued.

Gradually vegetation began to appear. Before the day was over they climbed a steep rise. At the summit they gazed in wonder at a valley as green and inviting as the desert was bleak and uninviting. Shining like a jewel set in greenery, sparkled a small shimmering lake. They hardly could keep the animals in check as they scrambled down the slope toward the unexpected oasis.

"Oh-oh!" Deacon uttered. "Someone's already here." But it was only an empty camp with a couple of lean-to shelters erected under a tree. "From the look of what these folks left behind, they reckon ta be peaceful -- maybeso, trappers're hunters," Deacon said. "We'll camp yonder so's not ta disturb 'em,"

Toward evening a group of dust covered young men appeared. Joe judged that most of them were still in their teens. They introduced themselves as Applegate road builders. "We been cuttin' brush, blazin' trees an' removin' rocks to make the way for the hundreds of wagons we expect to come this way," one youthful road worker explained.

Accompanied by the road builders, Joe and Deacon pressed on toward the Siskiyous. In the lands of the Modoc and Klamath they sighted rings of smoke puffing skyward, something Joe hadn't seen since leaving the land of the Pawnee. "The Injuns're spreadin' the word we're comin'," Deacon observed.

They passed black lava beds where the young road workers said Modoc warriors often were seen. They came to forests of tall evergreens to see dusky figures flitting among the dark forest shadows. Joe's hand went automatically to the scab at his throat where Hare Lip's knife had cut the skin. The ghostly apparitions sliding through the trees reminded him of the set-to he had with the two rascals after Hawk Beak's gold. He didn't need to go through something like that again. This time Michael and his band of Snakes wouldn't be around to save him.

That evening several Modocs appeared out of the shadows. Deacon calmly raised his hand in greeting. He fished in a pocket and handed each man a dust covered twist of tobacco. The young road builders watched nervously, fidgeting with their axes and what guns they possessed. Without saying a word or changing an expression, the Indian men took the gifts and blended back into the shadows.

"I don't like it," Deacon said later as they walked out to bring the horses and mules nearer to camp. "These bucks ain't dumb. They kin see these pilgrims're so skeered they're about ta wet their pants. One false move an' we could hev a Injun war on our hands. Then where'll our wagon train be?"

The farther they traveled the more apprehensive Joe became. The weather added to his worries. Almost every morning ice crusted the water containers. An early winter would certainly catch the wagon train in Siskiyou snows. On the far side of the mountains the road dribbled away to become a blazed path. The Umpqua Canyon, through which the trail passed, was a mass of boulders and loose rock. The usually sure footed mules slipped and stumbled. It was plain to see, although only about three miles in length, this strip of trail could be disastrous for team-drawn wagons.

In the evening they camped with Jessie Applegate and Black Moses Harris. Applegate's calm manner infuriated Joe. "This track through the canyon isn't fit for mountain goats," he accused.

"That's why we asked for your help," Applegate replied, unperturbed by Joe's outburst. "We know it's bad. We hoped you'd show us a more passable route."

"But-but," Joe stuttered in his rage. "You told our people the passage was good. You're a worse liar than Steph Meek."

Deacon held up a big palm in caution. "Let's face it, pardner. The fat's in the fire. The wagons're too far along to turn back. We'd best do as Applegate says, search fer a better passage an' pray ta God we find it."

For days Joe and Deacon searched the Siskiyous for routes that would avoid Umpqua Canyon. None were discovered that could be readied in time for the arrival of the wagons. They returned to Umpqua Canyon determined to smooth out the canyon floor -- to provide at least a tolerable passage for the wagon column that would soon appear. Applegate workers frantically pried away boulders, shoveled dirt into low places and cut brush and trees to level and clear the worst of spots. Their efforts turned the terrible stretch of trail into a rough, but passable track. If teamsters were careful and the wagons not too heavy, they could make it safely through the three mile stretch. This, however, did not please Deacon.

"A good rain'll wash this away like we had never been here," he said. He glanced up at the gray sky and spit in disgust.

"Yep," Black Moses Harris agreed, "but what else kin be done? We did the best us poor mortals kin do. Now, we gotta think on how we kin best help these folks when they git here. They'll be short of everythin', includin' temper. Shouldn't wonder they'll be in a mood ta lynch ol' Jess like they were fixin' ta do fer Steph Meek."

"I'm not doing any good here," Joe said. "I think I'll ride back and prepare the folks for what's ahead."

Black Moses nodded. "Good idea. Whilst yer gone Deacon an' I'll mosey to Jason Lee's settlement fer supplies. The folks'll be down ta eatin' ther boot straps, if I'm any judge."

Jason Lee had been appointed by the Methodist Missionary Society to serve the Flathead or Nez Perce. Instead of stopping in the homeland of these natives, Lee traveled westward to select a mission site at French Prairie in the Willamette Valley. Here he became more active in getting homesteaders established than evangelizing the natives. The mission, with its inventory of trading supplies, was a natural place to go for help.

After bidding Deacon and Black Moses good-bye, Joe rode south on the Applegate Trail. Surprisingly, he found the route back easier and shorter than he remembered. He crossed the Siskiyous and rode into the land of the Klamath and Modoc before meeting the first wagon -- one of a dozen that had forged ahead of the others. The Jennings party, now with the Dunbar train, had fallen behind, he was informed.

Swallowing his disappointment, Joe hurried on. He had the nagging feeling something had gone badly wrong. Late the next day he met the Pringle-Brown party. Virgil Pringle pulled his oxen to a halt, his attire as ragged and dirty as a Digger Indian. The weary, defeated expression spoke more than words of the ordeals suffered.

"Hard crossing?" Joe needlessly asked.

"Tolerable. What's it like ahead?"

"Not good, not for wagons, anyway."

"There aren't many whole wagons left," Pringle said.

"Have you seen the Jennings' wagons with Dunbar's group?"

"Far's I know they're still rollin'. Did hear they lost a driver and most of their livestock. Diggers ran a lot of loose critters off. Fellow by the name of Abernathy went after them. The Diggers were waiting in ambush . . . killed him dead. "

Before Joe could fully absorb the tragedy, Pringle produced another surprise. "Yep, the Jennings people also had a wedding. Your sister, Tildy, and her beau got hitched. Reverend Josephus Cornwall tied the knot. 'Bout the only good thing that has happened on this stretch."

The news staggered Joe. Tildy had made it plain she was not going to get married until they arrived in the Willamette Valley. From the way she spoke he wondered if she would even marry Sandy then. Macon Laird was the one she truly loved. For some reason he was left with the impression that she and Macon had a secret plot to get together later. Apparently that was not so. Joe spurred Blaze ahead, leaving Pringle still talking.

It was nearly dark before Joe came upon the Dunbar group. The Jennings' wagons were at the end of the column. Just as he caught sight of them a gust of wind swirled around forming a miniature tornado. Brush, twigs, leaves and dirt went flying. Out of the dust and debris plodded Sandy. At the sight of Joe Sandy's tired, red-rimmed eyes brightened. "You're a sight for sore eyes," he said. Granddad sat on the jockey box, looking old and strained. His eyes also lit up when he saw Joe. "I say, where did you come from?" he jokingly asked. "We were just wondering when and where we would see you again."

Joe glanced around for Tildy. "She's driving the second wagon," Granddad said. Joe reined away and waited.

The second wagon was some distance behind the first. At first he didn't see her. She was walking in the shadow of the wagon. A drooping sunbonnet hid her face. Her clothes were disheveled, dirty and torn. She looked even more wan and pale than when he last had seen her at the Raft River camp. She glanced up and gave him a weary smile.

"Oh! You could not have returned at a better time. We are truly at the end of our tether," she said. "Guess you know Saul Abernathy was killed. Poor brave soul. He tried to save our stock. Sandy told him not to go after them, but he wouldn't listen. He chased the Indians into a draw. We found his body pierced with arrows . . ." Her voice cracked.

Joe wrapped Blaze's bridle reins around the brake handle and swung down. He took Tildy in his arms and gave her a comforting hug. "It's all right, Sis. Saul did what he thought was right. What's done is done. There have been a lot of mistakes made on this trip. We're going to have to forget them and go on. Now, dry your eyes and tell me about your wedding."

Immediately, Joe could have bitten his tongue in two. Instead of drying her tears, Tildy began to sob as though her heart would break; tears coursed down her dust coated cheeks, leaving twin channels of mud.

"You will think me cruel, but it was something I had to do . . . I'm with child," she whispered, although there was no one but Joe to hear.

The painful parting of the lovers and memory of Tildy asleep alongside Macon flashed into Joe's mind. "Macon's?"

Tildy sadly nodded. "And neither Sandy nor Macon must ever know. Do you understand? Promise me you won't ever tell." She spoke so fiercely Joe was stunned.

LAND WITHOUT A COUNTRY

XXII

*Mother thinks if she should come here she would
be afraid of the Indians . . . .They never were
more peaceable than now.*

Narcissa Whitman, September, 1846

The fall of 1846 was far less depressing for Narcissa
Whitman than previous autumns. No threats or grumbling came
from Tiloukaikt's camp and Buffalo Horn remained on his home
grounds on the lower Umatilla. "I have never felt more con-
tented in my work . . ." Marcus Whitman wrote the Mission Board.
Narcissa echoed her husband's feelings by writing a friend, ". . .
we feel that our influence for the good was never greater among
them (the Cayuse) than now."

During the first weeks of September, tattered, mud spat-
tered covered wagons began to appear, but not in the numbers
expected. The Applegate Road had diverted many emigrant families who normally would have taken the Blue Mountain route.
Most of those who did take the route, went straight to the Umatilla
Crossing, and by doing so bypassed Waiilatpu. One of the families who appeared at Waiilatpu was the Walls. Dad Wall drove
alongside the hill behind the mission compound, studying the
thick rye grass that stood higher than the wagon bed, and silently
marveled at the sumac bushes that were beginning to change color.
For almost the first time on the journey, he smiled.

"This is our new home, Brother Whitman's Presbyterian
mission," Dad Wall notified his flock. "Here we'll make our
mark fer the Lord. We're goin' ta civilize these Cayuses or my
name ain't Wall. See to the horses an' lend a hand ta yer mom,"
he ordered his older sons, Robin and Roy.

Hardly did the dust of the Wall wagon settle when another newcomer arrived, riding a tall black and leading a rust
colored pack mule. The stranger also noted with interest the tall

coarse rye grass and the striking red and yellow sumac that bordered the far side of the mission grounds. He swung down, beat the dust from his clothes and walked around to inspect the mission compound. He met John and Francis Sager, who had been milking the cows in the nearby pasture. The boys came toward him swinging buckets and snapping like two quarreling dogs. They had had a milk fight, squirting streams of the white liquid at each other until their clothes and hair were sticky and stained. They knew Narcissa Whitman would give them a good scolding as soon as she set eyes on them.

When they saw the stranger they stopped to stare. He was tall, square shouldered, and walked as if marching to the beat of a drum. In greeting, he raised a hand that was almost a military salute. "Hello, men," he said, "I trust I'm not intruding. I just rode in and was looking around, hoping there was some place here I could put up for the night. The name is Macon Laird."

The boys gave each other a knowing glance. This man was their salvation. By bringing him to the mission house Mother Whitman would be far less likely to scold. She always took pleasure in meeting men of what she called "breeding" and from the looks and sound of him this stranger had "breeding." "Come with us. We'll introduce you to the Whitmans. They never turn a needy traveler away," John Sager assured the newcomer.

The judgment of the Sager brothers was indeed right. Narcissa Whitman barely gave their sticky, milk-stained clothing a second glance. The courtly manner and obviously cultured speech of Macon Laird entranced her. She not only arranged a room for him in the nearby emigrant house, but also invited him to partake of the supper that she and her orphan helpers -- all of whom gave him approving glances -- were about to place on the table. Little David Malin plucked at his coat sleeve and showed him where to wash.

"River water but sure takes off dirt," David said, putting out his small hands to reveal their well-scrubbed surfaces. "Father Whitman says cleanliness is next best to godliness."

"I am certain he is quite right," Macon said, marveling at the manners displayed by the children. Not only were they clean and respectful, but they were industrious. The girls, arranging the food in family style on the table, moved from sideboard and kitchen stove as quietly and efficiently as well trained palace servants. The lad named David Malin was the exception. The handsome stranger fascinated him. The boy chattered away like a magpie. He pointed proudly to one item after another, giving a running explanation of each and describing everything he could remember about it until Narcissa Whitman finally shushed him.

"It's time to eat," she said. "Children, take your places at the table."

"I must sit by my new friend. We have lots to talk about," David said, his high voice rising in pitch.

"All right, but it seems you are doing all of the talking. You've hardly given our guest the chance to say a single word," Narcissa said not unkindly. "Now, you be quiet until after the blessing."

David took Macon by the hand and led him to the head of the table. "You can sit right next to Mother and Father. They will want to visit."

The Whitmans did indeed want to talk to Macon Laird. Seldom did a person of his obvious gentility grace their table. After the long prayer that not only called for blessing the food but also every member at the table and for Michael Two Feathers who was on the trail east and for the mission's Cayuse flock, Marcus Whitman said a loud "Amen" and looked to Macon who less loudly repeated, "Amen." "We're Presbyterian," Marcus stated as if that explained the long prayer.

Macon nodded. He knew the missionary expected him to announce his religious affiliation. "I happen to be Church of England," Macon obligingly said. "I hope you won't hold that against me." Before the missionary couple could respond Macon, who had heard the name Two Feathers mentioned, could not restrain his curiosity. "In your prayer you spoke of a person,

Two Feathers, a native I suppose?"

"Yes, Michael Two Feathers. He has been practically a member of the family," Marcus replied. "Why do you ask?"

"I met a young man with the same name at Fort Hall. Nice looking chap, wore two feathers in his hair -- came in with a band of Snake Indians."

"Snakes!" Narcissa exclaimed. "That wasn't our Michael. He's Nez Perce."

"Wait a minute," her husband cautioned. "I can't recall anybody but Michael with the name Two Feathers. Did you notice anything about him that was special. Was he with two missionary men, Coleman and Taylor?"

"I don't recall anyone named Coleman or Taylor. But I must say, a white man named Joe Jennings introduced Two Feathers as his brother. Bit strange as Jennings' sister and his grandfather didn't appear to know the fellow."

"Ah!" Narcissa uttered. She and her husband glanced at each other.

"So the Jennings family was at Fort Hall," Marcus said thoughtfully. "That must mean Joe found a way to bring them west. They should be here any time. Then perhaps this Two Feathers' mystery will clear itself up. Snakes! What in the world would Michael be doing with a band of Snakes? Where were Coleman and Taylor? Surely, they didn't abandon Michael."

"I am afraid you won't see the Jennings soon. They aren't coming through the Blue Mountains. A fellow by the name of Applegate claims he found a better route -- one that follows the California Trail and turns north in a region called Black Rock Desert. From there they go northwest to enter Oregon in a region inhabited by Modocs and Klamaths."

"Oh!" Marcus muttered. "So Applegate found the shortcut he was talking about? I hope and pray it works out well."

# # #

Gradually, Joe Jennings learned of the fearful toll the wagon train had paid in coming from the Raft River turnoff. Bad water, little pasture, Indians who peppered the wagons with poisoned arrows, and the ever-present choking dust and heat. Dead livestock, broken wagons, discarded belongings and several graves, among them Saul Abernathy's, were left to mark the grim passage. Lawyer Quinn Thornton lost his wagons and almost all he owned. Others fashioned two-wheeled carts from broken wagons and proceeded with bare necessities.

The wagon train rolled through the parklike lands of the Rogues. Gun in one hand and goad stick in the other, weary teamsters urged staggering teams through thick timber and over hillsides choked with brush. So formidable was the way some refused to continue, stopping by a bouncing stream -- Cow Creek. Storm clouds threatening a gully-washer urged the travelers on. They labored down miles of rock-strewn creek bed. The worst appeared over, then abruptly the lead team halted. The teamster cursed. Ahead lay deep, dark, boulder-laden Umpqua Canyon.

"My God!" Alphonse Boone cried. "All this way to land in a hell hole like this."

Willie Smith called his brood of nine children, one a daughter sick with fever, together. "Looks bad but we'll get through somehow," he promised. "Let's ask the good Lord for guidance." He sank to his knees on the rocky canyon floor. "Lord have mercy," he called out, then clutched his chest and toppled over, dead from a heart attack.

Two days earlier two other deaths had occurred, yet the loss of Smith, who had been so energetic and alive, was a stunning blow. Any one of them could be next to leave this world. No one realized it more than Joe Jennings. He walked helplessly among the wagons avoiding everybody, loath even to attempt words of encouragement. To add to the travelers' problems, dark clouds overhead signified snow. Snow and a hard freeze could finish off the sick and the elderly and make the passage through the canyon near impossible for team and wagon. Instead of snow, a heavy rain began to fall.

The camp fell quiet, except for the downpour of rain and

the screams of the Jones woman. "If yuh hadn't been so bull-headed," came her wild voice, "we'd ajoined the Donners an' Reeds when they took Hastin's Cutoff fer California as I wanted. By now we'd be nice an' warm feastin' on Captain Sutter's fat beef 'stead of starvin' ta death. Three people dead in the last three days an' we jest got inta this hole in the ground, an' thet's only the beginnin'."

Joe wished there was a way to hush the woman. It was bad enough to be aware of the death toll without hearing the Jones woman rail about it. He returned to the Jennings' wagons, built up the fire and held his hands out to catch the warmth. Rain plunked against the lid of an iron kettle and sizzled on live coals. Trickles of water raced down the steep canyon walls to form rivulets that trickled through the wheels of the parked wagons. It took pitchy splinters to keep the fire alive. The warmth of the pitch-fed flames and weariness of the day's toll, made him drowsy. He jerked awake from a doze that had become a deep sleep to find Lawyer Thornton feeding the low flames with slivers of pitch.

"Couldn't sleep," Thornton said. "Thought you wouldn't mind sharing your fire." A flare of flame revealed the man's gray, stubbled face, his shrunken, bloodshot eyes and a mangy spot on his fur cap. All his lawyer pomposity was gone.

Stiffly, Joe got to his feet. Though the rain still pelted down, the blackness of the sky had given way to a dull gray. Dawn was about to arrive. "My God!" Joe exclaimed. Water, the color of creamed coffee, spread over the canyon floor to disappear into the blackness of the far shore.

Alphonse Boone came out of his tent. His cheeks, where they showed above his wet beard, had the color of dead ashes. "When we arrived the stream was a trickle. You could've crossed dry shod by keepin' to the boulders," he groaned.

"So I heard," Thornton grimly answered. "If the train had followed Reverend Cornwall down the gorge while the water was low we wouldn't be caught in this trap. I can't understand how a grandson of the famous frontiersman, Daniel Boone, was duped into taking this hellish trail in the first place."

Thornton mopped his face with a soiled handkerchief. "Being a lawyer and my wife a schoolteacher, we didn't presume to be authorities on wilderness travel. That's why at Fort Hall I waited to hear your decision. Following you cost us everything: wagons, cattle, law books -- everything! It only will be through God's mercy if we come out alive."

"Look here, Thornton," Boone said sharply, "I didn't tell you to follow me. You've only yourself to blame."

The camp came to life and folks made ready for the crossing. The Pringles walked by, bent against the storm. Tabiatha Brown, Virgil Pringle's mother-in-law, followed close behind. The old lady led two horses and managed a cane. She waved a cherry greeting. "Now that I've lost my oxen I'll have to leave my wagon," she called out. "But I'm still countin' on the Lord's help. He'll see us to the settlement."

In a nearby tent the Boones held a sharp exchange. "If it comes to the oxen dying, we'll walk," Chloe Boone stated.

"Chloe, quit gabbin'," Al Boone snapped. "Come here an' sort things. Mary's not able an' Lucy don't know how."

The sound of the Boones' voices scarcely died away before Teamster Newton yelled for help to unload his wagon. "Oxen'll be hard put to pull it empty," he declared.

Boxes and barrels of belongings floated away as Newton's wagon emptied. Men stood thigh-deep in the water heaving on the wheels, but the oxen were powerless. The wagon would not budge. Slowly, the oxen crumpled to lay where they fell. First one, then the other, dropped its head to be swallowed up by the coffee colored water. Newton stared at the islands of goad-marked hides. Tears began to trickle unchecked down his seamy cheeks.

Boone blew his nose. "The poor critters are just tuckered out." Suddenly, his head jerked upward . . . "Who'n tarnation?"

Upstream came a horseman hunched against the storm. "It's Deacon Walton!" Joe announced. "Help has arrived!"

The burst of excitement abruptly faded. Deacon and the

white mule, Lightening, were alone. Sensing the travelers' disappointment, Deacon quickly offered comfort. "Help's on the
way. Applegate and Black Moses'll be along in two shakes with
vittles an' stuff; all we could get in trade fer our mules an' more."

Tildy brushed at her tears. "Deacon, you're an angel without wings."

"Yep, St. Peter couldn't find a pair big enuff ta lift me
carcass off the ground," Deacon joked. He glanced at the sad
condition of his friends and shook his head. "'Pears yuh've fallen
on hard times."

Tildy gave a choking laugh. "Yes, you might say that."

"Tabiatha Brown and the old sea captain are riding their
horses into the flood waters," Granddad announced from his perch
on the jockey box. "And Phrena Pringle is following her mother's
horse on foot -- has a big load balanced on top of her head. If she
can walk through the canyon, surely we can do it too."

"Mr. Jennings, there'll be no need fer yuh ta go walkin',"
Deacon cried out. "Yuh'll ride the trustiest steed this side of
Missouri." He gave the shivering Lightening an affectionate slap
on its skinny neck.

The forlorn band of travelers collected what essentials
they could take along. Tildy placed another quilt on a bulky pile
of bedding. "Sis, we can't take any more covers," Joe objected.

"It's the Lone Star Granny made for me," Tildy cried.
Her approaching motherhood was beginning to show. The sight
made Joe turn away. If he felt badly, she must feel terrible, and
her trials only had begun.

Before Joe completed sorting out what to take, the flood-
stranded party was on the move. Deacon, with a frying pan clanking against the hand ax at his belt, and Lightening with Granddad
aboard, splashed into the stream. Tildy and Sandy, leading a
heavily laden mule, waded away to disappear into the thick mist.
On a partly submerged sand bar, Henry Smith knelt in the mud
above where his brother lay buried. His wife, a baby in one arm
and a bundle in the other, stood helplessly by, her dripping bon-

net hiding her peaked face. "Brace up, Henry. Save your wife and baby from this hell hole," Thornton's raspy voice ordered.

"We can't leave Willie here. High water'll wash him away. Besides, all I've got in the world's in that wagon yonder," wailed Henry Smith.

The sound of feet squashing through the mud, a man's wild curse, another's pleading prayer, a woman's scream, the crying of children and the clink of frying pan against the ax at Deacon's side, combined to drown Thornton's rejoinder.

Willie Smith's widow stood at the water's edge. She carried a great bundle on her back and a tiny baby in her arms. Two little ones clung to her long, wet skirts. Two boys with bundles and a gun waited at her side, their frightened eyes fixed on the cold, muddy water.

Somehow, Joe piled the two boys on Blaze. Granddad took the baby while Deacon and Joe each carried a tot. Shivering and sucking on a thumb, the child Joe carried stared stonily at the camp left behind. Joe glanced back, but the Thorntons blocked his view. Lawyer Thornton and his wife, armed with stout sticks, felt their way through the muddy current. Their dog, Prince Darco, waded shoulder deep at Mrs. Thornton's side. He growled menacingly at an ox weighted with bedding and youngsters that lumbered too close to his mistress.

Animals and travelers struggled through the treacherous canyon. Partly submerged chests, trunks, abandoned farm equipment, bones and slippery hides of dead oxen left by the first train, paved the path with obstacles. Benumbed in mind as well as in body, the settlers slipped and stumbled three miles in deadly cold waist-high water. When it seemed they could not take another step, a gleam of light sent a tantalizing signal of relief and warmth. Someone had built a fire to guide them to shore.

The travelers took heart. Everything suddenly appeared brighter. The canyon walls that rose beyond the storm clouds, broke away, exposing blue sky just as the breaking clouds had done minutes before. On a patch of ground ahead, a huge bonfire lighted a sagging tent and three battered wagons. "The Cornwall camp," someone shouted.

A sharp, anguished cry made everyone look back. Beyond the ox laden with bundles and youngsters, Thornton frantically clung to his wife, who had fallen. Water tugged at her long skirts, pulling her from his grasp. He seized her inert body only to fall on his knees. He struggled upright and pulled her to a boulder. With her body cradled above the rushing water, Thornton grabbed up his wife's trailing skirts to expose streams of water pouring from holes in her high-topped shoes. The old dog, his forepaws on the boulder, tried to lick her face.

Thornton pushed the dog away to take off his wife's shoes and stockings. Joe perched the child he carried on the boulder. He held the lawyer steady while Thornton ripped open his wife's bodice and unbuttoned his own clothing so he could press his wife's bared, shrunken breasts against his own flesh to pass on the warmth of life. Joe averted his eyes as Thornton kissed his wife's corpse-like face and sobbed a prayer.

Gradually, Thornton regained his composure. Weighted by a pack and his wife, who he wrapped in his great coat, he struggled toward the inviting fire. One coat sleeve dragged in the water beside the dog. Joe helped him up the bank made slippery by the sodden garments of those who already had emerged from the cold, muddy stream.

The chilled waders huddled near the fire, their clothes sending up a fog of steam. Youngsters who hadn't whimpered in the icy water, began to cry. The torture of warm blood flowing through their veins was more than young flesh could bear.

Granddad bowed his head to thank God the worst was over. A man cursed fate for reducing him and his family to their unhappy state. Thornton stood silent. His shrunken eyes watched his wife, who sat in Mrs. Cornwall's favorite chair, her feet on an alder chunk near the fire. The lawyer looked more like thanking God than cursing the fate that had dropped him on Umpqua River's far shore.

"Boulders bigger'n wagon wheels." A stretch of the Applegate Trail in the land of the Umpqua. Photo from Catherine Cornwall DeMoss' research papers, taken 1946 - one hundred years after her father's family passed this way.

"Easy driving down the small stream as the Applegate road-explorers saw it in midsummer." This is a photo of Cow Creek Canyon, a section of the Applegate Trail, taken in August, 1946, when waters were low, one hundred years after emigrants journeyed along the same route.
Catherine Cornwall DeMoss Papers

XXIII

. ... by assistance obtained from the settlers and a
great deal of fatigue and exposure, all have reached
the settlements except my own family and one other . . . .

Rev. J. A. Cornwall, 1847

There was little time for the Umpqua Canyon survivors to rejoice or grumble. More and more stragglers climbed the slippery bank to stumble into Reverend Josephus Cornwall's camp. More and more fires had to be built and firewood chopped. To Lawyer Thornton's disgust, while the rest of the men labored, Alphonse Boone sat with the women and children to sip hot broth. He had not given up on saving his possessions.

"I'll return to the wagons as soon as I rest," Boone said. "The girls can stay while I go back for more."

"Risky with Injuns 'bout," Deacon cautioned.

Boone remained undeterred. "I'll leave one of my guns with Chloe. She can handle the Injuns. Blast it, where's that scallywag Moses Harris you said was comin'?"

Idly, Joe observed the camp activity and listened with half an ear to the conversation. Reverend Cornwall's wife, Nancy, watched wistfully as Pringle led his oxen away to find pasture. The Cornwalls had saved their wagons but lost their oxen. Without them they faced spending the winter deep in Indian territory.

"Don't worry, Mom. We can ride the mules out," young George Cornwall tried to comfort his mother.

"Probably what we'll have to do," his minister father agreed. "No chance of getting the wagons out."

"What'll happen to your beautiful library?" Nancy Cornwall asked. Her husband had brought along a prize collection of books that he hoped would help launch a college.

Willie Smith's widow, who rocked her cross-eyed baby, glanced up in disgust. "How can you think of books when I ain't got a single diaper for this child's chapped bottom.

"Forgive me for such a thought," Nancy Cornwall begged.

"If all these folks hev ta worry 'bout're diapers an' books they ain't down an' out yet," Deacon quietly commented.

The following morning the Jennings family, Widow Smith and several others bid the Cornwalls, who remained stuck in their camp on the Umpqua, good-bye. Joe helped Granddad get astride Deacon's faithful mule, Lightening. The tails of Granddad's coat, still weighted by dampness, were pulled back to lap around the legs of the little Smith girl who perched behind the saddle. The front folds protected the small Smith baby. Tildy and Mrs. Smith rode Blaze. The rest of the group plodded behind with rifles ready. It was feared the small, defenseless party might invite Indian attack.

Soon they came to a small stream that wandered back and forth through a narrow valley. Into the muddy waters the travelers splashed to climb the far bank. Teeth chattered and clothes dripped. Sandy Sanders, walking by Joe's side, estimated they forded the stream thirty times that day. The travelers struggled on, deaf to the sound of water squashing in worn footwear -- the plop, plop of animals' hooves pulling out of the mud, and the whimper of tortured little ones.

Finally, Joe, leading the way, called a halt. Walkers fell to the ground, almost too weary to set up camp. Near dawn they were awakened to a choked, heartbreaking cry. Into their midst stumbled a woman. Her long black hair fell loose over a red flannel nightgown. "Injuns murdered my husband!" she screamed. "Three of them demanded grub. When we didn't have any they took my husband's gun . . ."

Though the woman choked and said no more, everyone knew what had happened. This was Mrs. Newton. Her husband had decided to camp away from the rest so their thoroughbred mare could pasture on clean grass. Concern for the horse had cost him his life.

The commotion aroused the camp. Tildy prepared broth

for the bereft woman. Phrena Pringle and Mrs. Smith crowded around to console the new widow. Scared to death themselves, the only comfort they could give was hand wringing and mingled tears.

In the half-light of the cold November dawn, Pringle, Sandy and Joe found Newton's body. They decided to dig a grave close to camp so they could watch over the women and children and still take turns using the shovel. The ground was frozen and rocky. Already tired from the previous day's travel, the two men were exhausted before they had a pit sufficiently deep to protect the corpse from wolves. When the body had been wrapped in a blanket and lowered into its last resting place, Granddad Jennings said a prayer. At the end of the brief ceremony Virgil Pringle wiped the rain from his head and replaced his hat. "At least the man is out of his troubles."

After filling the grave, Joe went to saddle Blaze. The horse was gone. During the burial Indians had stolen him. Joe swore so bitterly Granddad chided him. "That kind of language won't bring the animal back. I've been taking it easy, anyhow. It's time I walked." Instead of leaving, the travelers decided to remain in camp and rest.

That night it was agreed to double the watch. Two men would take turns circling camp and tending the fire. Wretched over losing Blaze, Joe drifted to sleep listening to the lonesome moan of the wind in the tall firs. It seemed only minutes before someone shook him by the shoulder.

"Reckon it's midnight. Anyways, I'm so done in I can't keep awake." Joe opened his eyes to see Pringle's floppy hat.

Joe wiped the mist from his face and got up to pile more dry limbs on the fire. Indians for miles around were certain to see the fire, but it was the only protection against the deadening cold. Joe circled his side of the camp, stopping repeatedly to listen to the hoot of an owl. The spooky call was a reminder of unpleasant memories -- Indian raids, battleground deaths and even the mad Nez Perce woman who had stabbed him, marking him for life. Joe turned his thoughts from the past to the future. They, too, depressed him. The end of the trail would offer nothing. Bithiah would not be there to welcome him. Instead the Abernathies were apt to blame him for Saul's death.

Then there was Sandy's and Tildy's marriage. Would it work or would they go their separate ways? In spite of her transgressions with Macon, Tildy had a strong sense of fair play. She surely would stand by Sandy while rearing Macon's child. But what would prevent Macon from showing up to expose Tildy's deception? It could result in the ruination of three lives, four counting the unborn child.

Deacon, who manned the opposite guard post, interrupted Joe's thoughts. He slithered out of a shadow to stand by his side, Hawken in hand. "Any Injun sign?" he asked.

"Not unless that owl is an Indian passing signals."

"If we hev nothin' more ta worry about than the croakin' of thet innocent creature, I'll be gettin' meself a few winks." In a nearby clearing Deacon flopped on a bed of dead ferns and pulled a canvas cover over his frost-whitened beard.

Joe continued his patrol. The light of a half moon cast eerie shadows among the evergreens. His senses told him something was amiss. This was the danger period, the hour before dawn. He couldn't understand Deacon's lack of vigilance. Joe let his gaze rest on the blurs that were oxen contentedly chewing their cuds. If danger threatened they were unconcerned. He glanced to where Deacon lay. The old canvas cover made him appear lifeless as a corpse. Lightening, ghost white in the moon light, stood behind Deacon's form. The mule's ears pricked forward toward the far side of camp. Joe glanced where the ears pointed. For certain there was movement. He dropped to a knee, and brought the Hawken to bear. An arrow whistled overhead, thudding into a tree trunk. A gun shot shattered the predawn. Half a dozen figures scampered across a moonlit space and into the blackness of evergreens.

"Run, yuh varmints!" Deacon yelled.

"You old fossil! You were supposed to be asleep. And why didn't you tell me those were Indian hoots?" Joe demanded.

"Shucks, I figgered yuh knowed thet. Anyways, yuh did right good, got 'em ta expose theirselves without harm ta yerself."

"But-but I was a sitting duck!"

"Tut-tut, with me watchin' there was nothin' ta fear. As the Good Book says, 'They thet was against thee shall be as nothin', an' as a thing of nought.'"

Joe jerked the arrow out of the tree and shook it in Deacon's face. "Does that look like a thing of nought?"

The gun shot had aroused the camp. Shivering from cold and fright, everyone gathered near the fire for warmth and comfort of companionship. As fears lessened, hunger appeared.

"I'm 'bout as starved as a shoat with a broken snout," Pringle said. "My stomach growls so I can't hear myself think."

"Quit bragging," his wife snapped. "If you had enough brains to think, we wouldn't be in this fix."

"We're all so hungry we could eat the cover off a wagon," Deacon said. "Maybeso, we should try an' shoot somethin' fer the pot."

When the morning mist cleared, Deacon and Joe trudged north to where game trails led off into the higher slopes. The two hunters hardly had crossed the first brushy knoll when a faint tinkle like distant sleigh bells could be heard. They stopped to hold their breath and listen. The only sound was the chatter of scolding magpies that had yet to fly south for the winter.

"We're so hungry our ears're ringin'," Deacon said. They crested the next knoll. Again they heard the sound. "Look!" Deacon exclaimed. "I tol' yuh help was on the way."

At the turn in the trail a bell mare hove into sight. Following her came several flop-eared mules. Behind the mules plodded four red and white spotted steers. In the background men's voices goaded the animals along. Three mules passed before the lead driver appeared. "It's starvin' Captain Dunbar folk," driver Kuykendall called to his two companions.

"Yuh guessed right," Deacon said. "We got starvin' kids of the Dunbar party an' others hungry as toothless coyotes."

"Anybody in yer camp make pan bread?" the driver asked.

"My sister makes the best pan bread ever," Joe said.

"Settled then. You furnish the cook. We furnish the flour an' beef tallow -- some meat besides. Me an' my partners didn't stop to eat this morning. Got the train underway to try an' hit Cap Dunbar's party for breakfast. Which way is yer camp?"

The three Magi bearing gifts of gold, frankincense and myrrh could not have inspired more emotion than did the three bearded settlers. Mrs. Pringle wiped away tears with her apron. Tildy let tears flow unchecked. Virgil Pringle had a coughing fit and turned away to blow his nose. Granddad Jennings sat with a smile. He believed all along rescue was at hand.

After the first burst of emotion, the women bustled about, getting in each other's way. They giggled and stopped to sort out the duties. Tildy was to make the pan bread. Widow Newton said she would fry the meat. This left Phrena Pringle and Widow Smith free to fix food for the children.

His hunger satisfied, lead driver, Kuykendall, leaned back to pick his teeth. "You people should head for the upper valley as fast as you can," he advised. "Try and make it over the Calapooyas before the deep snow falls."

The next day Deacon reckoned the Jennings party covered twenty miles. The following day a brisk wind and driving rain slowed travel to a crawl. Mud lay shoe-top deep in the track. The rain turned to snow. The wind whipped it into the travelers' faces and rolled it into drifts. Pushing against the wind became so exhausting, Tildy begged to camp for the night though it was only mid-afternoon. She insisted they take shelter under a snow-weighted cedar that stood by the trail near a dead pitchy snag. No one had the heart to go against her wishes. "This'll make a fine camp," Sandy praised the decision.

"Yep, plenty of firewood an' close ta the trail so ol' Mose Harris'll spot us when he passes," Deacon approved.

"Still counting on the black bearded packer to pick us up, are you?" Tildy asked in a voice that revealed her exhaustion.

"Miss Tildy, Mose'll do jest thet. Yer brother knows this same black whiskered packer saved starvin' folks on Meek's Cutoff 'bout this time last year."

It was fortunate Tildy forced them into an early protected camp. An east wind kicked up. It cut through the cedar branches to cover everything with a damp coating of snow. Tildy wrapped the five star quilt around Granddad's head and shoulders. This done, she clutched her shawl about her and went to Sandy's side to wrap a blanket around the two of them.

Though there wasn't much danger of Indian attack on the bitter night, no one got much sleep. The cutting wind and numbing cold forced the travelers to keep a roaring fire going. Toward morning the wind died to a whisper. The half frozen group began to stir. After breakfasting on cups of hot water, they broke camp. They traveled a few hundred yards only to stop again. Tildy took the shawl from her ears to clear it of snow and heard the ting-a-ling of bells. Lightening's ears tilted forward to pick up the sound.

"Packers' bells! Glory be!" Deacon shouted. "It's thet angel of the trail, Black Moses Harris." Tears rolled down the man's broad cheeks to find a hiding place in his tangled beard.

# # #

Deep snow had come to the Northern Rockies. As the blanket of white became deeper and deeper, wrapping all things of Mother Earth in its cover, Michael Two Feathers' optimism began to fail him. The lodges of the Snake village were snug but stuffy, the air heavy with the odors of fish, green hides, smoke and human flesh. He lived cheek to jowl with the family of the young maiden who shared his sleeping pallet. Their talk was mainly of past hunts, raids and village gossip. Except for what game they might trap or shoot the next day, no one gave the future any thought. After a few days Michael found himself irritated by every word uttered.

The nights were even worse. There was a dearth of blankets and robes. To keep warm the entire family huddled together on the same sleeping pallet. Snores and other bodily noises were so annoying Michael found himself lying rigid as a hitching post, straining to shut them out. Each move a sleeper made affected them all. There was a constant hauling and pulling on blankets, each one attempting to keep his or her share.

In other ways life with the Snakes was not as pleasant as he first had thought. The people were nice enough to him but it did not take long to see that their peaceful, tranquil temperaments were easily pierced. Little spats and snide remarks brought to surface long-standing animosities over some matter that had occurred in the distant past.

Although many things annoyed Michael, there was still a certain satisfaction in living and working with these people. His friends taught him many things he needed to know if he was to live the life of his native people. The band had traveled north to the headwaters of the Snake River in time for the salmon run. They stopped to camp at a falls where the roar of the water was so loud it awakened babies from their sleep. It seemed to Michael a poor place.

"Why camp here?" Michael asked an elder.

"To pass the falls salmon leap into the air. We catch them before they drop back into the water and swim away," the elder explained. Michael noticed that when the salmon did arrive many of them bunched up below the falls, trying to gain strength to make the leap to continue on their way to spawn. With scoops, nets and even hands, the fishermen were able to keep a steady supply of fish pouring ashore where they quickly were cleaned, cut into strips and laid on racks to dry.

Among the workers who toiled at the task of cleaning and preparing the salmon for the drying racks, were Hare Lip Bruce and Hard-Bitten Smith. All the way from Fort Hall they had performed the role of slaves. Under the direction of the women, they did the heavy chores involved in breaking camp in the mornings and setting up camp at the end of the day's journey.

After several weeks on the trail the two prisoners began to lose their paunches and double chins. Although reluctant slaves who had to be prodded into doing their work, they received the same rations as their captors and never were beaten. Only at night were they kept bound, hand and foot.

"We do not want to harm these people," Michael had said to his Snake Indian friends when they first brought the captives into camp. "We will teach them to respect us. We will teach them to appreciate our way of life and all the things Mother Earth does to keep us alive. We will see that they have everything they need, but they must work for it."

Not all members of the Snake band agreed on this way of handling the two rogues. A group of young men spoke of burying them up to their ears in the sand and letting the scorpions and ants slowly eat their flesh away. Others wanted to have them run the gauntlet and whack them good with whips and clubs. A delegation of women came to ask that the two men be given to them. They would cut off their private parts and feed them to the birds.

All of the options were discussed loudly in front of the prisoners, who at the time were bound and gagged. They struggled and fought against the rawhide lines that held them, their eyes popping out until they could have been knocked off with sticks. Michael did not interfere. It was the Indian way of having fun. Not until the band of Snakes was well on its way to the fall hunting grounds were the white men unfettered and allowed to march alongside the women and pack ponies. Now they were in flat sagebrush land, so hot sand lizards panted from the heat. If the captives attempted to escape it would be easy to hunt them down.

The fishing season had gone well. Row after row of orange flesh hung on racks that lined the river banks. From early morning until late at night the harvest had continued. Mother Earth had sent this wonderful gift but allowed the people only a certain amount of time to reap the benefits. Once the wave of

salmon had moved on, the fish spawned and died. After spawn-
ing the flesh was unfit to eat except for buzzards and scavengers
who Mother Earth sent to keep her surface neat and clean.

Michael kept a close watch on the two white men who
stubbornly resisted their lowly position as slaves. He seldom
spoke to them but often wondered why they were so intent on
running down his brother, Joe. They had been as persistent as a
pack of starving wolves on the track of fresh blood. He thought
back to the time in Fort Hall. Joe had known these people were
camped nearby but ignored them. Did he not know the danger
he was in? It was a good thing he and the Snake band had trailed
the ruffians to the Raft River Crossing. No telling what they
might have done to Joe if they hadn't interfered.

In general, meeting up with his Boston brother had been
a disappointment. It had not been the best of times to meet. The
emigrants had been re-provisioning and trying to decide which
trail to take. His new sister, Tildy, and Grandfather Jennings
hardly acknowledged his presence. Instead of extending him a
happy, exciting welcome into the family, they had acted as though
he was a stranger, someone they were polite to but did not want
to know better.

Of course, he was Indian. What else could he expect?
They thought him an "uncivilized heathen," someone not worth
wasting their breath on. It was another reason for choosing the
path of his native ancestors. Here among the village of Snakes,
he was deemed a person of worth. Yes, he would remain with
them although he did find some of their customs loathsome.

XXIV

We don't chop down the trees. We only use dead wood.
But the white people plow up the ground,
pull down the trees, kill everything.

Anonymous, Wintu

The Season of First Snow had arrived. The lodges of the Waiilatpu camp of the Cayuse were coated with white. Except for spirals of gray smoke, the village blended into the landscape until it almost was invisible to travelers passing on the Walla Walla Trail a short distance away. Tiloukaikt, headman of the Waiilatpu band of Cayuse, sat inside his lodge, smoking his long-stemmed pipe and staring into the fire. There was grim talk the Season of Deep Snow would come early and remain late this year. He had urged the people to enlarge the underground storage places where they kept squash, root crops, potatoes and other edibles that perished in cold weather.

Some did as he instructed, others said he talked foolish. This Season of Deep Snow would be like the one past when the white stuff barely dusted the ground. "If we are wrong, a little hardship won't hurt. It's time some of us lost a little fat," Feathercap, one of Tiloukaikt's more severe critics said. "Living near this mission has made us like wild creatures that have been tamed. We don't know what it's like to fight for things any more."

Another area of Tiloukaikt's leadership that frequently came under question was that of his vigilance. He always kept men watching the approaches of the village. He wanted to know who came and went, especially to and from Missionary Whitman's compound. Today a watcher rode hurriedly up to his lodge, announcing Buffalo Horn and two hairy faces riding up the trail from Fort Walla Walla. "One hairy face has a long, pointed nose just like a red fox!" one watcher exclaimed. "Like the fox, he has a sly, hungry look. He is one to watch."

The three riders rode in, dismounted and called out they had tobacco and had come for a smoke and talk. Always interested in a gift of tobacco, Tiloukaikt stepped out and bid them to enter. He glanced at Buffalo Horn, headman of the band of Cayuse that made its home on lush pasture lands along the lower Umatilla River. There had to be trouble in the offing, otherwise Buffalo Horn never would have made the journey. They sat and passed the pipe.

Throughout the smoke Tiloukaikt studied the two white men. They had a different look than the newcomers who had come down the Blue Mountain trail. Their expressions were intense. They held themselves erect and aloof, but under his gaze they shifted uneasily as horses did when encountering a rider they did not trust. Indeed, the one man did have the face of a fox, with long nose and equally long jaw. The nose, especially, attracted Tiloukaikt's attention. It was the color of the vegetable the missionaries called tomato. Obviously, the strangers were bursting with words to say. What message did Fox Face and his companion bring?

Instead of putting the pipe away when the first loading was ashes, he filled the pipe again and started another round. Tiloukaikt did this for two reasons. First of all, the tobacco the men brought was pleasing to his palate, but mainly he wanted more time to think. What mischief did these men have in mind? Were these the hairy faces the Delaware Tom Hill had spoken of -- Redcoats who would start a period of unrest that would drive the mission people from their homelands? That had to be it -- the tense hands, eyes that never remained still, the shifting around as though their pants were filled with red ants. He finally carefully knocked out the ash and placed the pipe back into its bag. "Now, we speak."

Buffalo Horn cleared his throat. "These people come from across the big water called ocean -- not our big water where Father Sun sleeps, but the great water where Father Sun rises. They come to help free our homeland of hairy faces who come from beyond the River of Many Canoes. Our Redcoat friends bring guns, powder, shot and men to fight alongside our warriors. Should Cayuse people accept this help or should they not? My band say 'yes.' Five Crows' people say 'yes.' Stickus says 'no.'"

Buffalo Horn paused. Stickus! The name stuck in his craw. He was Christian -- Missionary Whitman's lap dog. "We come to hear your desire," Buffalo Horn continued. "Does your band want to be free of these missionary people with their false words, sheep, cattle and grunting, smelly creatures called pigs?"

Tiloukaikt stared into the fire. Why did these people come to them now? There was a time when they would have been welcomed with open arms. And a time might come when their gift of arms would be accepted. At the moment it was bad medicine to stir up the people when they should be getting ready for the long, dark Season of Deep Snow.

Buffalo Horn frowned. "You see what these mission people do to our homeland. They build wood and stone lodges and fences. They bring creatures called sheep that eat grass down until there is nothing left. They have a noisy thing called saw-mill that swallows trees like frogs do flies. Without grasses what do we feed our herds? Without trees to nest in, what will happen to birds? If there are no pine seeds for squirrels and chipmunks, where will they go for food? No trees . . . no grasses . . . no birds . . . no creatures . . . what kind of homeland will the Cayuse have? I say we welcome these Redcoat people. They come to protect this land we call home."

"Your words are good, but does making war solve our problems or make them worse?" Tiloukaikt questioned.

"What else is there to do? Every Season of Falling Leaves these hairy faces spill down the trails like salmon coming home to spawn. Unlike the salmon they do not die at the end of the trail. They stay alive and multiply. Already their numbers are greater than ours. If the rumors we hear are true, more are on the way. If these people are not stopped they will take over our home-land and everything we have."

Tiloukaikt remained silent. With all of his great horse herds Buffalo Horn could move his people around as much as he pleased but the Waiilatpu band; it was something different. Now that the missionaries had taught the people to till the ground and live off the harvests, they were tied to the land. Let Buffalo Horn and Five Crows go on the warpath. No! That would never do. It would bring the Blue Coats down on his own people, too. That was the trouble with the hairy faced ones, they were unable to tell good people from bad people. If Buffalo Horn and Five Crows went on the warpath, the entire Cayuse tribe would be blamed.

The two Redcoats had been silent but suddenly the man with the long red nose who looked like a fox raised his hand to speak. "Our great queen who rules many lands and has many warriors is grieved to see what these hairy faced invaders do to your homeland. They are our queens's enemies as wells as yours. Soon they will take over Hudson's Bay trading posts which have served your peoples for many many moons. Our queen does not like this. She wishes Hudson's Bay to continue to trade with you and all Indian people as they have in the past."

Red Nose paused to determine the effect of his words. Tiloukaikt's inscrutable expression was not reassuring. He plowed ahead anyway. "Our people do not seek land to build stone lodges or missions or bring creatures to eat your pasture lands or have these noisy things called sawmills eat your trees. It is our plan to keep these people away. We want your people to live as you always have. When the land is free of these people our queen will keep warriors here to see your homeland remains free."

Tiloukaikt stared into the dying campfire. The man spoke with a split tongue. He wanted the American hairy faces gone so the Redcoats could possess Cayuse country. All hairy faces were alike. They wanted to possess whatever land they could. It did not matter to them who lived there, even if it had been a people's homeland since the beginning of time.

Tiloukaikt suddenly felt depressed. What was worse, Redcoats or Blue Coats? One or the other was certain to eventually rule this land. As Buffalo Horn so wisely said, hairy faces, no matter what color coat they wore, were as intent on their goal as salmon coming home to spawn. A sudden thought came to Tiloukaikt's mind. Perhaps his people should join with the Redcoats and do away with these hairy faced settlers. When the Americans were gone then they could face the Redcoats. There were fewer of them and their great queen with her warriors was far away, across the big water.

For the first time he looked Red Nose full in the face. Never had he realized how much these hairy faced creatures resembled animals. Some had faces like dogs, others like rodents, birds, and, indeed, this one had the face of a fox -- cunning, crafty, shifty green eyes . . . This was not a person one could trust. But he came to his lodge with his neighbor and tribesman, Buffalo Horn; he must treat him as a guest.

"Your words rest heavy on my mind," Tiloukaikt finally said. "This matter is not to be taken lightly. It is proper I place it before the council of elders and our people." He rose to his feet. The meeting was finished.

# # #

The bedraggled remnants of the Dunbar wagon train gathered on the bank of the Willamette River near an abandoned cabin -- Skinner's place, Moses Harris called it. While the survivors debated their next move, Orris Brown unexpectedly appeared with team and wagon. He and his family had elected to keep on the Old Oregon Trail and had arrived in the Willamette Valley weeks earlier. Tabiatha Brown greeted her son, Orris, with tears. "Lord be blest," she cried. "I knew all along we'd make it. Though I have barely a shoe or dress to my name, it's the happiest day of my life."

Those who had oxen and riding horses made ready to accompany Orris Brown to the mission settlement, roughly sixty miles north along the river. The foot weary survivors who did not have means of transport, decided to build a boat and float down river. The strokes of dull axes, the thud of mauls and the crackling of falling timber, echoed against the butte that rose behind Skinner's cabin. Nails were not available so the boat builders used buckskin thongs to hold the timbers together. The result was a queer craft. Deacon said it looked a cross between a raft and bateau. Regardless of its appearance, it floated. "We'll call it *The Last Chance*," someone proposed.

Under a gray, snow-threatening sky, women and children huddled to watch the men stow scanty possessions aboard the strange craft. As soon as the womenfolk found a place for themselves and cautioned their children about the dangers of falling overboard, the men took their places, wielding poles and makeshift oars. Perilously, the craft heeled to one side, then righted itself and careened downstream. Deacon and Joe, who still had mules to ride, remained behind. They helped push *The Last Chance* away, then stood on the bank to wave good-bye. No one waved back. The women and children were too frightened to let loose of their grip on the rough boat rail. The men were too absorbed in keeping the craft in the middle of the stream. Just as *The Last Chance* rounded the bend to disappear, Tildy looked back and waved.

"Glad somebody remembered us," Deacon said. "They ain't gone but a minute an' I'm already lonesome as a misplaced shoe. Now what're we ta do? Fer certain there's no future hangin' aroun' here." He glanced up at the scudding clouds overhead. "Howsoever, me thinks we'd best go nowhere at present. 'Less I miss my guess it's plannin' ta snow."

They hobbled the mules in the lee of the bluff behind Skinner's cabin to protect them from the chilling wind, then moved their gear into the weather-beaten shelter. While they cut a supply of firewood, snow flakes began to tumble down. It snowed through the night. The next morning they built up the fire, then broke a trail to the draw to tend the mules. In the protected area the snow lay level, six or more inches deep. The mules were nowhere to be seen. Deacon ran through the clearing and into the trees. He soon reappeared, his face red with cold and fury.

"The blisterin' Injuns took off with the critters," he stormed.

While still bemoaning the loss of the mules, Deacon slipped on a snow covered rock and twisted his knee. He lay half buried in the snow, swearing so artistically Joe thought he was joshing. "Well, yuh goin' ta give me a hand or ain't yuh?" Deacon snapped. "I'm as helpless as a headless chicken."

Joe helped Deacon hobble into the cabin. The injured man sat down with a groan and pulled up his pant leg. In the short time since the fall his knee joint had ballooned. "Sometimes a knee sprain is worse than a break," Joe commiserated.

"For certain, I ain't fit ta travel . . . be lucky to crutch aroun' in a week," Deacon moaned. "I feel worse'n a skinned cat, mostly 'bout losin' Lightenin'. Damn those redskins, they're probably roastin' the poor critter fer breakfast right this minute."

"They're luckier than we are," Joe said callously. "We haven't enough food to keep us another day."

The stranded men decided the most sensible plan was for Joe to go for help. It would be a long bitter walk to the settlement, but better than starving in Skinner's cabin. Joe cut a pile of firewood and stacked it near the fireplace. The weather cleared, but it was so cold even wood seemed frozen. Brittle branches snapped with reports like pistol shots.

"Worse than a Cheyenne freeze," Deacon said. "Think yuh should walk out? Frost bite comes on mighty fast."

"We have no choice," Joe replied grimly.

"'Tis so, 'tis so. It's do or die."

After doing what little he could to make the injured man comfortable, Joe made ready to leave. He took a small pouch of jerky, a hand ax and blanket roll. It was more of a load than he wanted to carry, but he had to be prepared to spend a night on the trail. He debated over taking the rifle. Noticing his indecision, Deacon spoke up. "Take yer Hawken. An' be damn sure ta keep yer powder dry. Yuh gotta be on guard fer Injuns. Then there's the wolves. In this cold snap they'll be hungry and mean. God bless yuh. If I don't see yuh again, good-bye." Deacon laid back and covered his eyes with his arm. With that disquieting blessing and farewell, Joe departed.

The miles passed slowly. The sun seemed barely to move. Then late in the afternoon it quickly dipped toward the western horizon. The only sign of life was the chirp of small birds and cry of distant wolves. Darkness abruptly fell. But the brightness of the snow and half moon overhead made the trail easy to follow. Joe continued to plod ahead without conscious thought. The crunch, crunch of snow; the constant effort of placing one foot ahead of another; and the softness of the blanket of white, all sent a message to stop.

To ward off the hypnotic spell, Joe slapped his face. He felt nothing. This alarmed him. Frost bite was not a pleasant prospect. With a free hand he rubbed his face with snow. The flow of blood caused his face to burn and tingle. Sharp shooting pain from the temple scar where the Indian woman stabbed him made his eyes water.

For a while the pain seemed to give him added strength. It also affected his mind and hearing. Cruel, ravenous cries followed him. Frightening howls and yelping snarls became louder and more persistent. Suddenly Joe's cold, benumbed mind realized wolves were on his trail. He attempted to put new life into his stony legs. The effort was fruitless. He never could outdistance the famished creatures. He took the Hawken from its sling. The loaded rifle gave him little comfort. His hands were too numb to reload. The single charge in the gun would kill only one wolf.

He glanced over his shoulder. The yelping beasts became bounding objects, dark against the snow. He raced for the nearest tree. It went up and up without a limb. He turned back to face the wolves. The yelping was so loud it nearly drowned the roar of his gun. The scream of the wounded animal diverted the pack. Joe ran for all he was worth. Stumbling over his benumbed feet, he nearly fell. He glanced back to watch in horror as the ravenous animals snarled and fought over the kill, tearing their dead companion to pieces as effortlessly as if the carcass was a bundle of rags.

After what seemed hours, Joe scrambled to safety on the limb of an oak. His lungs burned like he had been breathing fire. The morsels of raw meat only had whetted the appetites of the pack. The wolves came to yelp and leap up the tree trunk. Sensing their prey was out of reach, they howled and snapped at each other, their pointed teeth pinpoints of light in dark furry masks.

Panting with exhaustion and unnerved by the harrowing experience and narrow escape, Joe leaned his head on the tree trunk to rest. Though the wolves kept up an unearthly din, he gradually fell into a trancelike sleep. Uncannily, the furry creatures below began to stand on their hind legs. They seemed to hold torches and speak.

"I remember him. He was sweet on Bithiah . . . ." The voice came from a distance as through a fog. Joe's fingers, and feet were centers of pain. His body was afire. "What in the world is he doing treed by wolves in our pasture?" the female voice that first spoke, asked. "Look at him. He's nearly frozen to death, yet his skin is so hot it almost burns my hand. What're we to do. He needs a doctor, real bad."

It was like a dream to hear a voice discuss him as though he was not there. In spite of the terrible pain and fever, Joe lay still, enjoying just being alive.

"It's too late for a doctor," a man's voice cut in. "We'll have to do for him the best we can. He's Saul Abernathy's friend, Joe Jennings"

"Ah! Yes, I always wondered what happened between those two. . ." the female voice said. "It almost was unseemingly the way Bithiah rushed into marriage with Luke, him with a family and his wife barely cold in the grave."

"Well, I suppose . . ."

Joe never learned what the man supposed. He suddenly

remembered Deacon who waited at Skinner's cabin. He struggled to get up. Hands gently pushed him back.

"Young man," said the male voice, "you're burning up with fever, and your poor feet . . . they're two blocks of ice."

There was something familiar about the man. Then Joe remembered. This was Luke Olafson's older brother, Manny. Ah! Fate was filled with irony but he couldn't worry about that.

"There's no time to lose," he blurted. "My friend is at Skinner's cabin, hurt and soon to starve. We must go to him."

"You're not going anywhere, not on those feet. We may be forced to amputate . . . ."

The fever turned to a terrible chill. All of a sudden Joe was back in a tent by the trail watching white, crawly maggots swarming over a gangrenous leg. Edwin Bryant was standing over him shaking his head. "It's too late to amputate," he said, his eyes bleak with pity.

XXV

"The poor Indians are amazed at the overwhelming numbers of Americans coming into the country. They seem not to know what to make of it."

Narcissa Whitman, 1847

On the Columbia River plateau the winter of 1846-1847 was more severe even than that of '43. Snow lay three feet deep on level ground. For weeks the Walla Walla and Umatilla Rivers were frozen so thickly it took an ax to break holes to get water. Indian lodges were little better than ice boxes. Lodge fires burned day and night; still occupants died from the cold. Wild animals fared no better. Wolves and coyotes that normally prowled in packs to seek food, only had to wander game trails to find deer, elk and other game frozen to death -- the meat so ice-solid it broke the scavengers' teeth.

The Sager brothers, wishing their old friend, Michael Two Feathers, was there to help with the chores, trudged daily through the snow to care for the Whitman mission livestock The hay and fodder that had been harvested in the summer was carefully rationed among the cattle, horses and sheep. Even so, a large number of sheep, calves, cows, foals and horses did not survive.

The Indian people, who did not have the luxury of a surplus of fodder and grain, saw their horses and cows die by the hundreds. The Spokane and Nez Perce, who lived in the higher and more northerly regions of the plateau, suffered the most. Missionaries working among the Spokane reported one Indian stockman saved only two head of cattle from a herd of fifty. The Hudson's Bay fort at Colville was hit nearly as badly with twenty horses surviving out of a herd of two hundred and twenty.

The Cayuse also suffered. Tiloukaikt and his band at Waiilatpu saw nearly a third of their animals succumb to the freezing cold. It was rumored Buffalo Horn's losses were even greater.

Only Stickus on the upper Umatilla fared reasonably well. Unlike most Indians, who saw the storing of surpluses a sign of greed, Stickus did not feel that way. He had gauged the long winter well and set aside ample supplies to see his people through the winter. This did not endear him to members of the other bands. He was beginning to act and think too much like the hairy faced ones.

The intense cold and snow brought activity to a near halt at Waiilatpu mission. In the fall the number of emigrants passing through Waiilatpu was small. It seemed only the desperate ones made the side trip to the mission -- those too sick and infirm to continue the journey or those who had run out of provisions. Six families settled in to stay through the winter. Three births were recorded and three deaths also would have occurred if it hadn't been for the medical and nursing care the Whitmans were able to provide.

One of those who was saved from the grave was a man found on the trail. He had been attacked and left for dead. A hunter from Tiloukaikt's village found the body in a snow drift, the surrounding area stained with blood. Besides suffering from exposure, the man had been beaten badly around the head, his face was an unrecognizable mask. Dr. Whitman cleaned and stitched the wounds and forced some medicine and broth down the patient's throat. He stood back and frowned. No Indian person did this. The man had been brutalized. It had to be the work of a ruthless, sadistic white man, someone who had laid in wait or overtaken the rider and slashed him with a murderous weapon.

"Whether he pulls through or dies is now up to the Lord," Whitman said to himself. He remained by the stricken man for some time. There was something familiar about him but neither he nor Narcissa were able to put a name to the patient. The stranger was in a coma for nearly a week. Over and over he kept mumbling to himself. Those who nursed him strained to hear what he said but without success. Besides Narcissa, Catherine and Elizabeth Sager took turns sitting at the sick man's bedside.

Once he opened his eyes to see Catherine Sager. He tried to sit up and said several words that were spoken with such intense feeling they brought tears to the teenage girl's eyes.

"What did he say?" Elizabeth Sager asked.

"He called to someone, 'Oh, I love you. I love you,' he cried, then went back to sleep."

"How romantic, just like a fairy tale. I wonder who it is he loves so much."

Hearing that the sick man had spoken, the Whitman family gathered around. "I know he is going to get better," Elizabeth said. "He has to get better. Someone misses him terribly."

Dr. Whitman agreed. "I do believe he's on the mend. As soon as he is able to speak we will try to find out who he is and pass word along to his loved ones."

Little David Malin walked up to the bedside and put his hand on the sick man's arm and uttered a little shriek. "Why, don't you know this man? He's my friend, Mr. Laird."

"How clever of you, David, of course it is," Narcissa exclaimed. "What in the world was he doing on the Walla Walla Trail? Why should anyone wish to do a gentleman like him harm?"

From then on David insisted on sitting by his sick friend, only leaving at meal time. "My friend is better," David said at the breakfast table one morning. "He wakes and talks. He asks for somebody called Tilly. What kinda name is that? And he talks about Pasha an' a bad man who'll do bad things to our mission."

"Hmm!" Father Whitman grunted. "Perhaps I should sit with him for a while, maybe he'll speak to me, too." But it was another two weeks before he had an opportunity to have a satisfactory talk with the injured man. In the meantime visitors from the Willamette Valley arrived with news of the Donner and Applegate disasters; the latest on British-American treaty negotiations setting the permanent boundary of Oregon Territory; and the unsettling rumor that British agents were attempting to resist the boundary treaty negotiations by fomenting unrest among the natives.

A man who had been a member of the '46 wagon train that disdained the Applegate shortcut and crossed the Blue Mountain instead, returned to search for stock lost on the outward journey. Still trying to solve the mystery of missionaries Coleman, Taylor and Michael Two Feathers, Marcus Whitman asked him about the crossing.

The man shook his head. "'Twas ill-fated from the first. Sinister happenin's took place every time a body turned 'round. Afore the wagons pulled outta Independence thar was a killin', youngish Nigra slain in cold blood. A man named Trimble got hisself killed in Pawnee country. A liar named Hastings hornswoggled people inta takin' a cutoff ta California. Me hear tells they was swallowed by the snow in the high mountains.

"At Fort Hall there was a ruckus with a band of Snake Injuns. Mighty funny business. A train captain knew the Snake leader, called him 'brother.' The Snakes followed the train ta the River Raft an' surrounded the Dunbar wagons -- took two men prisoner. Far as anyone knows, they ain't been seen again."

A rider from the Willamette Valley offered more information. "The Applegate boys decided they'd take it upon themselves ta be trail blazers -- figured on a route thet'd bring emigrants inta the Willamette Valley from the south. The people who took the trail lost 'most everything they had in the desert, then ran inta the Umpqua at full flood. Only a few wagons got through. They say some people, like the Cornwall family, were forced ta spend the winter there. Of course all of this is second hand. Maybe 'twasn't as bad as we heard."

Maybe worse, Whitman thought to himself. What happened to Coleman and Taylor? Were they the two men taken prisoner by the Snakes? The poor fellows, they were already nervous enough as it was, responsible for taking an Indian lad all the way to New England. He had not a word from them. What had happened? Why didn't anyone write?

The first day Macon Laird showed signs of regaining his strength, Dr. Whitman encouraged him to speak. "You saw Michael Two Feathers at Fort Hall. Did he seem all right?"

Macon Laird gave the missionary a blank stare. Desperately, he attempted to clear the fog that clouded his mind. The last he remembered was Radley's outthrust jaw and long red nose and the evil man's raised arm. Then came the blow. He shuddered. Maybe he was dead. The man with the kind eyes was St. Peter interrogating him at heaven's pearly gates. No, he was alive. His head ached like it would split open. He groaned and closed his eyes.

Missionary Whitman scolded himself. "I'm a doctor. I should know better than to force questions on him. This man suffers from a concussion . . . perhaps brain damage or loss of memory. He should have peace and quiet." He took a cold compress and carefully laid it across the injured man's forehead and went out closing the door softly behind him.

Daily, the doctor came to gauge the injured man's progress and daily he was encouraged. Finally, one morning he found Macon sitting on the side of the bed. He was going through his clothes.

"Feeling pretty skookum, are you?" Marcus Whitman asked. "That blow on the head was a bad one, sure didn't come from falling off a horse. I hope one of our locals didn't attack you. They have been peaceful, but outsiders come now and then -- try to rile them up. Could be one of them was around again. Did you by chance get a good look at him?"

Macon Laird looked at the doctor as if he didn't comprehend. "Ah, yes, the attacker . . . clubbed me with his rifle barrel . . . probably trying to rob me. I see my pockets have been rifled. I shouldn't complain. You folks have been awfully kind to me."

Narcissa found her husband sitting with an open Bible upside down in his lap. "What in heaven's name is wrong? Has your English patient taken a turn? Hasn't he spoken sense yet?"

"Yes, he's come around and is quite lucid," Marcus answered. "I can't make him out. He knows who knocked him on the head but he won't say. Why would he do that? Furthermore, there's talk the British are reneging on the boundary treaty. There's a clique connected with Hudson's Bay that insists land north of the Columbia River should rightfully belong to Britain. I can't help but think this man is part of that plot. Why in the world is he wandering around up here in the dead of winter all by himself if he isn't up to mischief? Ah, these mysteries: Coleman and Taylor; Michael and the Snakes; this man and the British threat. If that isn't enough worry, I'm told Tiloukaikt and Buffalo Horn met with a couple of strangers. What was that about?" Whitman sighed. "All we can do is look to the Lord and hope for the best."

#

Marcus Whitman was not the only one with tortured thoughts. Deep in the Rocky Mountains Michael Two Feathers was trying to find solutions to problems that had been nagging him for weeks. The Snakes had weathered the Season of Deep Snow well. They had wintered in a cul de sac, protected on three sides by high mountains. Here the piercing winds of the north were diverted away. It was still numbing cold but by keeping campfires burning day and night the lodges were liveable.

Food also was plentiful. Before the first snow they'd had a successful buffalo hunt and, for a while, elk and deer were plentiful. They dried a great quantity of meat and were able to keep a store of fresh frozen meat for weeks. The salmon harvest also helped fill their larder to overflowing.

It was the livestock that suffered. Grass and low growing bushes the animals usually foraged on were buried under layers of snow. It did not take long for the edible leaves, bark and tender branches of trees to be stripped clean. The men ranged farther and farther to cut branches and search out underground storage pits of roots and seeds buried by rodents to find sufficient food to keep the horses alive. A swamp with dead bulrushes was another source of fodder that took hours and hours to collect.

But it was not the hard work or fear of starvation that

worried Michael Two Feathers. It was his future that had him concerned. He had tried his best to be happy with the Snakes. They were friendly, actually overly friendly. He hardly could go anywhere without one or more of his friends tagging along. It was the sameness that wore on his nerves. Every morning they got up to greet Father Sun then went about their chores, the same routine day in and day out. For the men it was the never-ending search for food for the horses. That in itself was not bothersome. One was in the fresh air and surrounded by all the beauty only Mother Earth could provide. It was the people -- the same every-day talk. He knew ahead of time the exact words they would say.

It was the philosophy of the people that disturbed him most. They did not look to the future. They lived one day at a time and were satisfied. Tomorrow, the day after, the next season -- the people would be taken care of; hadn't it always been this way?

The youthful maiden who shared his blankets was like all the rest. He attempted to talk to her, discover her interests. She would giggle or look at him blankly, as if he spoke foolishness. Never would he get used to it. He wanted someone he could confide in, someone who had thoughts broader than what happened that day in camp. More and more he thought of Little Fox. Although he only had sheared sheep with her and ground her corn, there were unspoken words. She understood him. He knew in her quiet way she loved him. How pleasant it would be to share life with her.

The daydreams of Little Fox brought to mind again and again the desire to return to Waiilatpu, but could he? What explanation would he give the Whitmans for not going east with the missionaries, Coleman and Taylor? By now the Mission Board would have labeled him incorrigible, not acceptable. He should take his courage in hand and tell the Whitmans the truth. Even if they did not understand, he would have the worry off his mind.

Then there were the two hairy faces they had kept enslaved. He had done his best to teach them that the native way of life was good. For certain they had gained much knowledge but the lessons had been harsh. The women had ordered Hare Lip Bruce around with such persistence and ferocity, instead of having the appearance of a bushy headed squirrel, Hair Lip had turned into a timid field mouse.

Hard Bitten Smith also had changed markedly. His female masters had become so irked with his indolence, they shaved his hair so they could pull him by the ears, giving him the resemblance of a badly shorn sheep. At the same time the two slaves had become slim, hard-muscled, clear-eyed men, a far cry from the pre-journey paunchy, irascible rouges.

Late in the season, just before the Snake band made winter camp, Michael had taken the two slaves a day's ride from camp. He kept their weapons but gave them two horses to ride and sufficient provisions to see them to the nearest trading post and turned them loose. Instead of being grateful, they left with hate in their hearts, snarling like wild animals. They were enemies for life. That was another reason he could not return to Waiilatpu. They were certain to come after him with a vengeance. They might not only harm him but the Whitmans, too.

"Ah!" He had not only brought shame to the Whitmans' but, danger as well. He dared not return to Waiilatpu . . . but where was he to go? He was a half-blood. He did not fit in anywhere. He had tried to walk the path of the white man and was shunted aside like a worn out moccasin. He had tried living with the Snake people and found their way of life impossible. Michael groaned. He was locked in a prison from which there was no escape.

XXVI

*"I arrived in the Wallamette Valley on the 30th of September,
and my calculations are all defeated about Oregon.
I found it a mean, dried up, and drowned country."*

Hezekiah Packingham, 1847

Joe Jennings and Deacon Walton, who had been rescued from either being eaten by wolves or a snowy grave, spent the winter and into the spring, recovering from their ordeals. For both men it was a time of torture, and not just because of their injuries. Inactivity made them as grouchy and cranky as sore-nosed bears. At mealtime it became a joke between Tildy and Sandy, into whose cabin the grouchy ones had moved, which one of them had the courage to feed the caged animals.

Even after they had healed sufficiently to get around, the men continued to quarrel, snap and growl. Tildy understood. As long as he lived, her brother would never get over the ignominy of being beholden to the Olafson brothers who now counted his former love Bithiah Abernathy as a member of their family.

However, there was little time to brood. Settlers who entered the Willamette Valley via torturous Applegate Road the winter of '46 spent the following summer struggling to raise new homes and get crops under cultivation. Some had success, others gave up and made plans to retrace their steps across the plains. Pringles, Boones and Cornwalls took up homesteads in the upper Willamette Valley.

Thorntons, and others, including George Curry, Edwin Bryant's friend, became residents of Oregon City. Gossip had it that George had been smitten by Chloe Boone and forsook his companion Edwin Bryant to follow his sweetheart into Oregon Territory. Always looking for new challenges, George Curry took on the task as editor of the *Spectator*, the Territory's first newspaper.

In his role as collector and dispenser of news, George Curry made an attempt to visit every family in the valley. In due course he appeared on the doorstep of the Sandy Sanders' home. Now the Sanders-Jennings family had grown to six: Sandy, Tildy, Granddad, Joe, Deacon Walton and a healthy, handsome baby boy, Baby John.

"Stay and sup with us," Tildy and Sandy invited George Curry, after the preliminary small talk was concluded.

"Yes," Granddad Jennings echoed. "We'd like to hear what's going on in the outside world."

"There's so much going on I don't know where to begin," Curry said as everyone was seated in the tiny living room. "One of your wagon train companions, J. Quinn Thornton, has Oregon City in an uproar. He's been attacking Jessie Applegate. Claims Jessie is no better than a heinous pirate who promoted the southern route to line his own pockets. Jessie don't much care but his friend, Nesmith, took offense. He rode in and challenged Thornton to a duel. Thornton's been walking around town armed to the teeth, but makes certain he doesn't run into Nesmith."

"Thornton should be happy he can still walk and talk," Granddad said in disgust.

Curry kept his audience fascinated. He reported the boundary dispute between Great Britain and the United States had been settled. "They agreed on the 49th parallel," he said. "There is a great deal of grumbling on both sides. The Americans wanted the boundary even with Russian holdings on the north coast. British supporters argue the Columbia River is the natural geographical boundary and they have a point. A number of the settlers above the Columbia River are Canadians. They will now have to change their stripes and swear allegiance to the United States."

The most interesting and heart-rendering news was of the Donner and Reed party. When the wagon train left Fort Bridger, Lansford Hastings, who promised to guide them over his short-cut to California, had gone ahead leaving word for them to follow. The travelers approached Weber Canyon where the passage narrowed until wagons had barely room to squeeze through and then it narrowed even more. Teamsters were forced to winch their wagons to the canyon rim. In the process a wagon slipped and pitched onto the canyon floor a hundred feet below.

After leaving Weber Canyon they entered Bossman Creek, so choked with brush and trees every foot of passage had to be chopped clear. To escape the obstructions of the creek bottom, they climbed the wall of the ravine. The incline was so steep, only by locking the wheels could they keep the wagons from rolling back on those below. They topped the summit only to encounter another canyon with walls equally steep.

"Imagine!" Curry stopped to exclaim. "It took them twenty days to travel thirty-six miles and the worst is to come. Reed quarreled with a teamster -- knifed him. Outright killed the fellow."

Deacon grimly shook his head. "I figgered thet shortcut'd lead ta trouble."

"Keesburg, the German, wanted to hang Reed," Curry continued. "Instead, they banished Reed from the train. He went on to California by himself."

"How did the Donners fare?" Tildy asked.

"Last I heard the rest of the wagon train was snowbound in the Sierras. Perhaps by now they've been rescued."

James Reed's display of arrogance, Virginia Reed's perky cheerfulness, Margaret Reed's sadness and Tamsen Donner's apprehensions, vividly came to Joe's mind. After they suffered through the ordeal of Hastings' Cutoff, to spend the winter buried in snow . . . ! The very thought made his frostbitten toes burn and tingle.

The conversation turned to Tildy's newborn, John Aloysius. "Named after his grandfather, John Jennings, but where does the Aloysius come in?" Curry wanted to know.

"It's my first name," Sandy said, blushing furiously.

"Hmm!" Curry grunted, writing on his note pad. "Oregon air must bring out the male strain. Just visited the Luke Olafsons in Tualatin Plains. They have a strapping lad, too. Several months old now, born on Valentine's day. Easy to remember his name; they call the sprout Valentine."

Curry turned to look at Joe who had made a choking sound. "I suppose you'll be taking a homestead?"

Joe shook his head. He had no desire to make a home for himself, certainly not where any day he might run into Luke and Bithiah and Valentine! "I haven't any plans. Should visit Whitman's mission," he said. Above everything else he had to make peace with Michael and bring him into the family. How he was he to do that? He hadn't the faintest idea but surely the Whitmans would have word of him.

"Take care," Curry said. "Trouble's brewing on the plateau. There's talk of raising a regiment to guard the Oregon Trail. It also is rumored the mission at Waiilatpu is to be closed."

"Is the situation getting that serious?" Tildy asked. A frown creased her forehead. She was concerned for Macon Laird, Joe thought, another reason to leave the Willamette Valley, find Macon Laird -- catch him before he disrupted Tildy's life again.

After supper Curry thanked Tildy and Sandy for their hospitality. He promised to send them a copy of the *Spectator* announcing the arrival of their son.

"Did you know it's rumored George Curry is courting Chloe Boone?" Tildy asked, watching their visitor ride away.

"No," Joe absently answered. If Curry's information of the plateau was true, he should go to Waiilatpu regardless and help the Whitmans. If they abandoned the mission it would leave Michael without a place to call home. Sooner or later he was certain to get fed up with the Snakes. His education and years of mission life would make him dissatisfied with their haphazard existence. Should Michael leave the Snakes, as he surely would, where else could he go but back to Waiilatpu?

Joe inwardly groaned. If only the situation hadn't been so chaotic at Fort Hall. Michael's introduction to the family had been an unmitigated disaster. Tildy and Granddad were so distracted they didn't know whether they were coming or going. Their minds refused to accept the fact that Michael was one of them. Michael, who was so sensitive to the thoughts and feelings of others, had to be offended.

Joe groaned again. He was at fault more than anyone for not making Michael feel welcome. The news of Bithiah's marriage to that odious Olafson had had him so upset he could think of nothing else. To make matters worse, in the meantime he hadn't done anything to clear up the situation -- make Tildy and Granddad understand that Michael was truly their own brother and grandson. He had been too concerned with everyday affairs, like getting his frozen feet well, making certain Tildy remained happy and that Granddad stayed healthy. Somehow he had to put everything right. He could start by finding Michael, but did he dare leave? The family would want an explanation. Some weeks later Deacon provided an excuse.

"I think I'll take off," he announced to Joe. "Kin yuh believe it, winter's 'bout ta set in. Been here 'most a year. If'n I wanta keep the ol' woman happy I'd best show up onc't in a blue moon. She'll be expectin' me ta git ta bargainin' fer a man fer Mornin' Star. I figured you an' me could come ta terms but yuh've been a real disappointment. I'd best look elsewhere -- maybeso, thet brother of yers, Michael Two Feathers, 'd be a prospect. He must be eighteen, young but gotta a good head on his shoulders. Probably tied hisself up with a Snake lass, whadayuh think?"

"He had better not," Joe said gruffly. At the moment he couldn't think of anything worse. It was going to be hard enough to get Michael accepted into the family -- if he had a native wife and youngsters . . . ! He shuddered at the thought.

The Jennings family took Joe's departure well. The fall harvest was in. The house Sandy built for Tildy and Granddad was completed. Joe's frost bitten-fingers and toes were pretty much healed and Tildy was so happy to be rid of the scruffy mountain man she would have given up her prized Lone Star quilt to see the last of Deacon.

Still, it took a while to outfit themselves. Replacing Blaze and Lightening, stolen along the trail in the '46 crossing, was difficult. After the hard winter available horses and pack animals were scarce. Joe finally acquired a black mare and roan pack horse. For Deacon he purchased a long-legged, flop-eared mule that immediately received the name, Zebra. Dark stripes crisscrossed the animal's withers.

Astride the black mare, appropriately named Blackie, Joe turned for a last look at the log cabin Sandy had prepared for his bride. On the doorstep Granddad held his namesake, Baby John, flanked by Tildy and Sandy. The lean-to room that had been added to accommodate Deacon and himself, the rail fence they had helped build and especially the waving people, sent a message of happiness and satisfaction. After the many hardships and disappointments and near break up between Tildy and Sandy, everything had turned out fine, or so Joe thought at that moment when he and Deacon turned to ride up the Willamette Valley.

The sun was setting into the waters of the Columbia River when they approached the ferry landing opposite Fort Vancouver. A bearded man dressed in slick buckskins watched the gold and crimson of the sky reflected in the water. "They always say hereabouts one of the finest sights is watchin' the ol' Columbia swaller the sun," he said, waving a dirt encrusted hand at the fiery orb. "Here comes the ferry . . . no time ta dawdle. Switzer's so cantankerous yuh gotta git 'board the minute he lands or he'll send the ferry back whilst yer still diggin' in yer pocket fer the fare."

When the animals were aboard and the ferry underway, Joe studied the far shore. Silhouetted against the darkening sky was a British sloop of war. The loquacious stranger spoke up. "The Redcoats've had this monstrous boat here fer months. Don't know perzactly what they're afeered of, 'spect us ta attack the fort with huntin' guns?"

In the dim evening light the palisaded fort that overlooked the river was barely visible. As the ferry neared the far shore the cannons mounted in the bastions that guarded the front entrance came into view. Their cold, menacing presence gave Joe the shivers. Was the boundary question settled for certain or did these people still have hopes of maintaining their rule over the land north of the Columbia River?

Joe and Deacon rode off the ferry and up to the fort gates. The walls of hewed logs, fitted closely together and buttressed on the inside, gave the fort an impression of impregnability. Buildings lined the inside walls, making the fortification appear even more formidable. The most imposing building stood opposite the entrance, a two-story structure where the fort factor lived and which contained the common eating hall and bachelors' quarters for commissioned officers and clerks.

Deacon, who often had traded at the fort, pushed up to the trading window to inquire about friends and when the table would be set for the evening meal. Eating in the dining hall was a new experience for Joe. He spent much of the time observing and listening to the diverse group gathered around the table. The conversation consisted mainly of workaday complaints voiced by Hudson's Bay personnel.

"It's not what it was when White-Headed Eagle -- Dr. McLoughlin -- ruled," an accountant who had grown gray bending over company books, complained. "Balances are now on the wrong side of the ledger."

"Can't be any other way, as I see it. Instead of gettin' ready for the trappin' season Injuns spend their time hangin' around wagon trains lookin' fer a few crumbs and a chance to leer at the women," a red-whiskered man responded.

"It's not the redskins' fault. With American trappers takin' pelts at any season regardless of how many kits are left to starve, there's little left to trap," grumbled another, giving Deacon and Joe a pointed glance.

"You're jolly well right," spoke up a youngish man with a pale, peaked face and white collar. "Things have come to a pretty pass when an honest Englishman can scarcely call his soul his own without being contradicted by some lout from the States."

"Yes, and after all Doctor McLoughlin did to save their hides. If it hadn't been for him the lot of them would have starved to death or been tomahawked by the Indians," another clerk chimed in.

Joe and Deacon studiously ignored the brazen attempts to draw them into a quarrel. Instead, Joe covertly studied these men who represented Britain's claim to this part of the world. They seemed the ordinary men found in similar trading posts across the west, certainly no threat to American settlers. Of course, they did not represent the military.

Finished eating, Deacon brushed off his beard and announced he was off to see if the animals were safely housed for the night. "Can't tell," he said, giving the Bay men a sly glance, "these honest Britishers might take a fancy ta ol' Zebra."

Joe started to follow when a familiar figure entered the hall -- Macon Laird. Joe hardly recognized him. The Englishman was thin, haggard and walked with a limp. He came to the long table and glanced indifferently at the diners. His gaze met Joe's. Recognition brightened his eyes. He limped forward to grasp Joe's hand.

"Fancy meeting you here," Macon said, lapsing into his British reserve. He sat down, clumsily hitching his stiff leg under the table.

"What happened to you?" Joe couldn't help blurting.

"Got a bit careless. Where you bound?"

"Up river -- Waiilatpu."

"Dangerous," Macon said. "The pot's brewing up there."

"Yes, I've heard the Indians are upset."

"You have heard true. Outside mischief-makers are heating things up."

Joe's senses came alert. "What do you mean by that?"

Macon looked ill at ease. "A faction is attempting to discourage American immigration and close the missions. If American missionaries close the missions it will show the government can't protect its people. Settlers north of the Columbia will look to Hudson's Bay and the British for protection. Since most of the settlers north of the Columbia are Canadians, it would be the natural course for them to take. When they ask for protection, the military will step in. It's a strategy our empire builders have used time and time again. As your friend, Marcus Whitman, says, 'This is a land without a country.' Until a bona fide government is recognized, the boundary settlement means nothing."

"How do you know all this?"

"I was sent to forestall the bloody business, but I'm powerless. The people who sent me are now out of office. I'm stranded like a shipwrecked sailor."

"I still don't understand. Are you telling me you have been mixed up in some underhanded international intrigue?"

"I guess you could put it that way."

"After what we've been through, shouldn't I know?"

"It's a long story and very involved."

"I've got the time," Joe snapped.

Macon hitched his leg around to a more comfortable position. He pursed his lips as if pondering on how to begin.   "I guess you could say it started with the Irish potato famine in which a million or so people died of starvation. Our prime minister at the time was a man named Cobden. Cobden was very upset by the Irish tragedy and vowed it would never happen again.

"To prevent future famines, Cobden envisioned a land where thousands of bushels of surplus grain could be harvested each year. He settled on Oregon Territory as the place where that could occur. He didn't care who grew it or ruled the land, all he wanted was a source of grain. He selected me as courier of documents that would put what he called his granary scheme into motion. Instead of discouraging American settlement of the region, he wanted to encourage it. He saw American farmers turning this land into the granary of the world and by doing so solve the food problem for peoples of all countries.

"Cobden's foes thought he had gone out of his mind. Pelly,

the Lord Governor of Hudson's Bay hated it -- did everything he could to stop it. And he had powerful allies, including the Duke of Wellington, but Cobden went ahead anyway."

"Those rascals trailing you were sent to stir up the Indians, and you came to keep them peaceful, is that the general idea?"

Macon nodded. "Something like that. The documents I carried instructed Hudson's Bay's trading posts to maintain the peace and do what they could to assist homesteaders."

"The bird who killed Pascoe was after you?"

"He was after the documents. Actually, the papers are worthless. Cobden was ousted as PM. With Cobden gone I had no official capacity. But they did not give up. Caught me on the trail -- stole the papers and gave me the beating of my life."

"Hmm!" Joe uttered a sympathetic grunt, then a terrible thought came to him. Was Macon on his way to see Tildy? "What are you doing here?" he bluntly asked.

"Waiting for a ship to London."

Joe breathed a sigh of relief. Tildy, Sandy and Baby John were safe. He also was angered. Macon, who had played so loosely with Tildy's feelings, was leaving without giving her a thought.

"How is Tildy," Macon asked as if reading Joe's mind.

"Fine."

"And her son?"

"How did you know she had a son?"

"He that travels far, knows much."

Macon's expression also told Joe the Englishman knew who had fathered John Aloysius Sanders. He could have guessed the birthing date but how did he know it was a boy? Had he and Tildy been in touch? Were they planning to get together and sail away on a ship? Joe inwardly groaned. Was the apparent domestic bliss he just left a big hoax? He gave Macon a searching glance but the newly scarred handsome face was as inscrutable as a blank wall.

XXVII

*"The doctor's hands were more than full among the Indians,
for sometimes five died in a day. My dear sister
Whitman seemed ready to sink under the immense
weight and care resting upon her . . . "*

H. H. Spalding, 1848

The end of the Season of First Grass was near. The warmth of Father Sun bathed the hills and valleys. Rivers and creeks swelled into rushing streams. Birds of all kinds winged in from the south. Bulrushes, reeds, wild flowers and bunch grass became vibrant with color. Fresh scent of evergreens sweetened the air. It was a time when all things of Mother Earth rejoiced in being alive.

The village of Snakes entered into the spirit of the season. Shaking off their lethargic winter existence, men and boys took long sweat baths, afterward jumping into icy creeks. The women scrubbed the children, aired the sleeping robes, packed the winter clothes and cooked a great feast with freshly slain game. Elders sat in council, smoked and made plans for breaking camp. Departure from winter camp always followed the same pattern, a journey to new hunting, fishing and gathering grounds. The trek took them down the Snake River to Fort Hall and beyond to a region two day's travel north of Fort Boise. Here they stayed the summer, digging edible roots, picking berries and harvesting seeds of various kinds.

Anticipation of the journey created an air of festivity. The people became gay and mischievous, joking and playing tricks on one another. Laughing children skipped around camp with a train of dogs yapping at their heels. Pack horses were rounded up and driven into makeshift corrals. The long winter layoff left the animals unruly. They had to be reintroduced to halter and pack saddle. Chasing, roping and breaking the wild creatures added to the excitement.

After the horses were settled, the business of packing and loading began. Lodge poles were taken down. Some were left; the best kept and made into travois. The camp was cleaned and a last minute hunt for fresh meat for the trail was made.

The hunting trip was the opportunity Michael Two Feathers had been waiting for. When the hunters scattered to flush out game, he reined his black and white pony up a forested ravine. For a while he rode, then stopped to see if he was followed. When satisfied he was alone, he turned to ride north and never looked back. It was an unkind and cowardly way to leave, but if he told his Snake friends of his plans it would have resulted in an uproar. They would have attempted to restrain him any way they could. When their efforts failed accusations would be made, feelings would be hurt, his sleeping partner would wail and carry on obligating him to stay, or worse, take her along.

Still Michael felt disgusted with himself. He had his freedom, but it did not bring him joy. Why didn't he have the courage to tell his friends he was leaving instead of running away like a coward? The people had accepted him as if he were one of their own. Now, he had turned his back on them, leaving behind feelings of betrayal, disappointment and heartache.

Michael's journey took him by three mountain peaks the Snakes called the Hoary Headed Fathers and which French trappers named The Tetons. The valley west of these mountains consisted of a smooth plain crisscrossed with streams. Everywhere deer, elk and an occasional small herd of buffalo appeared. In the sky two hawks circled lower and lower. The sight of the abundance of wildlife brightened Michael's spirits. After being closeted with the over-attentive band of Snakes all winter, it was soothing to be alone, listening to breezes whisper in the trees, scoldings of blue jays and the chatter of magpies. He forgot everything but the peace that surrounded him. He wished moments like this could last forever.

He came to the ridge of high mountains some called the

Backbone of the World, on to Lost Trail Pass and down into Bit-terroot Valley. His people knew this country well. His uncle, Vision Seeker, had spent a Season of Falling Snow and Deep Snow in this region with three hairy faces, one of them his father, Little Ned. Vision Seeker had not intended to stay with the hairy faces, but a sudden storm laden with snow had trapped him. It turned into a good thing for Vision Seeker. During the long winter the hairy faces taught him mysteries of the Bible and the ways of talking paper. Before the Season of Melting Snow was over he could read and write the hairy faces' language. At the time he was the only one in the Lapwai band of Nez Perce who possessed these skills.

Thoughts of Vision Seeker and of his father brought a feeling of homesickness. How he would have liked to have lived in those days before the time of missionaries and wagon trains. Life was so simple then. One was not troubled with making the decision of which path to take. The path to the future was marked. All one had to do was follow it. Everyone trod the same trail.

Up the Bitterroot and into Flathead country Michael jour-neyed. Flatheads and Nez Perce were long-standing friends. They traveled together, hunted together, went on the warpath together, intermarried and counseled each other. Recently the friendship had become strained. The Flatheads chose the religion of the Long Robes -- Jesuits, they were named. A Father de Smet es-tablished a mission among the Flatheads. The Long Robes' pres-ence was a personal affront to Missionary Spalding. He accused them of not teaching the true meaning of the Scriptures. Both Missionary Whitman and Spalding believed Catholic teachings smacked of Satanism.

The Flatheads did not permit these differences of opinion to interfere with their hospitality. They received Michael Two Feathers warmly. He was the grandson of Lone Wolf, a Nez Perce man they respected. They had traded with Lone Wolf, hunted with him and accompanied him to their first hairy faces' rendez-vous. At one time there was talk of marriage between a Flathead maiden and Many Horses, Lone Wolf's first son. Now Many Horses was in the Great Spirit land. The matter was never spoken of again. The Flatheads did not forget Lone Wolf's second son, Vision Seeker, who as a youth, could see into the future.

"What does your uncle foresee now?" an elder asked.

"I do not know," Michael answered. "I have not seen him for a long while."

The elder looked at him strangely. One always kept in touch with one's family, especially an important person who could see into the future. Had this Michael Two Feathers done something that made him an outcast? They wanted to ask but that was not polite. Seeing they could not learn more, the elders lost interest in the visitor. Parents who had eyed him as a potential mate for their daughters also dismissed him -- the great herd of Appaloosas that Lone Wolf possessed would not be available when it came to making a marriage bargain.

The mystery surrounding this man who rode alone into the Flathead Valley on a colorfully marked black and white pony, did intrigue the Flathead youth. The newcomer had the bearing of a person with considerable knowledge and experience. They were planning a buffalo hunt. They asked him to join them. Michael refused. He had no desire to kill precious buffalo, he said. He had no one to skin or butcher his kill, and what would he do with the meat?

The Flathead youth were aghast. Every young man wanted to run the buffalo. A coveted coup was to kill a buffalo and make a necklace or other ornament of the horns to remind everyone of the hunter's great hunting ground skills. Perhaps a foray into enemy lands would interest the youth.

"Let us raid the Blackfeet," a flathead youth suggested. "It is always good to add more horses to one's herd." But the thought of riding into the land of the Blackfeet and stealing horses did not appeal to Michael either.

"One can ride only one horse at a time. I have no need for a great herd," he said.

Now it was the youths' turn to dismiss him as an object of interest. They glanced at him with disdain. What kind of a man was this who cared nothing about making coups on the hunting ground or battlefield? Quite aware of his shortcomings, Michael rode away from Flathead country. He had proved a disappointment to the missionaries, now he was in disfavor with Indian people, too.

Michael journeyed down the Bitterroot Valley and up the summit to follow the Lolo Trail. This was the trail he had traveled while a baby in his mother's arms. All the way along the Kooskooskie, the river white folks called the Clearwater, Michael rode in a cloud of gloom. "Just what am I good for?" he wondered. "Where do I fit into this world that is divided into people who follow the old ways and those who have left them behind?"

The sight of his old home at Lapwai brightened Michael's spirits. Grandfather Lone Wolf and Grandmother Quiet Woman greeted him as though he had dropped from the clouds. Lone Wolf, whose eyes had become clouded with a film of white, came close to see better. "Our boy has become a fine young man," he announced to his mate.

Quiet Woman pulled Michael to her and ran her fingers over his head and face. Michael was shocked. She was blind. "Of course he is a fine man. He is of the Lone Wolf Clan."

His uncle, Vision Seeker, greeted Michael next. The look of approval in the wise dark eyes made him want to cry. These people loved him so and he had let them down. He had done nothing worthy of such great love. After they visited for a while, Vision Seeker took him on a walk along the Kooskooskie.

"Your presence is good," Vision Seeker said. "You bring happiness to Lone Wolf and Quiet Woman. They will depart for the other side carrying good feelings in their hearts."

Michael gave his uncle a startled glance.

Vision Seeker motioned toward the river. "Life is a stream like the waters that rush by. See the waters bounce and swirl, going one way, then another. Is that not the way we live, going from place to place, changing our paths from time to time? And, like the stream, when life's energies weaken we slow to flow into the Great Beyond much as the water gently enters the great water called ocean." Vision Seeker fell quiet. Not until they turned to walk back to the long lodge did he say another word.

"You wonder why I speak as I do. It is no wish of mine to bring messages of heartbreak but days that break one's heart have come. A storm of death blows across the homelands of our peoples. Like wind driven fire it leaps from one village to the next. Already this wind of death has struck Cayuse lodges -- measles, the white man calls it. It comes in darkness of night and in light of day. It strikes the strong and the weak. People can flee but there is no escape; there is no cure. Lone Wolf and Quiet Woman are in its path . . . . Again Vision Seeker fell silent. Just before re-entering the long lodge he spoke again. "You journey to Waiilatpu. Travel with care. I foresee danger . . . ."

"My friends . . . the Whitmans; they are in danger?"

The look in his uncle's eyes gave him the answer.

"I must go. I owe them much." He said a hurried good-bye to stunned grandparents, ran for his black and white pony and galloped away.

Vision Seeker started to call Michael back but what could he say? As he had foreseen, the youth had tried the life of his native forefathers and was disappointed. He wanted to give the path of the white world another chance. Returning to help the missionaries in the measles crisis would pave the way back into the white world, or into the next, if he came down with the disease. Either one probably was better than the path he now trod.

#

Indeed, the fall of 1847 found the Whitmans in dire straits. Emigrant wagons had begun to appear in mid-August. The watchful Cayuse descended on them like a swarm of locusts. Beggared by the previous severe winter, they stole anything they could get their hands on. Food, pots, pans, anything left about camp was taken. Marcus Whitman caught a group of thieves leaving an emigrant camp. At his wits end, he chastised them, telling them stealing was wrong, a sin against the Ten Commandments. The culprits, wrapped in blankets, listened in silence. Then from beneath the blankets one utensil after another began to slide out and drop to the ground until almost all the stolen items had been recovered. But this did not stop the stealing. Harassment of the emigrants by the natives became so prevalent one of the last letters Whitman wrote was to the Secretary of War stressing the need for military posts to protect those traveling the Oregon Trail. He recommended spacing fortifications fifty miles apart along the trail from Independence, Missouri to the Willamette Valley.

Harassment of the emigrants by the natives also was a great worry to Narcissa Whitman. Her sister, Jane Prentiss, was expected to arrive to teach in the mission school. Each wagon that approached brought Narcissa's hopes up, but her sister did not appear, and none of the new arrivals could give her any news. Nevertheless, Narcissa and her helpers cleaned the house thoroughly in preparation for the sister she never would see. She had little time to worry. The mission buildings were crowded to capacity. More than forty children and nearly that many adults were under her care.

This was the state of things when Michael Two Feathers unexpectedly arrived. Everyone was so thronged, as Narcissa expressed it, they hardly knew what day it was. Neither Marcus nor Narcissa inquired about his absence. They pressed him into service almost as if he never had been away. He quickly found himself overwhelmed with chores; many of them he felt should have been done by the emigrants. The manner in which they settled in and expected to be cared for disgusted him. Not only did they bring more work; they brought more sickness. John Sager took to bed with the measles as did his sister Catherine, Helen Mar and several other members of the mission family.

As Vision Seeker had warned, the virulent disease spread like a wind driven prairie fire. In the Indian village nearly every lodge held two or more deathly ill occupants. Every morning

Michael awakened to the keening of those mourning new dead. One day alone he counted five burial ceremonies in the Cayuse cemetery. Dr. Whitman was on call every hour of the day. People stood at the kitchen door, pleading with him for medicine or to visit a sick child that had slipped into a coma.

When the doctor visited the Cayuse village, Michael accompanied him to act as interpreter and help with the patients. Right from the start he kept an eye out for Little Fox, but in vain. His great fear was she had been stricken with the illness. He attempted to make inquiries among women for whom he had ground grain at the gristmill. It was impossible to get their attention. Everyone was too distraught to speak of anything except the terrible plague that had befallen the village.

"Not good! Take away! Mission man's medicine no good," a grief-stricken mother shrieked over the body of her sick child. Her dead baby sister lay on a sleeping robe nearby. Then one day a medicine man, painted and wearing an incongruous mask, blocked Dr. Whitman's path. "No more white man's medicine. Cayuse medicine best."

Dr. Whitman attempted to push by, but others came to the medicine man's assistance. There was nothing the doctor or Michael could do but leave. The result was disaster. The medicine men ordered the sick to the sweat lodges where they sat naked in hot steam, then ran and jumped into the river to cool. Many who might have lived, did not survive.

Near the height of the crisis the last of the emigrant wagons arrived. One wagon carried Joe Lewis, a person as deadly as the plague, itself. A Delaware half-breed, sick and badly clothed, Lewis came to the mission house seeking help. The Whitmans took him in, clothed him, fed him and found him passage with a family leaving for the Willamette Valley. In three days he returned. He moved into a lodge with another half-breed named Finley, married to a Cayuse.

From the very first Michael distrusted Joe Lewis. The arrogant half-breed was inquisitive to the point of being obnoxious. He continuously asked questions and entered emigrant camps and mission buildings indiscriminately and without invitation. He quickly made it known to Michael he hated "Whites." He claimed the only reason he left Waiilatpu was that the Whitmans had driven him away. After moving into Finley's lodge, the Finleys and Lewis made frequent visits to Tiloukaikt's village. Michael watched them come and go with rising alarm. Joe Lewis and his outspoken bitterness could easily inflame the Cayuse to violence.

During the fourth week of November Missionary Spalding arrived from Lapwai. He brought with him his daughter Eliza and a train of pack mules laden with grain. Michael helped unload the mules at the gristmill where the grain was to be ground into flour. This was Spalding's contribution in replenishing the fast disappearing food stocks consumed by the overflowing population of emigrants. The outside chores now fell to Michael. Most members of the mission family were sick, Helen Mar Meek's condition worsened until Narcissa and the doctor feared for her life.

The presence of Missionary Spalding gave Michael a measure of encouragement. Perhaps he would be able to persuade the Whitmans of the great danger hovering over their heads. In the camps of the Cayuse every day brought more deaths and more tension. It was only a matter of time before the terrified people would lash out in grief-stricken desperation at the only people they could blame -- the occupants of Whitman's mission.

Michael's hopes were quickly dashed. Spalding had less vision even than the Whitmans. He had no idea the Cayuse were near the breaking point and seemed to ignore the virulent measles epidemic. Although the mission school was closed because of the plague of sickness, Spalding left his daughter in Waiilatpu to attend classes when school reopened.

Before Spalding returned to Lapwai a messenger arrived from the camp of Five Crows on the Umatilla. Five Crows beseeched Doctor Whitman to come and save his people. "Many,

many sick peoples, some die," the messenger reported.

On a rainy, windswept night, the doctor and Spalding saddled their horses and rode toward the Umatilla. Michael quickly caught Magpie and soon followed. Why hadn't he thought of it before? Stickus, the leader of the upper Umatilla Cayuse, was the person to warn the missionaries. Stickus was one of the first Cayuse to become a Christian and was a loyal supporter of the Waiilatpu mission. Whitman was certain to listen to him.

Unbeknownst to Michael Two Feathers, the gaze of two dark eyes followed horse and rider until they disappeared into the darkness. The Delaware half-blood, Joe Lewis, smiled with satisfaction, the thin cruel lips drawn back over eye teeth resembling the fangs of a wolf. Everything was good; one more troublesome member of the mission family was leaving. All he had to do now was wait for the right moment . . . an incident between an emigrant and a villager . . .a measles death in a prominent Cayuse family . . . Yes, everything was going in the right direction, just the way he had hoped.

XXVIII

*"The storm is lowering; the heavens grow black; the counte-
nances of the Indians forebode evil . . . ."*

Catherine Sager on eve of massacre, 1847

Joe and Deacon left Fort Vancouver early in the morning,
riding east on the Columbia River's north bank trail. At first
Deacon set a jogging pace. After passing through the cleared
area around the fort, he reined Zebra to a walk. "Mighty good ta
be outta civilization, ain't it?" he said. He stuffed a wad of tobacco in his mouth. "Seems a lifetime since a body could freely
chew an' spit. Ain't perlite ta do it 'round houses'r campsites, or
even parade grounds like they hev at the Fort. No one minds out
heya." He aimed a sluice of tobacco juice at a bare tree branch
and missed.

Joe paid little attention to Deacon's rambling talk. His
mind was busy mulling over the conversation with Macon Laird.
Where were the British troublemakers, and what were they doing now? Macon Laird hadn't said or didn't know. Joe had been
so relieved to learn the Britisher was leaving for England he hadn't
bothered to learn more. Was Pascoe's killer spreading his poison
among the Cayuse, Walla Walla and Nez Perce?   If the people
were as upset by the measles epidemic as rumored, the killer
could easily set the whole plateau country aflame.

"What yuh mopin' 'bout?" Deacon turned in his saddle
to ask. "Yuh should be happy ta be on the trail again."

"You're quite right," Joe replied, clearing his mind of the
evil that might be occurring. He shouldn't dampen Deacon's
high spirits. His bearded, tobacco-chewing companion was happy.
He was on his way home to his family. For a moment Joe tried to
imagine what it would be like to have a loving wife and children
who believed you to be the most important person in the world.
If he had grabbed onto Bithiah like he should have, he would

have known by now. He'd had his chance and booted it. He shook his head in disgust. He had to quit thinking about of what could have been. There was no future in dwelling on the past.

The lofty firs, the bigness of the river and the power of its surging current echoed by towering cliffs, made Joe suddenly feel insignificant. What impudence to believe ordinary humans could conquer this wild and overwhelming land.

Joe felt less irrelevant when the gloom of the gorge gave way to the glare of a cloudless sky, and the trail emerged from tall timber to wind through hills sprinkled with stunted pine. By the time they arrived at The Dalles Crossing, his thoughts turned to the trip ahead. He bargained with an old Indian canoeman to paddle them across river. Holding onto the halter ropes, they urged the animals into the water. The current caught Zebra first. The old mule's head went beneath the surface. For a moment it appeared the animal would be swept away, taking Blackie with it. The roan pack horse snorted, jerking its head so violently the lead rope slipped from Joe's grasp. Before either Joe or Deacon could stop it, the pack animal wheeled about and was gone.

Joe swore. He had paid a pretty penny for the animal and the roan carried most of the provisions.

"Yuh wanted ta travel light, anyways, didn'tcha?" Deacon asked.

On the far side of the river the two riders inventoried their supplies. Little foodstuffs remained. "We'll be all right," Deacon assured. "Jest havta pull in our belts a notch."

Joe was irked. "A start like this doesn't bode well."

Joe and Deacon rode toward the Methodist mission at Wascopum. Parked near the weathered buildings were several battered prairie schooners; desolate and forlorn, their weathered canvas covers whipped in the breeze. Skinny, goad-marked oxen grazed on the hillside. They probably had been left by travelers who couldn't get their outfits over the mountain passes or were reluctant to raft them down river, Joe decided.

The scene painfully reminded him of Bithiah. The

Abernathy family had camped near the same spot where the wagons now stood. One of the last memories he had of Bithiah was of her peeling potatoes with Luke and the Olafson youngsters playing in the background. How silly not to have realized then the jig was up. Bithiah and her motherly instincts could not resist the pull of the motherless kids. Their need overpowered whatever love she had for him.

At the mission Alanson Hinman, the former Waiilatpu schoolteacher, opened the door and invited them in. A young man still in his teens rose from a seat by the fire and held out his hand. "I'm Perrin Whitman, Doctor Whitman's nephew."

Joe explained they were on their way east and stopped to say hello and see what news they had of the plateau.

"When Uncle Marcus was last here, he was so upset about the way the Cayuse were acting he didn't talk of much else," Perrin Whitman said. "I'm worried for his safety."

"Injuns causin' trouble, are they?" Deacon asked.

"They're giving the emigrants fits. At night they drive off their stock. In the morning they offer to find the animals in exchange for a shirt or blanket. The next night the same thing happens. Uncle Marcus said they drove away the stock of four families camped at John Day Crossing. When the men were searching for the animals the Indians stripped the camp of everything, even took the clothes off the women and children."

"You hardly can blame them. The winter devastated the natives," Hinman added. "Many lost their herds. Measles cut family members down like stalks of corn. They're desperate."

The disturbing news made Joe question the wisdom of following the wagon trail along the Columbia, but Deacon scoffed. "Two experienced frontiersmen like us ain't goin' ta let a few Injun stories make us turn tail."

Deacon was eager to get on. Already snow had fallen in the mountains. It would not be long before the trail east would become impassable. Reluctantly, Joe agreed to continue but when the gloom of dusk descended over the gray sagebrush covered hills, he wished they had remained overnight in Wascopum. All campsites they considered looked cold and foreboding. As they argued over where to stop, a covered wagon off to the side of the track came into view. The promise of trail side hospitality brightened Joe's mood. It was short lived. The wagon sat deserted. There was no sign of humans or animals.

"Wonder where the folks be?" Deacon said. "Probably lost their team an' begged a ride with friends. No use lettin' the place go ta waste. Let's make ourselves ta home."

A nearby draw provided water and grass where they hobbled the animals. Over a small fire they heated up what remained of breakfast pan bread. After eating, Deacon settled back and began to doze, but the deserted wagon gave Joe the shivers. The canvas cover popped and crackled in the wind as if protesting their presence. A chorus of coyotes yipped in the distance. The sounds soon disturbed Deacon.

"Don't mind the coyotes singin', but this dinged wagon's as noisy as a flock of crows. Maybeso, we should bed down in the draw near the critters. An' me thinks 'twould be wise ta set guard. I don't fancy bein' set afoot in Cayuse country."

The draw was as black as Blackie's hide. While Joe felt around for a soft spot to lie down, Deacon roosted on a hillock, his Hawken propped against a knee. Finally settled, Joe drowsily listened to the cry of coyotes and the cropping of Blackie and Zebra. He dozed off, only to jerk awake and reach for his rifle. The sound of fast approaching hoofbeats made Blackie's and Zebra's ears shoot up. Both Joe and Deacon grabbed for the halter lines, ready to stifle any sound from the animals.

"Fer sure it's a batch of Injuns," Deacon observed. "No sane white man'd be out in the middle of the night."

Soon sharp yelps of surprise and pleasure came from the horsemen. They had discovered the wagon. After a noisy period of plunder, the despoilers set fire to what remained. Torches of flames and burning cinders swirled skyward to light up the draw.

"Tarnation!" Deacon cocked his Hawken. "Jest young

bucks havin' fun, but I'm sure they wouldn't look down thar noses at liftin' a couple of scalps."

Before the fire died away, the horsemen mounted up and, with yips of satisfaction, galloped east. Gradually the sound of hoofbeats faded, leaving behind only the moan of the wind, cry of coyotes and crackling of the wagon fire. The next morning trampled grass, charred wood, ashes and twisted wagon iron, proved the night's events were more than a bad dream.

A long hard day's ride brought them to a shallow valley cut by a brush-fringed stream. Along the eastern bank thin columns of smoke mingled with the late autumn haze. The smoke and sound of yelping curs warned of an Indian camp.

"The Umatilla," Deacon announced. "Fer certain we're in Cayuse country." He reined Zebra down a gully, away from the trail. "I don't fancy ridin' inta thet Injun camp in broad daylight. We'd best hunker down 'till dark."

They ate the last of the jerky the roan hadn't carried away and waited for the Indian camp to settle for the night. A half-moon rose to set dozens of dogs barking. Yipping cries of coyotes quickly answered. When quiet descended, the riders cautiously approached the river crossing. The thirsty animals plunged their muzzles into the water only to be startled by a volley of yelps that made the men jump and the animals snort.

"Those Injun mongrels make more fuss than a jackass convention," Deacon muttered.

Carefully, they circled the Indian camp. When it seemed they were safe, Blackie neighed. A volley of neighs answered. Suddenly, horses were black against the horizon. They didn't take time to see if riders clung to their sides. They raced through the sagebrush. At the crest of a ridge they stopped to look back. All that was visible was the blackness of rolling clouds that suddenly covered the starlit sky. The only sounds were the roll of thunder and the heavy breathing of the animals and the ever-present cry of coyotes.

"I guess we're outta the woods now," Deacon said, brushing from his beard raindrops that had begun to fall.

At daybreak the gray Columbia River unfolded before them to finally disappear between high bluffs. Near midday they crossed the Walla Walla River to see the flag of a Hudson's Bay fort loom out of the gray sky. A brisk rain-filled wind blew the Hudson's Bay banner straight out. The beaver on the flapping cloth bounced up and down making the rodent look as though it were alive. Chilled to the bone, the riders cantered through the fort gates, anxious to get out of the damp, cold, cutting wind.

As they tethered the animals to the hitching rail, five horsemen rode away through the fort gates. The leader sat his saddle straight and stiff like a cavalryman on parade. For a moment the sun broke through the gray mist to shine on red waxed mustaches. Joe sucked in his breath. The man looked much like the trouble-maker Macon Laird had described -- Pascoe's murderer.

The fort overseer was a newcomer who introduced him-self as McBean. He wanted news of the trail. He didn't appear surprised to hear of Indians burning the abandoned wagon. "Leave anything unguarded and these Injuns'll be on it quick as a buz-zard on a carcass," he said.

When McBean learned that Deacon intended to take the trail east, he shook his head. "Yer liable ta loose yer hair." He guffawed when Deacon removed his cap to reveal a shiny dome. "They'll fer sure have a time gettin' a handhold on yer topknot."

"Do you know the riders who just left?" Joe asked.

"They drop in from time ta time. Only one I can put a name to, is Lewis, the half-blood."

"What does he do?"

"Nuthin' thet I know of. Hangs around the mission at Waiilatpu. Whitman takes in every stray dog thet comes along."

Deacon paid no attention to Joe's concerns. He began to collect his needs for the journey to the Sweetwater. While McBean was tallying Deacon's bill, rain began pelting down. Far into the night, the fort, sitting on an exposed point above the bend in the river, took a lashing from the storm. McBean invited the travelers to roll out their blankets in the cannon guarded west bastion. Here, among powder kegs and bags of shot, Joe and Deacon spent the night attempting to get comfortable. In the morning they stumbled out to face a wind that sliced through clothes like a knife.

"You can't take off in this," Joe insisted. McBean agreed. "Give it a day to dry. Creeks are up an' sagebrush wet and loaded with ticks. Lots of sickness around. Regular epidemic. Measles, it's killin' Injuns like flies. The poor things don't know what to do -- claim Doc Whitman's medicine kills 'em. Thar own healers don't do any better. I'm telling yuh true, these folks're at the end of ther tether. I don't know what's goin' ta happen an' they don't either."

"Must be hard on Doc Whitman," Joe said, thinking of the overworked missionary.

"He's in a fix. If he doesn't watch out a grievin' Cayuse'll kill him fer sure."

The next morning dawned cold and foggy. Deacon would not put off his trip another day. Joe rode with him to where the Walla Walla Valley widened onto a plain. Here and there beside the trail were plots of tilled ground. Cattle muzzled among dry corn stalks left over from the fall harvest. On the rolling land above the valley floor, scattered bunches of shaggy ponies dotted the brown and gray slopes. Beyond the hills, a haze cloaked the incline that led to the Blue Mountains. Except for the bitter weather, the scene was so pleasant and serene it was hard to believe anything but peace and contentment reigned in the valley.

"Here's where the trail splits," Deacon said. "I'm off to cross the Blues." He pointed to the distant mountains.

"Gee, old timer, I'll miss you," Joe said, taken aback by Deacon's abrupt departure.

"Yep, we wore out a lotta saddle leather together. Seems only yestiday when we first met in St. Louie. Yuh an' me're the last of Buck Stone's trappin' brigade. Who'd a thought they'd be gone an' we'd be left? All the more reason fer us ta keep in touch. Yer always welcome on the Sweetwater. Yuh know how my people took ta yuh. An' I'm dead serious 'bout Mornin' Star. She'd be heap of comfort ta yuh."

"Go on, you old scalawag. You hate to see a man free and single. Besides, who could stand an old bear like you for a father-in-law?"

Deacon chuckled. "Anyways, come fer a visit."

"I'll sure think on it," Joe said huskily. For a long while he watched the indomitable mountain man and his striped mule thread their way through the low growing junipers. When they disappeared from view he reined Blackie onto the trail to Waiilatpu. The brisk air of approaching winter made him think of his last parting from the mission. Narcissa Whitman had been depressed. "Autumn brings the chill of winter that kills the plants and turns the leaves and makes them fall. It is a time of death and decay," she had said.

Joe pulled Blackie to a stop. On previous trips the trappers always tried to arrive with gifts, though simple ones as the can of molasses on their first visit. One good thing about having wealth was that he could splurge on anything he wished. McBean would take a draft on his St. Louis bank. There were candlesticks, sweets and possibly a length of gingham that would do. Joe turned Blackie about and galloped for the Fort. On the way Blackie threw a shoe.

If Joe had continued on the trail he would have arrived in Waiilatpu at the height of what became known as the Whitman Mission Massacre. Instead, at the time the murderous killing was taking place, he was safe at a blacksmith forge in Fort Walla Walla having a shoe shaped for his horse.

XXIX

"We arrived at the lodge of Stickas, thoroughly wet . . .
We spread down our blankets by a good fire
in the lodge, and lay by till morning."
Henry Spalding, November, 1847

Michael Two Feathers arrived on the upper Umatilla well after dark to find Dr. Whitman and Missionary Spalding had been invited to stay the night at the lodge of Stickus. Rather than disturb them, he sought shelter in the lodge next to that of Stickus. In the morning he arose early only to find Stickus and his guests were holding a prayer service. Upon its completion, Stickus and his visitors sat down to a breakfast of potatoes, squash, beef and bread of which Michael was invited to partake. Before the men finished eating, a messenger from across the Umatilla River came to get Dr. Whitman. The doctor immediately set aside his plate and picked up his medical kit. Michael ran to bring in the horses.

"My dear Michael, are you planning to ride with me?" Marcus Whitman asked in a pleased voice. "You always seem to be on hand when I need you most." These words Michael would remember time and time again for the rest of his life.

Before day's end the doctor and Michael had visited three villages and countless lodges in each village. Everywhere they were welcomed with desperate but hopeful looks. From almost every lodge the doctor emerged looking wan and grim. When he bid his patients good-bye he forced a cheery smile that as the day wore on, became little more than an exhausted grimace. From lodge to lodge he went. Mothers waited at the entrances, some holding sick babies in their arms; others greeted him with tears, pulling the doctor inside to air thick with the fetid fumes of feverish bodies. On sleeping pallets, sometimes as many as four stricken people lay stretched out side by side like cadavers awaiting burial.

The measles epidemic spared no one; little babies, youth, adults in their prime and old women and men were all victims. The doctor did what he could to relieve the suffering, but as the day wore on Michael couldn't help but see the helpless expression in the good man's eyes grow more pronounced. Late in the day they recrossed the river and made their way to the lodge of Stickus. Almost immediately the doctor prepared for the ride back to Waiilatpu.

"There is very little good I can do here but call on the Good Lord for mercy," he said to Missionary Spalding who had remained in the lodge of Stickus. "These people have no resistance and I have no cure. About all I have done is instruct them the best I can on how to care for themselves. Whether they live or die is up to their Creator now." He accepted the food Kin-noo, Stickus' wife, handed him, thanked her, took a few bites and set the plate aside. "I had better leave before it gets any later. I have sick people at the mission who need my attention, too."

"But you can't ride back tonight," Spalding protested. "In the morning I will saddle up and go with you."

"No, you need to rest that sprained leg." En route to the camp on the Umatilla the horse Spalding was riding had slipped and fallen, landing on the missionary's leg. "Besides, I would like to have you stay, visit the sick and give them what comfort you can. Michael will be good enough to take you to the lodges, won't you, Michael?"

Michael opened his mouth, but no words came out. He had no wish to remain behind. He gave Stickus an imploring glance. Stickus understood. He followed his missionary friend outside. He took the reins of Whitman's horse and held the animal fast. "Bad mens wait -- kill mission people -- stay with Stickus on Umatilla . . . ." The Cayuse headman implored, struggling with the few English words he knew, but the anguished expression on his face expressed his plea far better than what he said.

"My dear friend. Don't fear. For months these people have threatened to destroy the mission. If this is the night it happens, I should be with my family. They will need me more than ever."

Stickus released the reins. Whitman lifted his hand in a farewell salute. "God watch over you," he said to Stickus. "You are indeed a good friend and a man of God. When the time comes it will be folks like you who will reign in heaven above. Whatever the good Lord has in store for us, I want you to know you are my brother in Christ."

The missionary urged the horse forward. The three men watched as the rider loped over a rise to disappear in the misty haze that hung like a pall over the brown/gray hills. Michael turned away feeling ill. The man should not be riding alone. He should have insisted on going along. He had the terrible premonition tragedy awaited Marcus Whitman in Waiilatpu. All evening the feeling persisted. He could see that Stickus felt tormented, too. Late into the night the Cayuse leader sat silent, staring into the fire. Only when the chill of the breeze off the Umatilla invaded the lodge did Stickus fold himself in sleeping robes. Even after hours on the sleeping pallet, Michael could hear him mumbling prayers.

As the good doctor had requested, the next morning Michael escorted Missionary Spalding around the camps to visit and comfort the sick. Their presence did little good. "Where is the missionary doctor man?" the people asked. Missionary Spalding could pray all he wanted, but they needed medicine -- not words to the white man's God. Late in the afternoon, after the last lodge had been visited, they came upon a member of St. Anne's, the mission the Catholics had opened a few days earlier on the middle Umatilla by raising a flag over a cabin given them by the Cayuse leader, Young Chief. A long time foe of the Catholic Church, Spalding's face darkened.

"The gall of these people," he muttered to Michael, "setting up a mission among our Cayuse. Ride on. I want to have a word with this misguided person." Little did Spalding know his talk with the priest, who he regarded with disdain, would keep him out of harm's way, probably saving his life.

Michael, who had no desire to get involved in what was certain to be an argument over some interpretation of the Scriptures, gladly hurried on. He arrived at the village of Stickus to find it in turmoil. He questioned the rider who guarded the trail. The man gave him a furious stare. "See for yourself," he said in a surly voice.

Michael knew something terrible was wrong and that in some way he was involved. He rode nearer. The clamor became more intense -- a wail of mourning, followed by the chilling high-pitched chant of death. Suddenly it dawned on Michael what had happened. The grandchild of an elder Dr. Whitman and he had tended had died. Hurriedly, Michael staked out his black and white pony well away from the village. It would be foolish to ride any nearer. He did not want harm to befall Magpie. Taking a roundabout route, he made his way toward the lodge of Stickus. At almost every turn he had to dodge back and change his course. The village streets were packed with wailing mourners. Frenzied shamans exorcising evil spirits danced around and in and out of the lodge where the child had died. Dogs, excited by the uproar, barked and howled, adding to the bedlam.

Then almost at once the tears and wails of mourning became shouts of accusation and anger. Urging them to follow, the shamans led the people through the village. An imposing tall stranger, wearing a long cape fastened around his neck and shoulders with shiny clasps and a black broad-brimmed hat pulled low over his forehead, began to harangue the mob. Standing alongside him was a member of Tiloukaikt's village acting as interpreter. Michael stopped behind a lodge to listen. The man was obviously an outsider. He was telling the people the disease that sickened and killed was brought by Missionary Whitman. "He wants you to die. The medicine he gives is poison . . . ." Some stopped to listen to the stranger; others swept by, much too distraught to waste time on outsiders.

Michael moved on. The man's voice was lost in the cries

and shrieks of the shamans. Shaking their medicine bags containing magical rocks, sacred feathers, rodent tails and other oddments with the power to counteract evil, they proceeded directly toward the lodge of Stickus. The leader of the band was to blame for bringing the missionaries to the village, and he had sheltered them overnight.

Michael arrived at the lodge and quickly ducked inside to warn his friend. Stickus motioned to his woman and said a few words Michael did not understand. Kin-noo ripped the robes from the sleeping pallet. She scraped away the boughs and bulrush mats beneath, exposing a layer of poles that covered a deep storage pit where the family stored vegetables during the freezing months of winter. Kin-noo pulled aside the poles. Stickus motioned for Michael to jump into the yawning black hole. Hardly before he knew what was happening he found himself in a well lined with turnips and potatoes, his back hunched up against a pile of squash. The covering of poles was quickly replaced as were the boughs, bulrush mats and the sleeping robes. In the darkness, with dust and dirt sifting into his hair, nose and eyes and the terribly frightening din overhead, Michael felt as though he had been thrust into the dark dankness of a grave.

# # #

By the time Joe had his mare shod and purchased gifts for Narcissa and the children at Waiilatpu, the sun was dipping low on the horizon. He decided to wait until morning to make the twenty-five mile journey to Waiilatpu. The weather was bad and there was no reason for him to arrive at Whitman's mission in the middle of the night. He spent a pleasant evening dining with McBean on sturgeon taken from the river below the fort by Indian fishermen. The next morning he was up before daybreak planning to get an early start. He ate a cold breakfast and had saddled up when a bedraggled man staggered through the fort gates. Anxious to be on his way, Joe paid him little mind until he realized he knew the man -- it was Dad Wall. He hadn't seen him since the previous fall when the trains split up at Raft River Crossing. The Walls had taken the northern route through the Blue Mountains.

For a moment Wall teetered back and forth, apparently too exhausted to speak. Almost incoherent and repeating himself, Joe finally understood him to say, "Mission folks've been murdered!"

McBean, who came running up, grasped Wall by his tattered shirt. "Git yerself in hand, man. What's this squallin' all about? Who got murdered?" he demanded.

"The bloody Cayuse hev murdered everybody at the mission," Wall sobbed. "I been on the run all night -- jest gotta away by the skin of me teeth." Over and over he insisted the Whitmans and everyone at mission house had been cruelly slain.

The horrendous news made Joe's blood run cold. It was beyond belief the Cayuse would go on a bloody rampage, killing the people who had done their best to save their souls. Yet, something terrible had to have happened. It was obvious Dad Wall had lived through a harrowing event. What in the world should be done? They couldn't stay behind the fort walls and do nothing. He glanced at McBean.

"Hmm!" McBean grunted. His fort staff consisted of himself and three employees. He paced back and forth looking grim. "This is a pretty pickle. If the Cayuse are on the warpath, that means the Walla Wallas, Umatillas and maybeso, even the Nez Perce are likely on the warpath, too. They'll be out to kill every white man on the plateau. We need help and plenty of it." He glanced around. Other than his three employees, only two Catholic priests who had stayed the night were in sight.

"The first thing we should do is find out how serious the situation is," Joe said. "I can't believe the entire plateau has erupted. This could be an isolated incident," he spoke calmly but his heart was in his mouth. The Whitmans, the Sager orphans, Mary Ann Bridger, Helen Mar Meek, little David Malin -- all of his good mission friends slaughtered? It could not be possible. "I must go to Waiilatpu," he blurted. "Someone has to go there and find out what has actually happened."

"Don't yuh dare leave here," McBean said. "We have got to hold this fort. Can't yuh see, hardly a person here knows how to handle a gun." He glanced disdainfully at the two priests. "We must provide a haven for people like this man, Wall. Where else can the poor souls go? Hey, Bushman," McBean called to his interpreter who was accustomed to dealing with the Cayuse. "Yuh know yer way 'round these parts. Scout a bit. See what's goin' on. Be careful. We can't afford to lose a single man."

Near mid-morning one of the priests' converts, an Indian woman, arrived to report the Cayuse were indeed on the "warpath." They were riding for the fort intending to kill all Whites. McBean immediately ordered the fort gates barred and the cannons run out. McBean, the two employees who remained, and Joe stood guard, waiting for the Cayuse onslaught.

Slowly the day wore on. McBean chewed his fingernails; the priests thumbed their beads and breviaries; Wall huddled in a corner, shivering from shock and fright. McBean had given him food, but he was in such a state he couldn't eat. The Indian woman who had reported the Cayuse threat sat stoically unmoved, attaching beads to a pair of moccasins.

As the hours passed and nothing happened, Joe began to feel the fool. The only information they had received came from a hysterical man and an Indian woman. He put his rifle aside and patiently questioned Wall. Haltingly, the bereft man repeated his story. Indians lurked around the mission all morning. Whitman paid them no mind. He had tended to the sick and held a funeral service. Upon his return he was struck down in the mission house kitchen. "From then on, they was Injuns everywhere," Wall's voice nearly broke. "Tomahawkin', shootin', yellin' -- 'twas like a glimpse of hell. Oh! God! I should be dead. I held 'em off with a rifle an' ran fer the river, dove in and swam like fury. Arras an' bullets plopped 'round like a shower of hail. On the far side of the river I ran -- lost 'em amongst the trees."

Joe could not tell if the man told the truth or created the

story to cover up for his desertion. He couldn't help but remember the man's intolerance of Negroes. Perhaps he was equally intolerant of Indian people. The massacre he insisted had taken place might be a figment of his imagination. There was only one sure way to learn the truth. Joe packed his things and saddled Blackie. He couldn't sit in Fort Walla Walla and do nothing. Many of the mission people at Waiilatpu were his friends. It was only right he be the one to ride there and see for himself what actually had happened.

XXX

The morning of the 29th of November, 1847, was a dark,
dreary day . . . "I had such a bad dream . . . I dreamed
that Indians killed Father and a lot of others."

Matilda Jane Sager, eight years old

A SURVIVOR'S RECOLLECTION OF THE WHITMAN MASSACRE

From his prison pit, Michael could hear the shamans haranguing Stickus, demanding entrance to the lodge. Stickus opened the lodge flaps and let them in. Added to the shamans' shrieks, came the dull pounding of medicine clubs, thudding against bags, baskets, the sleeping pallet and the earthen floor. Through a hole in the pit coverings, Michael could see the horned masks as the frenzied men searched for victims. Although it was cold in the vegetable pit, he broke out in a sweat. How could the searchers overlook the hole in the floor of the lodge?

After what seemed an eternity, the thuds and shrieks stopped. In hoarse voices the shamans informed their followers messengers of evil spirits had spirited the mission people away. Michael leaned back and relaxed. He dozed, then awakened to hear the sound of movement overhead. The covering was pulled aside. A hand lowered a bowl of mush. Michael ate but hardly tasted the food. Hours of darkness dragged by to be followed by a filter of gloom, thick with the sound of mourning. Another period of darkness dragged by then guarded movements came from overhead. Stickus hushed Michael to silence and helped pull his cramped body out of the pit. Through a slit in the back of the lodge they slid, stealthily making their way to a clump of bushes where Magpie stood bridled and saddled.

"Go! Leave Cayuse country," Stickus ordered. "Go to Nez Perce home. Too much trouble in land of Cayuse."

Michael gripped the hand that helped him mount the horse. Stickus was one of the few true friends he'd ever had. He urged

Magpie forward, keeping in the shadows of the brush and trees that lined the banks of the Umatilla. Now and again, he pulled up to listen for pursuing hoofbeats. Only lonely coyote cries rose and fell and quavered to mingle with the answering yelps of dogs at the Indian village.

When he had traveled what he considered a safe distance, Michael turned from the river to ride northeast, breaking a trail through fields of pungent sagebrush. At break of day he paused to give Magpie a rest and say the morning prayer to Father Sun. Late in the morning, certain he was safe from pursuers, he resumed his journey. As the afternoon sun began to dip toward the western horizon, he spotted a lone horseman. He quickly reined Magpie into a clump of high-growing brush. He dismounted and reached for Magpie's muzzle but before he could clamp a hand over the nostrils the horse lifted its ears and whinnied. The horseman reined to a stop and pulled his rifle from its scabbard. For a moment Michael's blood froze. He was unarmed; he leaped on Magpie and dug his heels into the startled animal's sides.

"Michael! Wait up!" It sounded very much like his brother's voice, but could it be? He was far away in the Willamette Valley. It had to be a Cayuse trick. He whipped Magpie into a dead gallop and looked back. The wind had blown the horseman's hat off, his short hair whipped in the wind. Michael pulled Magpie to a stop. There was no one else who rode with such abandon. It could be no one other than his Boston brother.

#

After recovering from the shock of their unexpected meeting, the brothers quickly went over what each knew. Michael reported first on the agonizing visit to, and narrow escape from, the camp of Stickus.

Joe shook his head. "I guess Dad Wall didn't exaggerate after all." He related what had happened at Fort Walla Walla. "No wonder he was half out of his mind."

Michael uttered a cry of dismay. Missionary Whitman must have had a premonition he was riding to his death, but there was no stopping him, short of holding the good man prisoner. He had said if danger threatened his family, he had to be with them.

For a long moment the brothers were silent. The horror of what they might find at Whitman's mission overwhelmed them. They each knew they should ride on, but dreaded doing so. "Well, we'll never find out what happened by sitting here," Joe finally said. They mounted up and slowly rode toward Waiilatpu.

The short daylight hours ended with the riders still on the trail. An owl hooted mournfully from a perch on a leafless branch of an alder. Cautiously, the brothers skirted the Cayuse village. It lay dark and quiet; even the usually noisy dogs failed to make a sound. Damp river air rose up in ghostly, foggy patches. Chilled to the bone, the riders crossed the river to circle around the mission compound. Ominously, it, too, was still; not a spark of light came from any building.

At the base of the hill, near the grave of Baby Alice Clarissa, the little daughter that meant so much to the Whitmans, the brothers dismounted to tether the horses in a cluster of trees. Silently but quickly, they crossed the open space to follow the rail fence to where it ended at the blacksmith shop. Michael held up his hand to signal Joe. His keen ears had picked up a sound, like the murmur of human voices. They seemed to come from near the blacksmith shop. Then he remembered . . . because the rest of the buildings had been jammed with travelers when they arrived, the Canfield family was forced to take shelter in the blacksmith shop. Michael crept to the door and softly called Joe Canfield's name. The door cracked open. A rifle muzzle slid out. Behind it appeared a pale face.

"Git outta hiya, yuh bloody Injun, afore I shoot yuh dead," a voice made squeaky by fright called out.

Joe pulled Michael back and took his place. "Easy does it. We're here to help you." In the dim light he recognized Robin Wall, the lad who had driven for him from Independence to the Raft River Crossing.

"Bless me if it ain't Joe Jennings," the voice squeaked with a cry. "Come in! Come in. We're frightened to death of anythin' thet moves," Robin explained. "Yuh cain't imagine what we've been through."

Relief flooded the small room that teemed with people. Crouched around the walls were small and large shapes, their white faces turned toward Joe and Michael. In a quiet voice Robin introduced Joe and put a name to each face. "You're like angels from heaven. How many're with yuh?"

"There's just the two of us," Joe explained.

"Aaah!" The groan came from a woman. "A lotta good two men kin do agin this horde a Injuns."

"First, tell us what happened," Joe gently requested. The woman was obviously on the edge of hysteria.

Choked with emotion, Robin related the day's bloody events. "It began yestiday, 'bout noon. Whitman had jest returned from givin' a Injun a Christian burial. A Cayuse from the village came to tell of three more deaths from the measles, one of 'em Tiloukaikt's child. Thet was the last straw. Death of the village chief's child was the worst thing that could'a happened, but things stayed calm 'til 'bout two when all hell broke loose. A party of Cayuses came demanding to see Doc Whitman: Tiloukaikt, Feathercap, Tomahas and that half-blood, Joe Lewis. They came askin' fer medicines. When the doc went to the medicine cupboard they clubbed him from behind with a tomahawk. We heard Mary Ann scream, 'They're killin' Father!'"

Robin stopped to regain his composure. "The Injuns went wild, slashin' an' killin'. It was awful. Everybody from the Cayuse village was standin' around on the hill watchin', makin' certain no one got away. They murdered Mr. Marsh at the gristmill. Teacher Saunders at the school, an' John Sager was killed 'bout the same time as Doc Whitman. Gilmore, the tailor, was wounded an' died later, an' three men butcherin' a beef was shot down in their tracks. Joe Lewis was like a madman. He shot Francis Sager dead in front a everybody. A bunch headed by Joe Lewis took the children from the classroom, lined 'em up to shoot 'em -- thet was when he shot Francis. Tiloukaikt couldn't even stomach the way crazy Joe Lewis was actin'. He said thet was enough, there'd be no more killin' of women an' children. They marched 'em over to the mission house. I guess they're still there. No tellin' what they plan to do with us; we hope they had enough killin'. After the last bunch of bloodlettin' they held council. Maybeso, thet's what they're doin' now, but they'll be back in the mornin'. You kin be sure of thet."

"Go! Bring men! Hundreds of 'em," Mrs. Canfield burst out. "It's awful bein' left here not knowin' what tomorrow'll bring. I never wanted to come to Whitman's mission in the first place. Can't stand the sight of it. The Injuns themselves are afeared to stay here after dark."

"Where's Mr. Canfield?" Joe asked, worried that the woman was becoming hysterical.

"He's gone to Spalding's mission fer help," Robin said.

"Lotta good that'll do," Mrs. Canfield screamed. "Mission folk're helpless as babies in dealin' with these Redskins. If they wasn't so hell bent on savin' the savages' souls we wouldn't be in this fix. We'd be outta this godless country. We'd be home, safe and sound. What we need are troops!" She began to sob, rocking back and forth.

"Ma Canfield wants me to ride to Fort Walla Walla, but I can't leave these women an' kids," Robin said, putting an arm around Ellen Canfield.

"It's useless to go to the Fort . . . hardly anybody there and they won't budge." Joe scratched his head frantically. Why couldn't he think? "I guess the best thing to do is ride for the valley. How many prisoners are being held, would you say?"

"Don't know -- upwards of fifty. There's a bunch of folks at the main house. I'd go about this rescue business keerful. You bring a whole bunch of men stormin' in here -- who knows what these bloody Cayuses might do."

"Yeah, might make that Joe Lewis really go berserk. I

wonder if someone they trust could reason with them, calm them
. . . McBean? . . . No, he's so antsy he'd make a mess of things.
If only the White Eagle McLoughlin was still in charge of
Hudson's Bay. He would be one these people would listen to. I
wonder if we could get him out of retirement? We can try, but if
we are to ride all that way we'll need spare horses. Any in the
mission corral?"

"Yeah, don't know how good they are. These Injuns been
takin' everythin' they can lay their hands on," Robin answered.

The corral held a few animals. In the darkness it was
difficult to tell much about them. The horses must have sensed
the butchery. They snorted and reared away, the noise reverber-
ating across the mission grounds. By the time they had halters
on two reasonably good looking mounts, Joe was bathed in cold
sweat. He and Michael led the horses out of the corral and started
away to where they had left their own mounts tethered in the
trees at the base of the hill. Robin caught Joe by the arm.

"I'd sure go with yuh but I'm afeerd fer the womenfolk.
There's talk these Injuns're plannin' to take 'em to their lodges.
They say if white men can bed their women, why can't they do
the same to ours. I sure ain't goin' to see Ellen ravaged by no
murderin' Injun."

"Of course you must stay," Joe said. "We'll be back with
help as soon as we can."

The mission grounds, usually so industriously active, lay
unnaturally quiet. Little wonder the bloody murderers deserted
the place after dark, Joe thought. He couldn't wait to get out of
there himself. Away from the corral the only sounds were the
moan and creak of bare branches in the wind. Again came the
ghoulish who-who hoot of an owl. Fearing it an Indian signal,
Joe motioned Michael to hurry. They collected Blackie and
Magpie, mounted up and, leading the spare horses, rode away at
a gallop. The noise was fearful. If the Indians didn't know of
their presence before, they certainly knew it now.

XXXI

"The last I saw of him he was standing on the river bank
crying as though his heart would break."

Matilda Jane Sager, eight years old, 1847

A SURVIVORS RECOLLECTION OF THE WHITMAN MASSACRE

There was no snow, but December 29, 1847 was a cold, cold morning. Pockets of fog lay in the hollows. The branches of leafless trees stood outlined against the sky like great bony skeletons. Rays of the early morning sun turned their tips to a weak shade of gold. Beyond the millpond a row of sumac bushes continued to cling to its fall brilliance -- a deep red, almost the shade of dried blood. No one had the time nor inclination to pay any attention to the scene painted by Mother Earth. The forty-seven survivors of the Whitman Mission Massacre who had been held prisoner, had been ransomed. Two teams and wagons waited in front of the Whitman family home to carry them to Fort Walla Walla, away from the bloodied mission grounds.

It was a joyful, yet solemn occasion. A month's cruel captivity had come to an end, but the survivors left behind more than a dozen bodies of friends and relatives buried in shallow graves that wolves and other predators would soon uncover and tear to bits. Besides thirteen murder victims, three others died while in captivity, including ten-year old Helen Mar Meek and six-year old Hannah Louise Sager.

Darkness had fallen when the two wagons arrived at the gates of Fort Walla Walla. The survivors, who had to pinch themselves to realize they were finally free, filed into Factor McBean's living quarters. Tears came to the eyes of more than a few as they entered rooms with blazing fires and tantalizing odors of hot food. Conditions were crowded, but no one minded. After a month crammed together like sheep in a corral and their every move watched over by menacing guards, this was heaven indeed.

The survivors had Peter Skene Ogden, Co-Director of Hudson's Bay Northwest trading empire, to thank for their rescue. He received news of the massacre on December 6. He set off on the rescue mission December 7 and arrived in Fort Walla Walla on December 19. He traveled upriver, unarmed with sixteen paddlers. Immediately upon arriving at his destination, he began to council with the Cayuse and Nez Perce. In an all day meeting he warned the Cayuse their crime was not only against the Americans but also against Hudson's Bay.

"We are traders, and of a different nation than the Americans. But we are of the same color, speak the same language, and worship the same God. If the Americans begin war, you will have cause to regret it, for you will be exterminated," he warned.

Tiloukaikt, the Cayuse leader and one of the murderers, stood up to reply. "Your words are weighty. Your hairs are gray. We have known you many winters. You have come a long and tiring journey. I cannot keep the captives back nor can I hold back the young men of my village. I give these people we hold over to you."

The prisoners were released six days later in exchange for sixty-two blankets, sixty-three cotton shirts, twelve muskets, six hundred loads of ammunition, thirty-seven pounds of tobacco and twelve flints.

#

Not far from the walls of Fort Walla Walla, Macon Laird, Joe Jennings and Michael Two Feathers watched the survivors' wagons roll in. The past weeks had been filled with frustration for Joe and Michael. They had ridden full out from the blood soaked Waiilatpu mission to The Dalles -- their destination the Willamette Valley to recruit help to rescue the hostages held by the Cayuse. Upon arriving at The Dalles, they were advised to leave their horses behind and push on by canoe. They were bargaining for a canoe and a paddleman when Macon Laird appeared. He already had received news of the tragedy. McBean had sent a man rushing to Fort Vancouver to warn of an Indian uprising.

McBean's quick action was prompted by a Cayuse youth who had bragged to Bushman, the fort interpreter, of "many, many mission people" taken prisoner. The young white women would make wives, the remaining prisoners would be butchered, he reported.

"No point in going down river," Laird said to Joe when they met at The Dalles. "I have just come from Fort Vancouver. I used the little influence I have on the HBC committee, told them if they didn't get up there and council with the Cayuse for the release of the prisoners, I would send a scathing report to my publisher uncle. He's in position to make our officials out here look pretty sorry. But I must say HBC responded with alacrity. A party of Hudson's Bay people should be along soon."

Joe stared across the river at the cold, bare, foreboding bluffs that rose up from the north shore. If Hudson's Bay officials looked sorry, what about our officials, he thought. Here we are beholden to a man who, a little more than a year ago, he had threatened to shoot down like a sheep killing dog. The irony of the situation made him feel ill.

Laird, unaware of Joe's painful thoughts, urged him and Michael to return with him to Cayuse territory. "Perhaps together we can persuade the peaceful Indians, like Stickus, to mount a rescue party or at least parley with the Waiilatpu band long enough for Hudson's Bay people to get there."

Reluctantly, Joe agreed. After all, the men who trailed Macon Laird and killed Pascoe had a hand in this, and they were British. It was only right that it should fall to the British to help pull the chestnuts from the fire.

But upon arriving in Cayuse country, the three horsemen found their efforts ineffective. The Indian people who had not been involved in the Waiilatpu killings were still reeling from the horrendous measles plague. They were much too distraught to speak of anything but how to keep the angel of death at bay. A few like Five Crows, reveled in the disaster, anxious to get his share of plunder. The prisoner womenfolk were looked on as part and parcel of the spoils. Five Crows insisted youthful Lorinda Bewley, who had helped around the mission, come and share his lodge. The irascible chief sent a slave to ferret her away. The kidnapping of Lorinda Bewley took place under the nose of the murderer, Tamsucky, who also coveted the young lady.

Against his father's wishes, Tiloukaikt's own son, Edward, claimed Mary Smith, a sixteen year-old, for his wife. These outrages were well known among the Cayuse, but even Christian Stickus, on the upper Umatilla, was hesitant to interfere. He had attempted to keep his friend, Missionary Whitman, safe, but he had not listened. Stickus did agree to ride to Waiilatpu and speak to Tiloukaikt. Tiloukaikt listened politely and told Stickus there would be no more killing, but a number of the young Cayuse, even his own sons, were beyond his control.

"This has been a bad business all around," Joe said to Michael and Laird as they prepared a scant evening meal in their camp outside the fort. "I am not only ashamed that I have been so ineffectual but ashamed of my countrymen. We have let our people down. We encourage them to settle this territory and do nothing to protect them."

"You have nothing for which to reproach yourself. You've jolly well done all you can," Macon said, his British accent strong. "If a group of armed Americans had come to the rescue, chances are the Cayuse would have slaughtered every one of the prisoners. Anyway, this terrible affair is as much the fault of the British as it is of your people. You must remember that red-nosed countryman of mine did his best to keep the pot boiling -- he and the Delaware half-blood, Joe Lewis. If ever there were born killers, they are good examples."

Joe thought of poor innocent Pascoe, a dagger thrust deep into the little black man's chest. Yes, perhaps if the Cayuse had not been egged on by evil men the massacre might never have happened. Also, they had suffered through a terrible winter and then came the onslaught of measles . . . . That was what broke and hardened their hearts -- the horrific disease that descended like a scourge of locusts. That certainly was the fault of the emi-grants, carrying death in their wagons like barrels of gunpowder sitting next to open flames.

Michael Two Feathers' thoughts were also on the disaster that had occurred. He thought back to the night on the upper Umatilla when the tall fellow in the long black cape had harangued the grief-stricken crowd into a frenzy. Was that the man Macon Laird said teamed up with Joe Lewis? Why didn't outsiders let natives alone? Whenever they appeared trouble soon followed.

Of course, Tiloukaikt and his followers did some terrible deeds. The tribe never would be the same again. He thought of Little Fox. What would happen to her? Where had she been during all of this? What had she thought when Edward, Tiloukaikt's son, took the white woman for a wife? Did this mean Little Fox was not spoken for? Certainly Edward, by going against his father's wishes, had spoiled any chance he had of bargaining part of Tiloukaikt's herd for Little Fox's dowry.

Michael forced the thoughts of Little Fox from his mind. He was in no position to think of marrying anyone. He didn't even have a home of his own. With the mission gone and Cayuse country in turmoil, where could he go? No longer did he have Whitman's mission as a refuge. And from what he had heard, conditions in the homeland of the Nez Perce were little better. The outlook was bleak for everyone on the plateau. He glanced at his brother, Joe. Would he return to the Willamette Valley and live with their sister, Tildy, and Granddad Jennings? Michael inwardly sighed. Life had become so uncertain he almost wished he had remained with the Snakes.

#

Even after the survivors were inside the walls of Fort Walla Walla, their safety was not assured. There was danger a gang of young Cayuse might take it into their heads to crash the gates, launching another bloody massacre. It would be another two days before the survivors could make their getaway. They had to wait for Reverend Spalding and his mission family, who were coming from Lapwai. Although so far the Nez Perce had been peaceful, Spalding and his workers were warned their mission might be next to suffer a blood bath.

Escorted by forty or more Nez Perce horsemen, Spalding rode into Fort Walla Walla on New Year's Day, 1848. He leapt down to throw his arms around his daughter, Eliza, who had been left in Waiilatpu to attend the mission school. He listened with admiration while survivors told him what courage his ten-year old daughter had displayed. No one got along with the Cayuse as well as did Eliza. Often during the hostages' imprisonment she had saved the day with her knowledge of their language. She was the only one of the captives who spoke it at all well.

At dawn on Sunday, January 2, 1848, the survivors of the Whitman Massacre boarded three bateaux. Although cold and rainy, the air was filled with a feeling of good cheer. "This is the way to start off the New Year," a woman in a bonnet that nearly covered her face remarked, "sail away from this awful land of the Cayuse. I never want to see it again."

"Things aren't as bad as that," Reverend Spalding said. "There are a lot of good people here. When this fuss is over I hope to return and save the souls of every one of them."

Suddenly a couple of sour notes disrupted the joyous departure. Michael, who had been assisting with the boat loading, reached out to give Ellen Canfield a helping hand. She drew back as if stung by a wasp. "Don't you dare touch me, Indian," she said so sharply everyone momentarily stopped to stare.

"It's all right, Ellen," Robin Wall said, trying to smooth things over. "He's a friend."

"I don't care. He's Indian, ain't he? I've had enough of them ogling and trying to get their hands on me," Ellen snapped in reply. Of all the females of her age she had been the only one not molested, probably because Robin was constantly at her side.

Michael turned away and went back up the bank, but he knew as well as everyone else did, from now on, because of what a few Cayuse did, every native on the plateau would be regarded with suspicion -- they might appear trustworthy, but one never could be sure.

The loading continued but not in the spirit it had begun. Then the second discordant note rang out clearly and loudly. The Hudson's Bay people refused to allow little David Malin to board the bateaux.

"He's not an American; he's Canadian," McBean insisted. Although voices were raised in protest, McBean would not listen. "He is one of us. His father was an employee of Hudson's Bay. He's a subject of the British Empire. He must stay."

The three bateaux pushed away. Horror-stricken, Little David Malin watched them go. His adopted brothers and sisters were leaving him behind. His sobs could be heard above the rushing waters. "The poor boy," the woman in the big bonnet cried, "to be left all alone in this God forsaken land. It's unforgivable. Please, somebody do something! The child is heartbroken."

Macon Laird, who had been sitting quietly on his tall black horse, quickly leapt down to encircle the crying boy in his arms. "I say, old chap. I didn't know you were British. I'm British, too. Don't carry on so. We British have to stick together. You wouldn't want to let the side down, would you? I'll tell you what we'll do. You stay with me and I'll let you ride in the saddle with me all the way to Fort Vancouver. After that we'll board a ship with wings that will take us across the big water to the land we call Great Britain. Think of the wondrous sights you'll see. You can bet your life, we'll have a jolly good time. Your troubles will disappear as though whisked away by a magic wand."

Little David Malin's sobs subsided as if Laird's magic wand had turned the dark cloudy day into the brightest day ever. A cheer went up from the people in the bateaux. The Hudson's Bay people also applauded. Little David Malin's plight had touched everyone's heart.

Joe looked on approvingly. If Macon Laird kept his promise to take the boy to Great Britain that would remove him from endangering Tildy's and Sandy's marriage. At the same moment a nagging thought pecked at him like the sharp bill of a flicker. Could Macon remain away from his blood son Tildy would be rearing? Every normal male wanted to see his first-born, and surely Englishmen were no different than other men.

Ah! He had to stop thinking such appalling thoughts. Right now everything was fine. He had accomplished what he had set out to do. Tildy and Granddad were safely ensconced in a Willamette Valley home. The losses Sandy Sanders had suffered in the crossing of '45 were pretty much replenished. No one could say he hadn't tried to do right by them .... But he had not done right by Michael. Promise after promise he had made to him and never kept a one.

Joe's ears burned with shame. Michael had to be sorely tried. He was seeing the last of his mission friends disappear into the Columbia River mist. He must think himself as homeless and friendless as little David Malin. What could he do to ease his pain? For a start they could travel to the Willamette Valley .... If only he could get Michael happily settled into the family ....

Joe shook his head. He would bungle the job again. What had his father, Little Ned, planned for his Nez Perce son? When he sired the boy did he foresee the troubles a half-blood would face, not completely accepted by either race?

It was an upsetting period for everyone in the territory. Even God appeared to have forsaken the region -- people were reeling from the dreadful measles epidemic and horrible mission massacre. Where were the murderers? In this immense area Marcus Whitman had called "Land Without a Country," thousands of hiding places existed. The Indian people's code of silence and emigrants continuing to pour into the territory in unprecedented numbers, wrongly could tip the scales of justice. Would bloodthirsty Joe Lewis, Tamsucky, Tomahas and others ever be found and brought to trial? But this is a tale for another time and another volume in the Lone Wolf Clan series of books.

LAND WITHOUT A COUNTRY

Afterword from L. J. Hunt

Today the mission at Waiilatpu is a National Historic Site. The Great Grave of massacre victims lies at the base of the hill overlooking the old mission compound. The mission buildings are gone but the Park Service has reconstructed the foundations with markers and audio aids. Strolling along the walkways one can easily visualize the comings and goings of Tiloukaikt, Feathercap, Tomahas, Five Crows, Stickus, Young Chief, Joe Lewis, Tom Hill and others who played key roles in the tragic history that took place on these hallowed grounds.

My grandmother, Catherine Cornwall DeMoss, was fascinated with the early history of the Northwest. During my childhood, Peu-peu-mox-mox, Walla Walla; Stickus, Cayuse; Timothy and Old Joseph, Nez Perce; Sacajawea, Shoshoni; and explorers Lewis and Clark were common names in our household. Legends of Horse Heaven Hills, Bridge of the Gods and the fisherwomen Coyote turned to stone were as well known to us as nursery rhymes. Perhaps of all the research Grandmother collected, the most cherished she garnered on a trip deep into the Blue Mountains to interview Joseph Kash Kash, grandson of Stickus, Marcus Whitman's loyal and faithful Cayuse friend.

Publishing LAND WITHOUT A COUNTRY is an act of love and respect for Grandmother and her dedicated efforts to unearth and preserve our early Northwest history and for the people who lived it. Catherine DeMoss's grandfather, Reverend Josephus Cornwall, and grandmother, Nancy Hardin Cornwall, were among the pioneers who endured the tortures of the Applegate Shortcut. They left Umpqua Canyon with only a mule, Nancy Cornwall riding, her husband and children walking. The children (one Catherine DeMoss's father) were so exhausted they clung to their father's coat tails to keep from dropping by the trail. Later the Reverend returned to the north bank of the Umpqua where his library and some household goods lay buried. He took them to a cabin near the present site of Oakland, Oregon where the Cornwall family spent the winter of 1846-47. Today the cabin site is marked by a granite shaft. Reverend Cornwall went on to establish a number of Presbyterian churches in the Willamette Valley, including one in Marysville, (now Corvallis) Oregon.

Other actual personages playing major roles in these pages are Colonel William Henry Russell, Governor Lilburn W. Boggs, the Alphonse Boone family, J. Quinn Thornton and wife, the Donners, Reeds, Mrs. Keyes, Pringles, Newtons, William Smith family, Black Moses Harris, Jessie Applegate, George Curry and Hudson Bay employees: Grant, McBean, Craig, Peter Skene Ogden and Dr. John McLoughlin, "White-Headed Eagle." Many of the incidents, including the boy whose gangrenous leg was amputated, are true, derived from Edwin Bryant's journal, WHAT I SAW IN CALIFORNIA, published in 1848.

The family life incidents of Marcus and Narcissa Whitman and their eleven adopted children were gleaned largely from letters of Narcissa Whitman and reminiscent accounts of massacre survivors, Catherine and Matilda Sager. The Sager sisters published vivid details of the massacre and its aftermath as did Reverend Henry Spalding whose daughter, Eliza, played a courageous role in keeping the captive survivors from greater harm. Fictional liberty was taken to give little David Malin a happy home. History seems to have left the homeless boy crying his heart out on the river bank at old Fort Walla Walla.

In the original manuscript of LAND WITHOUT A COUNTRY, author DeMoss gave credit to a number of descendants of the 1846 immigration who she personally interviewed. In 1918, as a guest at a pioneer reunion, she met Ernest Brown, great grandson of Tabiatha Brown, and Matilda Sager Delaney, a Sager orphan and survivor of the Whitman Mission tragedy. Later she was to count Mrs. Delaney's daughter as a valued friend.

The massacre at Waiilatpu ended one dramatic era of Northwest history only to set the stage for another -- the hunt for the murderers. That search would keep the Cayuse homeland in turmoil for a long while.

Mill   The First House   Blacksmith Shop   The New House

Artist's conception of the Whitman Mission in Waiilatpu prior to the massacre. From Marcus Whitman and Early Days of Oregon by William A. Mowry – Silver, Burdett and Company copyright, 1901.

ABOUT THE AUTHORS

Bonnie Jo Hunt (*Wicahpi Win* - Star Woman) is Lakota (Standing Rock Sioux) and the great-great granddaughter of both Chief Francis Mad Bear, prominent Teton Lakota leader, and Major James McLaughlin, Indian agent and Chief Inspector for the Bureau of Indian Affairs. Early in life Bonnie Jo set her heart on helping others. In 1980 she founded Artists of Indian America, Inc. (AIA), a nonprofit organization established to stimulate cultural and social improvement among American Indian youth. To record and preserve her native heritage, in 1997 Bonnie Jo launched Mad Bear Press that publishes American history dealing with life on the western frontier. These publications include the Lone Wolf Clan series: THE LONE WOLF CLAN, RAVEN WING, THE LAST RENDEZVOUS, CAYUSE COUNTRY, LAND WITHOUT A COUNTRY and forthcoming DEATH ON THE UMATILLA.

#

Dr. Lawrence J. Hunt, a former university professor, works actively with Artists of Indian America, Inc. In addition to coauthoring THE LONE WOLF CLAN, RAVEN WING, THE LAST RENDEZVOUS, CAYUSE COUNTRY, LAND WITHOUT A COUNTRY and forthcoming DEATH ON THE UMATILLA, he has coauthored an international textbook (Harrap: London) and authored four mystery novels (Funk and Wagnalls), one of which, SECRET OF THE HAUNTED CRAGS, received the Edgar Allan Poe Award from Mystery Writers of America.